# Another Life Lesson

**ELIAS PUBLISHING LLC**



Cover Design: Nikki Nally Art
Editing: Gilly Critque Service
Book Design and Typesetting: Enchanted Ink Publishing

The text type was set in EB Garamond


ISBN: 979-8-9935564-1-3 (E-book)
ISBN: 979-8-9935564-0-6 (Paperback)


Thank you for your support of the author's rights.

**WWW.MICHELLECAMPBELLAUTHOR.COM**

# *Another Life Lesson*

MICHELLE CAMPBELL

# CHAPTER 1

## Celeste

A REQUEST TO INTERACT WITH THEM WAS NOT A COMmon one. Few have done it throughout history, of course. Special circumstances only. Still, she knew asking was a long shot. Celeste was nothing if not an optimist, so she had to at least try.

She placed sweaty palms on the deep brown oak door, her hands the size of pennies in comparison, and pushed her weight forward. The door crept open with a grating that could make ears bleed, and Celeste found herself face to face with the Council.

The eight members sat along the long wooden table, matched perfectly to the door in size as much as in color, and silently watched as she made her way towards them. The distance between the door and the table seemed endless, and Celeste's breathing did little to calm her.

She wiped her palms on her long white dress and tried to take it all in. There was something off-putting about the divine Council members, in their all-white clothes and glowing white auras, surrounded by wood paneling, potted plants, and indoor/outdoor carpeting. It was as if one of them took notice of an office from Earth Magazine, 1960 edition, and never looked back.

The luminous white that surrounded each of the Council members, manageable to look at when one-on-one, was at least enough to distract her from the room. She resisted the urge to turn her hand into a visor and kept her composure, as much as anyone could be expected to in such circumstances.

"Hi," Celeste said, her voice wavering. She smiled, too brightly, and raised her hand in an almost salute. "Um, yes, hello. I just wanted to come and ask—"

"We know why you are here." A familiar cold voice boomed from the left side of the table. Celeste squinted and tried to focus on the speaker. That darn light.

"Now, Reginald," an airy voice chimed in, and Celeste's eyes followed the sound to the left side of the table, where she could make out the shape of Muriel. "Let her speak."

"Why?" he asked, as Celeste's head played a game of ping pong. "We do know why she's here, and the answer is emphatically no."

Silence filled the room as Celeste thought of the speech she spent hours preparing. She tried to get herself to say the words she had practiced. Then she tried to get herself to just say anything at all. She landed on simply shifting her weight back and forth as she waited, hopeful for pushback from the others.

Her eyes traced the figures behind the table. All sat in varying degrees of height, weight, skin tone, hair color, and age. A Soul could choose exactly the form they wished to take in their afterlife, and the variety was refreshing, given that one of the requirements to be a Guardian was an all-white wardrobe. A rule Celeste shamefully hated.

The eldest, Kinsley, cleared her throat and brought everyone's attention to her. She chose her appearance to reflect her status: a woman in her late sixties to early seventies, her brown skin enhanced by the glow and her white gown. She kept her gray hair short, exposing a long neck that added to her already regal appearance. Reginald had the ability to shake a room, but Kinsley commanded it.

Kinsley addressed Celeste directly. "You know it is common for the Humans to fall back a little–lose their way–as they say, but that does not mean we intervene. It is imperative that they find their way back on their own. That is the process."

Celeste stepped forward, just a hair, and opened her mouth ever so slightly.

"Precisely!" shouted Reginald, his butt leaving his chair by inches. Reginald also chose an older appearance. He kept his jet black and chrome gray hair clean and perfectly trimmed; his build was tall and imposing. If he were allowed to wear a black suit and tie each day, Celeste had no doubt he would. Instead, he was stuck with white trousers and a long-sleeved white tunic, giving him more of a relaxed and carefree look that far from fit his personality. "This is a ridiculous request. We are wasting our time even hearing it."

Celeste raised her index finger in protest. Her eyes were beginning to adjust to the glow, and she appreciated the small win.

"I agree," said Muriel, in her signature tone, which did little to soften the blow Celeste was feeling. "We are supposed to let them run their course. They need to learn their seven Life Lessons on their own to ensure the lessons are truly learned." She brushed her long, sandy-blonde hair over her right shoulder, her cream skin smooth and youthful.

"Then what are we here for?" Celeste asked. She touched her fingers to her lips, as if she could stop the words from coming out.

Kinsley raised an eyebrow. She said, "We guide. We send our Souls signs, we add a little shimmer to the more appropriate path, we ensure they are at the right location at the right time. Guiding and outright interfering in their life lessons are very different."

A fourth voice spoke up from down the table, and Celeste almost looked up to praise the Heavens before remembering she was already standing smack dab in the middle of them.

With his usual devil-may-care attitude, Benny said, "But it has been done before." He winked at Celeste before glancing at Kinsley.

Reginald scoffed. "Very different circumstances. Those people were set for greatness; they had to succeed." He crossed his arms over his chest and sat back in his seat for the first time since Celeste entered the room. She swore she saw his ears grow pink.

Benny leaned against the table to better face Reginald.

"Are you saying that some are handled with greater care, that not all matter equally?" He gaped mockingly. "Very disappointing, Reggie."

Celeste had to refrain from laughing at the casual use of the nickname. Benny continued to look down the table at Reginald, while Celeste's eyes lingered on Benny. He was middle-aged. Choosing to be old enough to solicit respect while maintaining a young-at-heart feel. His light brown hair was sprinkled with white at his temples and his ice blue eyes sparkled with each mischievous poke at Reginald. As terrified as she was to come to ask permission from the Council, the little comfort she did have was that he was right there with her. Their strong relationship wasn't unique to Celeste; Benny treated all his Trainees with care and support, but she did like to believe they'd be proper friends in any other circumstance.

Reginald stammered. "That-that is not what I meant, and you know it. But, yes, for certain people on Earth to succeed, sometimes," he turned to address Celeste directly, "very sparingly, we get involved when we know it is for the greater good. We had to go down and stop Fred from quitting his kids' television show in 1975. He was being completely ridiculous, wanting to take a break when so many children were relying on him. We don't get breaks," he said, gesturing to the room. "His work was far too important and–"

"Reginald," said Kinsley, dryly.

"Yes, yes, anyway. I am sorry, Celeste, but your Human's path to enlightenment, the divine, rapture," he twiddled his fingers in thought. "Whatever they choose to call it, is a personal journey. A very important one," he growled while glancing towards Benny, "but a personal one. We cannot interfere."

Benny threw his arms up. "You cannot pick and choose. Despite what you may think, Reggie, we are not actually Gods. A tier or two down from that, which is pretty damn impressive, but we are here to help, and help equally."

An eruption of grumbles came from the full length of the table, most seemingly against Benny and his support of Celeste going down. She wiped her hands along her dress once more.

Muriel gently placed her hand on the table in front of Benny.

"Then where does it stop?" she asked. "We can't go down and intervene for everyone."

Benny sighed, and Reginald smiled.

"We all know each Soul gets to live twenty-five lives," she continued. "If within those twenty-five lives, they do not achieve the Highest Self through the learnings of their seven Lessons, then they don't enter Enlightenment. Celeste, I know this is your first Soul. You've been with them through so many lifetimes, but it's not your fault. Sometimes we do all we can do, and still, they don't learn all their Lessons." All of the other Council members, except Benny, sat silently, nodding their heads.

"We are Guardians, not miracle workers, despite what the humans may think we do up here." Muriel finished her speech, uncharacteristically rolling her eyes.

Celeste stepped closer, fueled by Benny's support. "But they are so close; they're almost there, I know it. They are just stuck on this one lesson. I know I sound like a young Guardian who can't accept defeat–and perhaps there's a little truth to that–but that isn't what drives me. They're close. I know that if I can just be there physically with them, I can help them get there."

Norah.

Her Soul's name in this life was Norah, and she couldn't–wouldn't–let her fail. She had been watching and guiding Norah's many lives. Norah had grown and learned almost every Lesson there was. There was only one Lesson left that she couldn't seem to learn. True, it was the hardest, but Celeste couldn't sit back and watch Norah get further off her path.

Celeste, with the help of Benny, tried everything she knew to try, and nothing was working. She needed to step in and be able to help from a different vantage point. It was a need Celeste couldn't quite explain. Perhaps all Guardians felt this way about their first Soul, but Celeste simply could not let Norah fail.

It wasn't an option.

Besides, Silas would never allow her to live it down if she did fail. Her know-it-all fellow Trainee did whatever he wanted as if the rules didn't apply to him. He certainly had a knack for keeping his eyes on everyone else, though, and was the ultimate angel in the eyes of his mentor. Ugh.

Not every Guardian in training had a mentor who sat on the Council, and a mentor could have more than one Trainee, but, of course, Silas's mentor was none other than Reginald. Silas was infuriating. Smart, Celeste would give him that, but infuriating. She never understood how he even made it to be a Trainee.

Celeste found herself grumbling about how the next Guardian's Bingo night would be a nightmare.

"Celeste," Kinsley said, bringing Celeste's attention back to the room and the stern faces of the Council. "I understand you want to help your Human; you don't get to become a Guardian without the passion and love you have. But you knew watching them fail was a possibility. We understand the difficulty of this not only as Guardians ourselves but as members of this Council. We are the ones who decide whether or not a Soul has learned their Lesson in each life. That can be an extremely difficult task, but one we need to be able to remove emotion from and adhere to the rules. Coping with this was a part of your training," she said as she looked over at Benny. "Or perhaps we need to review our teachings with your mentor."

Celeste dropped her eyes to her twiddling thumbs.

"That won't be necessary. Benny prepared me perfectly I assure you. I will step back and watch over them, guide them from a distance, just as I am supposed to." Celeste picked her head up to address all eight members of the Council directly. "Thank you for your time."

She'd find another way. She had to.

She walked out of the room feeling even smaller than when she entered. She needed some fresh air, and thankfully, fresh air was very easy to come by.

# CHAPTER 2

## Norah

N ORAH GLANCED AT HER PHONE AS IT VIBRATED, YET again, on the desk beside her.

"Will you please answer that damn thing?" Barb asked from behind her. "What's that, the one hundredth time he's called?"

Norah spun her chair around to look at Barb, who was facing away from her, keying in the last patient's information. "It's the third time today, and I don't feel like talking to him right now."

Barb was the momma bear of the Greenville Diagnostics Center. Full of tough love and soft edges. When asked, she was as old as the hills and young enough to still kick anyone's ass who needed it.

Norah spun back around to face her workspace. "We're at work. I'm trying to do my job."

This got an uproarious laugh out of Barb, and the corners of Norah's mouth reached for her ears.

"Are you going to tell me what you are fighting about this time, or leave me to my imagination?"

"Now, Barb, why would you even ask me if you already know the answer?"

Norah heard a scoff from Barb and then nothing but the clack of her keyboard.

Chris and Norah fell back into what Norah thought of as the valley of their relationship. Peaks and Valleys. There would be a day, a week, even a month of good. They would go on a normal date, a dinner out with a drink or two, leave by a respectable hour, and he would either sleep at her place or she at his. They'd have a week of going on runs and eating lunches together, laughing at everything the other said. Inevitably, either consciously or subconsciously, Norah would do something to upset their Peak. She'd stay out too late, drink one whiskey too many, or spend days hungover and miserable, snapping at everything he did and said. They'd spend more time fighting than laughing.

Norah could hardly remember what she'd done this time. A product of how often they fought or a foggy memory from one too many drinks, she wasn't certain which.

She knew she should answer the phone. Talk to him about it. He did deserve that, at least. He wasn't perfect, but she unfairly pushed him away more often than she intended. He just happened to be someone who was harder to push away than most. It was only a matter of time before she pushed too hard and he would stop calling altogether. Sometimes she wished he would already; it would've made things that much easier.

"Alright, kiddo," Barb sighed, packing up. "It's quittin' time. You want to join me and Tina for a drink?"

Norah said, "Not today." She glanced over her shoulder and saw Barb shaking her head. "Now, Barb, why would you even ask me if you already know the answer?" she joked again.

"One of these days," Barb said as she headed for the door.

Norah's phone signaled a text message this time, and she stole a glance as she packed up her things to head home for the day.

Pizza at my place? Please...

IT WAS JUST AFTER SEVEN BY THE TIME SHE MADE IT OVER to his apartment. It was one of the few places she went that she had to drive to, and finding parking was always a pain, but if he was willing to set aside whatever it was he was upset about, the least she could do was go to him. It was late spring, but the sun set early enough to bring the cold air. Norah tucked herself into her jacket as she made her way to his block, noticing the unusual quiet of the city.

She passed the French bakery where she and Chris had taken a bread-baking class once, and she smiled at the memory. She passed the boutique she told herself she would check out a million times but never had, and the glorious butter smell of popcorn wafted out of the doors of Mr. Poppin's Popcorn Shop. Her stomach grumbled audibly.

When she passed the Mast General Store, she stopped to peek in the windows. The store was enormous and always had the most random and fun finds. She glanced wide-eyed at the window, displaying an RFID wallet. Chris was paranoid that someone would walk past him and steal all his credit cards. Norah teased that she was either going to get him an RFID wallet or a tinfoil hat to wear.

She checked her watch to see if she had enough time to go in, and looked back up at the display long enough for her eyes to fall on a sheet metal sign that read *Home is Where the Heart Is*. An image showed two small kids from behind, sitting on a porch step, laughing with each other. He with a blue baseball cap, she with her pigtails; two bikes were thrown down haphazardly beside them. A memory of Sam flying down the street on his bike, Norah beside him on hers, keeping in perfect pace with each other, came to mind.

The familiar feelings of loss and guilt gripped Norah's stomach. She stood a moment longer before turning from the display, the wallet forgotten.

She walked into Chris's apartment to the delicious smells of Antonio's pizza and buffalo wings, and the sound of Stevie Wonder crooning softly in the background.

"Hello!" she called out as Chris turned the corner into his living room. His eyes lit up with his smile, greeting her warmly. Norah felt the tension in her shoulders fade as he leaned in towards her for a quick kiss hello.

He took her jacket from her and led her into the small kitchen off to the left of the living room, and the delicious smells grew stronger.

"It just got here," he said as he collected two plates and some napkins.

Norah glanced over the pictures on his refrigerator she had seen a million times before. Chris and his dad, Chris and his sister Kate, Kate with her husband and two boys. Chris's whole apartment was full of pictures. Family, college buddies, old baseball team photos from high school. He even had a couple of pictures of him and her. One was tucked casually in the mirror of his dresser, and one was amongst the shrine of friends and family on his fridge, held by a Cancun, Mexico, magnet he got on his spring break junior year.

Norah could only think of one photo she had displayed in her apartment.

"Want me to grab the drinks?" she asked as she opened the fridge and quickly scanned its contents.

"Yeah, umm, I didn't grab any beer or anything."

"Oh, okay."

"Yeah, sorry. I just didn't feel like it, you know? There's soda in there. Can you just grab me water?" His eyes never met hers as he reached for the glasses.

"Yeah, of course, no problem. I'm good with water, too."

Norah took one last look at the shelves in the fridge before closing it.

Chris led the way back into the living room, and they sat together on the couch a few inches apart from each other. Norah considered scooting closer, but was still uncertain of the state of their Valley.

Norah reached for her plate right as Chris cleared his throat. "I know we haven't talked about the other night." Norah's eyes flickered down to her food as her mouth began to water. "I just wanted to check in with you, see if things are good?"

Norah furrowed her eyebrows. "Me? Yeah, *I'm* good. What do you mean?"

"You know you need to talk about Sam for me to understand when you react to certain things, right? I can only assume the other night was about Sam, but I also don't know what I did wrong if you don't tell me."

"Chris, what are you talking about?"

"Norah, you got mad at me when we got home the other night. I suggested we build a pillow bed in the living room to watch a movie. It took me a minute to understand your reaction, and I am sorry for my response towards you. If you'd talked to me, then I'd know better. I know Sam was more than your best friend—he was a brother to you. If I suggested something triggering, I'd understand."

Norah groaned and slammed her plate down on the coffee table in front of her.

"That's what this is about? I wasn't mad." Mad wasn't the right word, but she didn't know how to explain that to Chris any more than she had the night he wanted to watch the movie. She knew it was a poor reaction–could feel the tension she was causing–but didn't know how to stop it.

"You refused to answer me. You practically wouldn't look at me and left minutes later."

"It was not minutes. Can we please not do this? I just want to eat. I'm starving." She was doing it again, and just like before, didn't know how to stop herself. He was trying to talk through it like normal adults did, but she couldn't allow it. To let Chris in meant she'd have to face things she wasn't ready for.

Chris huffed, but kept quiet for a moment, picking at his wings. She took her first bite of pizza and reached inward for the courage to explain what had upset her that night. Why such a seemingly normal thing to do, like building a comfortable spot on the floor to watch a movie, triggered something so deep in her.

Norah looked over at him, eating his chicken wings a little more aggressively than usual, his six-foot-two-inch frame crouched low, his knees working hard to balance his plate. His ears doing a semi-decent job of holding his dark, wavy hair out of his eyes and away from his mouth, but not perfectly, as a few strands made their way loose. She had the desire to reach out and tuck them back, but stopped herself.

The guilt of her attitude settled deep within her. He was right; she was put off the other night by the suggestion. He couldn't have known it would upset her. She needed to apologize; she needed to explain why such a silly thing upset a nerve deep within her.

They would have liked each other in high school. He being one of those men who grew into his looks, and she was someone who never quite saw her own. He was the quiet reader; she the loud, energetic one, a trait of hers that drew Sam to her, as well. She'd always been a talker.

Yeah, Chris would have liked her.

"Do you remember how bad the pizza at O'Connell's was?"

Chris instantly exploded with laughter. "The worst," he said, his frame relaxing. The tension in his shoulders dropped, and his back straightened just a little. "Who in the world names a pizza place an Irish name?"

"Maybe they were trying to stand out, get some attention." She shrugged while taking another bite of her delicious, authentic Italian pizza. "Their tagline was *The Irish do everything better.*"

"That's hilarious." Chris settled his plate on the table as he reached for another slice.

"Wait," Norah said, thinking back. "I thought you liked it? I remember because I thought you were either crazy or had the worst taste in pizza. Thankfully, you got Antonucci's the next time we had it, so I was reassured," she said, emphasizing Antonucci's with her right hand raised, shaking in front of her, thumb pressed to all four fingers.

"That was one of our first dates, and I was so nervous to tell you how awful it was because you picked it and I didn't want to upset you." Chris smiled, chicken and pizza grease rimming his lips, yet somehow Norah still wanted to kiss him.

Norah nearly choked on her sip of water. "No way! I was saying how bad it was."

"Still, I didn't want you to blame yourself for picking a bad place."

# CHAPTER 3

THE FOLLOWING DAY, CELESTE STROLLED AIMLESSLY through the gardens, a common area that joined the Great Hall, and its looming "boardroom" (where she'd hoped to never have to go back to), and the Guardian Tower, where all the guardians watched over and guided their Souls.

Out of the two, the Great Hall was the building with walls; it was where the Council worked and held their more private meetings, such as the one Celeste found herself in the previous day. The area across the garden, where the Guardians and those in training worked, stood the Guardian Tower.

The Tower helped the Guardians align timing and structure to their day, but mandatory "office hours" weren't a true concept there. The work of a Guardian could be done anywhere within the Guardian afterlife, but having the Guardian Tower gave a distinct place to work to help encourage the divide between work and personal time.

The building was an open space with spiral staircases connecting the floors. With every day full of sunshine, surrounded by greenery and flowers so colorful and beautiful they exceed one's wildest imagination, who would build walls and block that out?

The garden was a central location of the Guardian area of the afterlife; across the way was a large field where everyone could gather, relax, and socialize a little. Beyond that were the living quarters. Everyone had their own room, but all—except the members of the Council—were restricted in how they could design it, as simplicity and uniformity allowed for fewer distractions. It was difficult work being a part of a Soul's life, and once you became a full-fledged Guardian, you were responsible for up to thirty Souls at once.

Celeste touched the soft pink petals of the peonies and leaned in slowly to inhale the sweet smell. She was stalling, and she knew it. Yesterday's blow hit her hard, and it was taking everything in her to regroup and get back to it.

She did truly love it here. Some said the downfall of choosing a job in the afterlife, especially one as stringent as a Guardian, was that you didn't get to choose your surroundings. Beyond just their living quarters, if Celeste wanted to, she could have made her eternal resting place into whatever her heart desired. She could have lived in the world of Don Quixote, going on adventure after adventure. She could have finally become a famous pianist, playing to a crowd in a grand town hall every night. A dream that followed her in most of her own lives, but sadly, she never did get the chance to learn. She could have settled nicely in a home of her choosing. Brightly painted with all the colors she could imagine, a large porch outside with an overstuffed chair for reading, looking out along a beautiful lake where the sun was always shining, with a big old dog sleeping soundly at her feet.

Here, not only were there restrictions on how her living space could be decorated, not only was she always to be dressed in all white (the aura didn't develop until after she officially graduated), but the worst of it all, they were not allowed to own any pets. Nevertheless, she wouldn't have it any other way. There was something about helping Souls crossover into their afterlife, one of their choosing, that pulled at Celeste the moment she got there. She needed to be there to help Souls, and she couldn't imagine herself doing anything else.

She dedicated all her time to the job. The others, Guardians and Trainees together, made the time to do things with each other, build friendships. Not Celeste. Other than the occasional forced fun activities, like the bingo nights, she dedicated everything she had to her first Soul. All Guardians took their position seriously; it's why they were the Souls chosen for the role in the first place. But Celeste felt a pull that the others didn't seem to. Lately, it had become all-consuming; even Benny began to show frustration at her relentlessness. Going to the Council was Celeste's last resort.

At this point, Norah may never cross over. Celeste didn't know what she was going to do.

Celeste caught the eye of a Guardian named Eli as he walked through the garden and smiled. He'd always been pleasant during their brief conversations. Perhaps this was her sign to expand her world here and make some friends. She'd never stop fighting for her Soul's success—she simply couldn't, even if she tried. But she *could* give herself grace. A familiar voice came from behind.

"Sorry about the big, scary room yesterday," Benny said, coming up beside her. "Even up here, we love to feel powerful."

Celeste gave a forced but warm smile. "Yeah, I wasn't alive during 'boardroom' days, but I see why Humans hate them so much. Simply watching from up here doesn't do the nerves justice."

Benny laughed. "We've definitely taken their intimidation tactics." He took a quick look around the garden. "What are you doing out here?"

"I'm stalling," she admitted, and Benny nodded in understanding.

"Yesterday was hard, and I'm sorry you didn't get the outcome you wanted. I see how hard you work, Celeste. I see how important this job is to you. It's why I was so happy to back you; that, and I was a little afraid you were going to kill us both with how much work you were putting in." She couldn't stop her laugh despite her mood.

"You are my most dedicated Trainee. I know you just want to do what's best for your Soul. They'll learn their Lesson, and if they don't, that's okay, too. We never want that, but sometimes we do all that we can, and they still don't make it over. It honestly seems like it is getting harder and harder to get them across; you can't beat yourself up over it."

Celeste deflated. "Isn't that part of the problem?" She grumbled. "We used to have it easier–not *easy*–but an easier time bringing people to enlightenment. When I first started, I'd watch the Guardians, and their jobs seemed so fulfilling. Now, we're lucky if we get someone past the finish line once every couple of hundred years. The Humans are too caught up in their material things, expectations from others, and themselves, their boardrooms. All of it stops them from seeing what's important."

Benny nodded, remaining silent, allowing Celeste to work through her thoughts.

"I know that it's not our job to intervene, and I don't want to hand them the playbook, but this one is so close. I know it. Norah just can't seem to get this one final Lesson."

"The final lesson is often the hardest," Benny said. "You are a great Trainee, and Muriel was right; we don't get to win them all." He leaned in and lowered his voice a notch. "As long as you are very careful and don't get caught, I am sure you can nudge this one over the line."

Celeste sat staring out ahead of her, feeling Benny watching her with that Benny smirk of his, allowing her to process his words. It finally came. "Wait, what? What are you saying?"

"Look, they allow Guardian interaction far more frequently than old Reggie wants you to believe. You're the hardest-working Trainee I have ever had. Hell, you work harder than some of the Guardians I know. If you feel at a loss, and I know you've tried everything you could, I think you deserve a chance to go down."

Celeste choked back tears. Benny recognized her hard work *and* was allowing her to go down to Earth. It was enough to overlook his use of the h-e-l-l word.

"Still," he continued, his tone firm, "it is extremely risky and I do understand why they can't let every Guardian go down."

Celeste picked her jaw off her lap and asked, "But how? I'm a Trainee, I'm Marked. The Council would know if I left."

"Actually, it's not just because you are a Trainee. Only members of the Council can go down to Earth or send another Guardian. That's where I come in. You can cross as long as I send you through and bring you back. It is like popping in and out of places around here, except I have to be the one to do it for you. Like you said, you're Marked. The Council would know."

It took everything in Celeste not to hug Benny. "I promise to be careful."

"And remember—when you go, you cannot directly interfere. I mean it, Celeste. You are still guiding, not handing them the playbook. Norah still has to learn the Lesson on her own."

"Okay, but we help from up here all the time. It's what we do."

"We put them in situations that prompt good and bad choices. You know this. We put up roadblocks to prevent them from going to see a bad ex. We throw up career opportunities that point them to their passions. But they still have to make the decision to go or not to go on their own. We cannot interfere to the extent that they don't work through the Lessons enough to truly learn them. The Council will infer that she did not learn the Lesson fully, and therefore, will not deem the Lesson complete."

And with this being Norah's last Lesson in her last life—Celeste's breath caught in her chest at the thought. Maybe it was too risky for her to go, but if she didn't go and Norah didn't learn the Lesson, she'd never forgive herself for not trying harder.

Benny continued, "And she cannot–*cannot*–learn who you are." Benny's face was the most stern Celeste had ever seen. "Humans aren't meant to grasp the enormity of the Universe and all that comes with it. To comprehend that they have a Guardian Angel who watches over them...they'd never handle it well. They'd never learn their Lessons, and this," he spread his arms out wide before him, "as we know it would be gone.

"The Council will know right away that I was involved because you're Marked. You are under my watch with this being your first full Soul Guardianship. If the Council finds out I let you go, we could both be in some very hot water for going against their orders."

"Then what do I do, exactly?" she asked.

"It would be best if you kept your distance as much as possible, but you'll obviously have to interact a little..." Benny tapped his chin while he pondered the options. "I need you to be as much of a bystander as possible. Be more *nosy neighbor who asks too many questions and gets on her nerves*, less *close friend*. Getting too close to Norah will cause too much room for error, and you cannot slip up."

"I promise; no direct interference, no obvious nudges. I promise."

"I'm going to give you three months." Celeste began to protest. Three months to help Norah on a Lesson she hadn't been able to get in all her lifetimes thus far didn't seem fair. Benny silenced her quickly. "Anymore than that, Celeste, and the Council will start to notice your absence. It's plenty of time to get her on the right path," he said, as if he could read her mind.

Celeste agreed, and then, she simply could not resist. She hugged her mentor.

# CHAPTER 4

# *Norah*

"BARB, DO YOU EVER GET THE FEELING THAT YOU ARE being watched?" Norah sat at work thinking about the feeling she had been unable to shake these last few days. The tingle at the back of her neck, the goosebumps along her arms as she walked down the street, the mysterious shadow on the wall, a flash of color out of the corner of her eye.

"Honey, it's been a very long time since anyone's eyes have lingered my way."

"Oh, please, you're a catch. What about what's-his-face?" Norah snapped her fingers while names ran through her head. "Frank! He comes in and always leaves flowers."

Barb scoffed. "Those are because of your brownies, not because of my failing looks. I'm good with it. I've got my Janet, Mariah, and Whitney to keep me company."

"Barb." Norah rolled her eyes playfully. "I get that you love your cats, but damn, don't you miss *it*?" Not the direction Norah had intended for the conversation to go, but if Barb could pester her about her personal life and lack of friends, Norah could poke at Barb for her lack of a man.

"Of course I do. What I don't miss is the headache that comes with it."

A woman approached Norah's window with a question about her insurance, and Norah's focus was pulled back to work.

For the next several hours, her mind kept wandering back to that feeling. She eventually chalked it up to the time of year–Sam's anniversary. Always an unsettling feeling, to say the least. This year marked the third anniversary. All those feelings that crept up the months leading up to the date should have started to become familiar, but becoming more irritable, the desire to be even more isolated, seemed to still sneak up on her. She anticipated the rush of her grief, pain, loneliness, and guilt that arrived with the anniversary date. She knew the obviousness of it all would once again catch her off guard.

For some people, there were moments in life that marked a before and after. Events that were so big, the timeline cuts to the years, months, days, and minutes before it happened and after it happened. The shift could occur with happy events, too, of course. Before and after getting married, before and after college, or after becoming a parent.

But it was different from the sad events. A weight to them that never let up. Events that marked identity differently from the happy times. Something in the way someone holds their shoulders, the way their eyes see and are seen, the hint of a pull in their laughter, as if they can't quite let it out too loudly. Sadness could change a person so fiercely that they are left with no other choice but the before and the after. A divorce. The sudden loss of a home. The death of a loved one.

Norah's mind drifted to Sam as she busied herself with the menial tasks of the day, organizing the various requisition forms for her boss, Dr. Ross, and filing the new patient and consent forms in their proper places.

*They stood together at the base of the tree, necks both straining to look to the tippy-top. Sam looked a little green in the face; Norah vibrated with excitement.*

*"Do we have to?" he asked.*

*"Come on, your dad said they used to do it all the time. I'll go first, and you can follow me up." Sam placed his hand on his stomach and took a deep breath in through his nose. "On second*

thought," Norah said, "you go first and I'll make sure you're good from behind."

"I don't know why I always get myself into things with you," he grumbled.

"Because I make everything fun," she said. He gripped the branch closest to him, his small hand making its way around only half its width. His sandy blonde hair lifted in the breeze. Norah was grateful for the relief from the hot summer sun. He heaved himself onto the first resting spot and waited for her to make her way up.

"See, easy," she said. "Let's keep going."

He scowled. She beamed.

"I'm right behind you. I won't let you fall. You trust me, right?"

They climbed up and up, and Norah could see he was getting a rhythm to it, each placement of his foot planted more confidently than the last. The heat continued to beat down on them even with the breeze, and he'll blame his sweaty palms for years, but he wouldn't blame her, never her.

It happened so quickly, she didn't have a chance to react, let alone reach out and catch him, something Mr. Bryers assured her countless times she would have never been able to do anyway. She watched in horror as Sam toppled down. He hit his shoulder hard on one branch, his knee on another, and his right arm broke instantly on impact with the ground.

Norah's heart raced as she climbed down as quickly as she could. Sam had the wind knocked out of him, and it took him a moment to catch his breath. The realization settled, and then came the pain. The bone stuck grotesquely from his skin, more blood than Norah had ever witnessed in her ten years.

Sam screamed in pain between choked sobs.

"It's okay, Sam, you're going to be okay," Norah said without a hint of a quiver in her voice.

She knelt beside him, doing her best to calm him down, never losing her cool as she got him to inhale and exhale. She forced *him to look at her directly. "I'm going to go get your dad, okay? I'll be right back." She ran down the street to the Bryers' house, where Mr. Bryers was trimming the hedges in the front yard. She explained quickly what happened, grabbing his arm to follow as she talked, and he ran back with her to help Sam.*

*It was that experience that inspired Norah to become a doctor. She would always remember the calmness that overcame her as she did her best to assess the situation. How the blood and bone didn't bother her, but rather fascinated her. How desperately she wanted to help Sam in that moment, and was frustrated at not knowing how to. She stuck by his side the whole ride to the hospital, as he was getting his cast, and begged to come to every doctor's appointment after that.*

Norah looked around the diagnostics center, at her desk, where she checked patients in and out every day. She never got to see them for medical needs or to help them with any real impact. She called their names back for their appointments, filed their paperwork, and answered the occasional insurance question.

It was only right that she was cut short in her career, only fair.

Sam had trusted her to climb the tree; he trusted her that he wouldn't get hurt, but he did. Yet, in all their years, he never stopped trusting her.

# CHAPTER 5

## Celeste

IT WASN'T EXACTLY MAGIC. IT OFTEN ANNOYED HER to hear it described that way when new Souls arrived. She couldn't move objects with her mind, or snap her fingers to clean up a mess, and although she could teleport in the Guardian afterlife, she couldn't while on Earth. But she did understand why they thought it was magic. There really was no other way to describe it. It was simply the way things worked. Everything Celeste needed, or imagined, was right at her fingertips.

A magic of convenience.

The apartment building, tucked neatly at the corner of Main and fifth, *conveniently* close to the coffee shop Norah frequented, had one empty apartment on the bottom floor. The landlord smiled politely and handed her the keys without a word about background checks and first and last month's rent.

Celeste placed her hand on the doorknob of the apartment, imagined the most perfect downtown apartment a girl could dream of, and opened the door to a fully-furnished space with all the colorful things Celeste loved. A teal pillowy couch fit the room perfectly, and a small fireplace was tucked into the corner with a purple reading chair diagonally across from it. Walls the color of watermelon and fuchsia with prints of strawberries and chunky floral art, and hanging plants in every free space. The kitchen brimmed with canary yellow, creamsicle orange, and cyan blue, decorated with her favorite Earth animal, the rooster, scattered throughout.

When Celeste needed clothes to wear, she envisioned a closet of the most fun clothes she could and opened it to more skirts and tops than she could ever need, bursting with all the shapes and colors one could dream of.

When she first arrived on Earth, she allowed herself some time to walk around the city. Well, walk was a strong word when she continuously found herself snubbing the sidewalk with her tennis shoe too hard, or tripping over a protruding tree root. She was there for Norah and only Norah, but, gosh, was it fun to be in the middle of a world she had only been watching from a distance for hundreds of years.

Celeste's last life ended in 1638.

The Guardians adopted their fair share of inventions and practices from what they saw on Earth. Good and bad–but not all things used on Earth were necessary in the afterlife, and getting to see it all up close was more exciting than Celeste expected. The smells alone were mind-blowing. There was something about the smoky burn of the exhaust on a car she rather enjoyed. But she was not so pleased with some perfumes people wore.

And speaking of automobiles, she frightened one woman nearly to death when she dodged a few cars trying to cross the road, unable to discern the speed at which they were going. Lots of Souls brought new music with them throughout the centuries. Sometimes bands came and played at Guardian Bingo night! But to hear a guitar riff of a bluegrass tune on one busy street corner, while a saxophone sang the blues on another in the middle of a humming city...well, Celeste didn't think there were many things quite like that.

She made a cup of tea as she walked around her tiny, but very own, space. Admiring all the things she was able to dream up. She hadn't realized how much she missed being able to decorate, and the world allowed for so many more options than when she was alive.

Her mind wandered back to when she first arrived in her afterlife, all those lifetimes ago. As soon as she learned of the role of the Guardian, she knew instantly that it was exactly what she wanted to become. She didn't realize until centuries later how much she'd missed getting to wear and surround herself with whatever color she chose, but still, she didn't regret her decision. Most Souls chose comfort; it takes a special few to dedicate their remaining existence to being a Guardian, watching over others. The most important jobs are the most difficult and the most thankless, but Celeste wouldn't change it for all the colors in the world.

She reflected on some of the rules she was originally introduced to: Guardians are to live a simple life to ensure little distraction and full commitment. They must wear all white. They have their own living space; however, their living quarters are in a shared area within the Guardian afterlife. All living quarters are to be up to code and minimalistic. No pets allowed, as taking care of another was far too great of a distraction. (Admittedly, that one gave Celeste a moment of pause.) While the Council believed in reducing distractions, friendships amongst your fellow Guardians are encouraged.

Each Guardian goes through a training period with one Soul, guiding them in their lives and Lessons, with the training and support from their very own Mentor. The Council tests Trainees' capabilities multiple times throughout their training by giving them various tasks to perform with their Soul. An example may be how well the Trainee transmits a dream to their Soul to guide a problem they are having. Another would be how well the Trainee plants an action of kindness for a stranger while maintaining the Soul's own free will.

Once the Trainee's Soul completes their Lessons and the Council deems a Guardian's training complete, a Guardian will be assigned more than one Soul to guide.

Guardians monitor their Souls during various periods throughout the Soul's day, frequency dependent on the Guardian's preference; however, Guardians must obey privacy rules.

Guardians are allowed to retire; everyone is entitled to the afterlife of their choosing, or request a new assignment should they feel they are not connecting with their Soul enough to provide the ultimate Guiding Experience. (Guardians can also be asked by the Council to retire or change assignments).

Lastly, under no circumstance can a Guardian be assigned a Soul they knew in Life.

This last one overcomplicated things. Clouds one's judgement. Or so they said. Celeste always found this to be the silliest of the rules. It was a very strenuous process to weed this one out, one Celeste never fully followed, but the Council loved their complex processes as much as they loved their big boardrooms. When they chose and assigned a Trainee their first Soul, they required the Trainee to report if they knew their Soul in one of their lifetimes, as a failsafe. If so, the Soul would be reassigned.

But, if the Council did find out that a Trainee knew them previously but didn't report it, this could have some pretty serious consequences, like a suspension from Guardian duties, or worst of all, being fired. Too much bias led to too much directing and not enough guiding. Yet another distraction they did their best to mitigate. It was important to begin with a clean slate when working with a Soul.

The typical training path was to work with the Mentor for one full Soul. Souls lived so many different lives, each with their own unique experiences, that a Trainee was able to learn a great deal from them, and the Mentor was there to guide them. Once the Soul has completed their Lessons (or it has been deemed by the Council that they are unable to), the Council members then hold a vote to decide if a Trainee has completed their training to become a full Guardian. Guardians can then watch over more than one Soul at a time.

A Guardian's role was to guide. Never interfere. All those gut feelings people get? That was their Guardian. It felt like a nudge, a sensation, when a person knows deep down what the right thing to do is. Guardians and Trainees couldn't interfere directly, so they had to mask it as their Soul's own internal feelings, as it was the only way to provide direction. The problem was this: Not only are humans stubborn, but they also trust others' opinions more than their own. Made a lot of work for Guardians, especially in the more recent years. Loads of distractions, less and less faith.

It was a frustrating process. But when Souls got it, when they trusted those feelings and instincts and allowed themselves to hear the right answers and to learn those Lessons. Ah! What an amazing feeling for the Guardians.

Celeste had watched over Norah for her previous five lives, her current one being the sixth. She was so close to being done with her training she could taste it, but her need to get Norah to learn the final Lesson went beyond her training and finally becoming an official, fully-fledged Guardian. She was genuinely proud of Norah and all she'd accomplished, all the Life Lessons she learned. Lifetimes of growth. Norah allowed herself to get stuck, that was all, and Celeste was there to set her straight again.

Celeste snuggled up in her purple chair, the warmth of the fireplace bringing comfort. The remaining chill of winter had crept back in once the sun went down, and a heavy sigh escaped her as her bones thawed. She hadn't taken into account the heaviness of gravity on Earth and what it would do to her old joints.

She closed her eyes and thought of how Norah was doing. The sound of the crackling fire lulling her to sleep. Celeste had been watching Norah for what felt like eons, but as for the Norah in this particular life, years. Thirty-two to be exact. Not every minute of every day, of course, but admittedly, Celeste kept an eye on Norah more often than most Guardians.

A Guardian could only check in on the Souls they had been assigned, and those they interact with, but essentially, that Guardian's Souls are the main characters. When watching a Soul, it was like looking at a giant hole in the sky or the floor, whichever angle one preferred, but always from a distance, wherever the Soul might be located. Like balcony seats in a theater, where the seat shifted around to see the whole stage.

Most Guardians loved their work, looking after their Souls, but had no problem shutting that part of the day off to enjoy a little of their own social life and have a bit of fun. Unless, of course, one was a certain Guardian-in-training named Celeste, who took full advantage of the time she had to check in on Norah as often as she could.

It was nice being down on Earth, to be so close to Norah.

Her eyes shot open.

Celeste was going to need to find a way to watch over Norah from her fireplace chair.

# CHAPTER 6

## Celeste

Over the last week, Celeste did her best to keep her distance. While mindful of keeping an eye on Norah, she didn't want to interact just yet. She feared saying or doing too much too soon and needed time to come up with a game plan on how to talk with Norah without oversharing.

But, without the vantage point of being high in the sky, so to speak, it was much harder to watch over her. A flaw Celeste hadn't thought about before defying the Council and putting her own personal longings first.

She hadn't been able to get any real intel on how things were going for Norah and thought that if she could just get close enough to overhear a phone call or a self-directed murmur, anything. She was desperate.

But that desperation led to sloppiness. That and the fact that Celeste was still trying to find her footing in all this gravity. Impossible.

And while Celeste fantasized often about meeting Norah, she never imagined it'd happen over spilled coffee in a coffee shop.

Celeste stared wide-eyed, but kept her lips glued shut, as the hot coffee rolled down Norah's arm and onto the floor.

Norah shifted her long, dark hair from her right shoulder to her left, doing her best not to give the liquid additional coverage. The shock of the incident no longer heavy on her face.

"I am so sorry," Celeste said, finally finding her voice. Cursing herself for tailing Norah just a tad too closely.

"It's no problem," Norah said, her attention on the barista as she asked for napkins. Her calm and reassuring tone filled Celeste with a sense of pride. She had witnessed some rather rude interactions since arriving on Earth, and Norah held her composure well. Especially after having had some crazy person dump coffee all over her.

So much for not getting too close yet. It was still okay; Benny said to be a bystander, he knew she would need to interact a little. The problem was, Celeste didn't trust herself not to do too much, an urge she was already having a difficult time containing.

The coffee shop quieted, all attention focused on Norah and Celeste. Celeste scanned the room, shrinking at their gawking eyes. It was 5:00 p.m. How many people needed coffee at 5:00 p.m.?

The young barista behind the counter handed Norah a handful of napkins as another none-too-happy barista came around with an additional stack to clean it up off the floor.

Celeste stood awkwardly, unsure of how to help, and Norah glanced up at her for the first time. "It's fine, really," she said.

Celeste, still feeling the sting of embarrassment, couldn't help but smile at hearing Norah's words directed at her. Surreal. Luckily, Norah had already shifted her focus to dabbing at the liquid on her shirt.

Her white shirt. It couldn't have just been a splash from the top, nope. This was a full-on dump and drop.

One thing she simply could not understand about the people down on Earth was why they chose 'style' over fun. She glanced down at her own ensemble. She was wearing green cotton tights, with a pink corduroy skirt and an oversized black knit sweater with a very exciting array of circles, triangles, and stars, all in varying sizes in every neon color one could think of. The offset of her blonde curls enhanced the vibrant feel. It was one of her favorite outfits so far.

People in the coffee shop began to shuffle back to their previous focuses, the excitement passing quickly.

This was a bad idea. The Council, the eight members who chose, trained, and oversaw all the Guardians, the ones who voted on if she was ready to even become a Guardian, had distinctly told her she was not allowed to come and interfere in Norah's life. She had disobeyed their direct order.

No, she had three months to get this right; she couldn't spend it second-guessing herself.

It would be fine; bumping into Norah didn't mean she would be Celeste's best friend and tell her all the secrets of the universe.

"May I buy you a new shirt?" Celeste blurted out.

She could mail it to her, still keep her distance.

She reached first for Norah's napkin pile, then towards the barista's to try and help in any way she could. They both had it covered.

Norah continued to dab away at the half-soaked shirt.

That was one of the many reasons why tea was the superior drink. It wouldn't have caused nearly the damage if it were tea she was dapping off her shirt.

"It's no big deal, really," Norah said.

Celeste chirped eagerly, "I am more than happy to!" She fiddled with the ends of her curls. She took a quick glance and pointed to the lanyard hanging from Norah's neck. "Is that where you work?" she asked, feigning innocence. "Can I drop something off to you there tomorrow?"

*What is wrong with you?* Celeste scolded herself. It was like she couldn't stop.

Norah looked at Celeste, eyebrows raised.

Celeste took a step back, realizing she had come on too strong. "I'm sorry. I just really feel terrible. I can be such a clutz."

The bustle of the coffee shop was back in full swing. Baristas called out names for order pick ups, and patrons began their murmured conversations again.

Norah smiled softly and gave Celeste her full attention for the first time since their collision. "It's okay, really. Things happen. I have a sweater to throw on."

Celeste took a moment for her pulse to settle. Norah stood in front of her. Real. She could reach out and touch her if she wanted. It was as if a gap that spanned centuries was suddenly closed, and Celeste was finally *home*.

A feeling Celeste hadn't realized she lacked until then.

Celeste may have always been able to see Norah before, but this was different. Tangible. She was shorter than Norah, which caught Celeste by surprise as she had been certain she was much taller. Norah's slim figure, wrapped in warm golden-brown skin and her long, dark hair were the antithesis of Celeste's fuller frame, light-pinkish complexion, and wild curly blonde hair.

Celeste had to stop herself from asking if Chris was still upset with her from a couple of weekends ago, from telling her how great he was, and not to give up on that one. She also desperately wanted to ask about Barb from work, as she was hilarious. Celeste really missed her cat stories. Or if Paul, Norah's unusually tall neighbor, was still having trouble with the mail carrier, odd that one. So much could happen in a week; she was certain she missed too much already.

These thoughts were precisely why Celeste needed to keep her distance between them.

Yet, Norah's big brown eyes stared back at her. Celeste. Looking back at her as if she were a complete stranger. A feeling in Celeste stirred that she couldn't quite put her finger on. Disappointment didn't feel like a strong enough word.

But then Norah tilted her head slightly, a faint pull in her brow.

*No. Wishful thinking.*

The past week was a lesson in humility. Celeste came charging down to Earth as if seeing was knowing. It was not. She learned a lot about how the physical world had changed since she was last there. Calling herself a clutz was rather generous. She also hadn't expected people to be so rude! She saw it happen often enough, of course. Guardians and Trainees alike would all gossip about it like one would when watching a reality television show, but when it was directed at Celeste, well, let's just say it was not a fun feeling.

But Norah, looking through her, was the most discomfort she had felt since arriving.

Celeste was there to do her job, and no matter how difficult it was, she could not afford to be so sloppy. Being as direct as running right into Norah and spilling her coffee all over her was unacceptable. She needed to find another way.

The behind-the-counter barista handed Norah a fresh cup of coffee, and Norah, turning to leave, glanced back at Celeste once more. "Well," she said as politely as one could after just having their coffee spilled all over them by a stranger, "bye." She waved and walked towards the door.

No hint of having just come across a multilife companion who looked out for her best interest.

Celeste stood and watched as Norah left the shop and stepped out onto the busy sidewalk outside. Celeste wished she could follow her close behind.

# CHAPTER 7

## *Norah*

N ORAH PARKED HER CAR ACROSS THE STREET FROM THE bar in the same parking lot she had parked in several times that month. Which was better than being there weekly, which had been better than daily. Growth.

Chris would be frustrated, she was sure of it, but as long as she stuck to one or two drinks, she'd be fine. He wouldn't even know. The month of Sam's anniversary hit her hard every year, and it felt as if it was getting harder and harder; she needed this.

She grabbed the sweater from her back seat in an attempt to cover up the stain along the front of her shirt and laughed out loud to herself. That was exactly why her wardrobe consisted mostly of dark colors. She probably should have been more reassuring to the poor woman; she didn't care about the shirt, and accidents happen. Norah hoped she wasn't too hard on herself about it.

Norah made her way to the door, still thinking about her encounter with the coffee-spill woman, an odd sense of familiarity hanging in the air. Funny how you meet people sometimes that bring that feeling of recognition to you.

*Perhaps I knew her in another life,* she thought.

Norah swung the door open, and a familiar sense of nostalgia hit her as it did each time. Entering the bar was like stepping back in time. The booths hadn't been updated in at least two decades; the varnish on the bartop was worn in all the right places; dust thick on the shelves, clear markings from where the liquor bottles rested making it that much more noticeable, and the smell of years old tobacco seeped from the walls, the only way to get rid of it would be to burn the place down and start new. She found comfort in the old, the established.

She walked in, allowing her eyes to adjust to the dark as she pushed down the feeling of guilt. She'd have one drink—it'd been one of those days—and then she'd go home. She thought the coffee would give her enough energy to make it through the evening, but she needed something stronger than coffee. She checked her watch. It was 5:15 p.m.. She had plenty of time to make it home and have a nice evening with Chris.

"Hey, Norah!" someone shouted from her right.

She turned to see Harry, one of her favorites, sitting in his corner seat. She waved and smiled brightly. "Did the coat and sweaters fit?" she asked.

"Like a glove." He smiled. "They'll be perfect for next winter."

She nodded as she continued to make her way to her seat. "Good. Let me know if you need more. We'll be doing the food drive at work soon; don't be shy with what you need."

"I won't be," he said, cheeks turning red as he sipped on his whiskey.

She pulled her chair and was greeted with a smile and a wave from the other side. "Hey, you're back," said Billy, the bartender.

Norah gave a closed-lipped smile and averted her eyes, settling into the stool. Billy slid a bottle of beer in front of her and began wiping down the bar. He was always moving.

She took her first sip and instantly felt her shoulders relax. She thought of how Jimmy, another regular here, once joked about never needing any vaccines because he drank the draft beer here. She opted for bottles, but still had the faint thought that perhaps she should be wiping the bottle tops before drinking.

Norah focused her gaze on the television above the bar, reading the caption with great intensity as some news anchor delivered the 5:30 news.

"Just getting off work?" Billy asked as he dried glassware.

Norah nodded and took another sip.

"You at the Greenville Diagnostics Center, still?"

Another turn of her stomach. Yes, she *still* chose to work in the medical field, no matter how mundane the work was or how low the pay. The one thing her parents ever did for her was pay for her schooling. She could have used her degrees for any number of things, as plenty of people don't complete their residency and continue on to successful careers. Shit, a lot of medical students don't even get matched with a residency, yet here she was by choice. Still, it made her uncomfortable whenever anyone asked her about what she did for work.

Sam would have been successfully building his career by now.

One beer turned into two as she sat quietly reading the closed captioning on the television. The bar slowly filled in around her as she replayed her work day. Two beers turned to three. She grumbled to herself about the one guy at the Diagnostics Center who went off about the wait time, but then reminded herself that the lab work was for his son, and he was more than likely a bit on edge. She thought of the one label she wrote out on a blood sample for nurse Amy, hoping her handwriting wasn't too difficult to read, and cursed herself for just not starting over.

A guy sat down at the very end of the bar and shouted towards her in greeting. "Hey, Dave," she shouted back.

"Wife misses those brownies you used to bring in here all the time, where ya been?" he asked.

"Oh, around," she said, unable to look his way. She took another sip of beer and thought about the time she tried to teach Chris how to bake brownies. He told her he wanted to learn to do something she loved, and it was the only thing she could think of to show him. Norah tried to stifle the smile that crept along her face. She'd finish this one and be done.

He'd get why this month was so hard if he understood how hard it was to lose someone you loved. Chris grew up in a perfect home with perfect parents and adoring siblings. He didn't understand what it was like to have found a family, only to have lost them suddenly. Especially when it was her fault.

Her cheeks grew hot as she recalled all the moments in the past year and a half where Chris begged her to just explain it to him, but it's not something she could explain. How could she explain that she was to blame for Sam's death and that she'd still have her best friend in her life if she hadn't been so selfish? He couldn't understand how difficult it was to do what most expected of her–to just move on.

Billy placed a new beer in front of her, and Norah took a sip as her mind wandered, as it always did, to Sam.

It was the summer they were both ten, although Sam relentlessly teased her that he was older by one full day. Mr. and Mrs. Bryers took them camping for the first time. Norah remembered the way Mrs. Bryers squealed at anything icky and smiled to herself.

*"John!" Mrs. Bryers shouted. "John, there's something touching my feet."*

*"It's a lake, Maureen, it's probably a pile of old leaves," he said, rolling his eyes with a smile. Mr. Bryers turned to Norah. "Or it's a water snake." He winked.*

*Sam heard him and gasped, dancing around in the water as if he were stepping on hot coals. Mr. Bryers and Norah both toppled over with laughter.*

*They stayed two nights, and there was a pit in Norah's stomach at the end of the second night because she didn't want to go home the next day. She spent a lot of time at the Bryers' house, but this was different. Tucked away in the woods, far away from everything, far away from her house, it was easy for her to feel as if she really was a part of their family. As if John and Maureen were her dad and mom, and Sam, her real brother.*

*"Sam," Norah hissed, trying her best to whisper, something she'd never been good at. She turned on her mini-flashlight but threw the corner of her pillowcase over it to dim the harsh light.*

*A murmur and stir came from the sleeping bag beside her.*

*She tried again. "Sam."*

*"Wha...?" He groaned.*

*Norah watched as he rolled himself toward her and tried his best to open his eyes. "Wanna make a pact?"*

*It took him a moment of blinking before he answered. "Sure," he yawned. "What kind of pact?"*

*"Best friends forever?"*

*Another yawn. Sam loved his sleep. "I thought we already were that."*

*"Okay, what about..." She hesitated a moment, thinking of a way to say it as she moved the light around to watch the shadows on the tent wall. "What about family forever?"*

*"I thought we already were that, too," he said, before rolling back over and falling quickly back to sleep.*

Norah half-noticed the energy shift in the bar as the lights dimmed in preparation for the evening crowd; the volume of the music loud enough people had to shout to be heard over it. The other half of her, the not-so-sober half, was still deep in her daydream.

"Do you think if I take this here rock," she said, as she peeled the soggy coaster from the bottom of her bottle, gripping the round edge with her thumb and forefinger, "I could skip it so smoothly across this lake that it will just jump all these years ahead of me?" Her words slurred as she added, "Take it all away."

With a quick flick of the wrist, the coaster launched inches away from the water's surface. It skimmed and bounced so smoothly, it appeared to be dancing with the sun-kissed ripples it left behind.

Norah lost her balance as she leaned a little too much into the throw.

"Whoa, there, Norah," Billy said as he dodged the coaster then reached across the bar to try and help Norah straighten onto the stool.

Norah brushed her dark hair from her eyes and tried her best impression of someone getting her shit together.

"Okay, okay," she said, drawing each syllable out as she tried to regain some focus. "I need to go, anyway."

She stepped outside to a much darker sky than when she entered, but the cool air instantly hit her face and sobered her a bit. Clear enough to realize she made a slight fool of herself, drunk enough still not to care. It was a good balance.

# CHAPTER 8

## Norah

Norah walked several blocks past her apartment before turning, making her way home. She hoped the extra distance would help to clear her mind—or rather, the alcohol from her system. Something about the crowds of city life allowed her to refocus. So surrounded by others that no one had the capacity to notice one individual. She learned quickly that springtime in the south still got cold in the evening, but on that night, she was grateful for it. She shivered enough to burn through the alcohol even more.

She found Chris pacing the hall outside of her apartment. Gone were the early days of his concern; now only anger hung heavy on his face.

She unlocked her door, and he followed her in. "I'm so sorry, babe." She did her best not to slur, tossing her bag down on the floor. "It was a shit day at work, and then I stopped for coffee on the way home, and some lady spilled my damn coffee all down the side of me. I stopped at the bar for one drink, and time just got away from me."

He breathed heavily through his nose as he scrutinized her up and down. "Norah, you promised," he said, running both hands through his dark hair.

"I'm fine, it's fine." She shrugged. "We can still have our night."

"I–I really can't," he said as he turned to continue his pacing.

"I'm sorry, really. Just let me take a quick shower. I'm good, I promise." She attempted to pull her right arm from her sweater, but became too entangled and gave up midway. Her elbow was bent, tucked to her side, and her wrist rested where her armpit should have been.

He threw his hands up at her. "Do you think being with you like this is fun for me? I want time with *you*, Norah, not drunk you."

"Jesus, Chris, calm down. It's fine."

He scoffed. "Calm down?"

"Come on, I've been good lately. But you know why this is a tough month for me." She managed to get her right arm all the way through her sweater, but kept the left arm comfortably in its place, afraid to start the mess over again.

Chris's whole body stiffened as his eyes darkened. "No, I don't, Norah. You don't talk to me about anything. No, I don't know."

She rolled her eyes, losing her balance slightly before righting herself. "Not this again."

"And you honestly think this is better? How do you expect us to have a relationship if you can't see what you are doing?"

Norah let out a cackle. "A relationship?"

"Oh, that's funny to you?"

She continued to laugh. "Fighting for a year and a half is most definitely a relationship." She was sober enough to see the hurt in his eyes before he turned away to reach for the door. "I'm sorry," she said again, throwing her loose hand up to stop him from going. "That was mean, and I am sorry. Of course, I don't want us to fight. I promise I'm okay. I want to hang out tonight. I'm going to go shower, and when I get back, we'll both be better, and we'll have a nice night together, okay?"

She walked away from him and made her way back to the bedroom, removing her clothes as she went, stumbling a bit right at the finish line, onto the bed. She sat hunched over, working her way to getting back up and into the shower. She needed to first catch her bearings. Sit for a minute. If she lay her head down for just two minutes, then she'd be right as rain. Just fifteen minutes.

IT WAS DARK OUTSIDE. HER HEAD THROBBED, AND HER mouth felt as if she had licked one hundred cotton balls before falling asleep. Her heart raced in that way that made her feel as if she'd done something wrong–if only she could put her finger on what. Sadly, the only thing missing was her need to pee, and Norah would have felt almost normal. She must not have been asleep too long.

She rolled off the edge of the bed, first her feet, then her legs, and finally, she managed to lift her head and chest from the mattress. She pulled on an oversized pair of sweatpants and grabbed the first T-shirt she put her fingers on from the bottom drawer. She went in search of the holy grail of water, stumbling her way through the living room of her tiny one-bedroom apartment, thankful for the clear path.

She made her way into the kitchen, unsteady hand reaching for the refrigerator, but stopped when she noticed the note stuck to the door.

*I've tried Norah.* It read.
*I've really, really tried. I'll call you when I'm ready to talk.*

She let out a heavy sigh, crinkled the little paper with one hand, and tossed it onto the counter.

Yet another loss that was all her fault.

The gravity of it would hit her tomorrow, but for now, she solved the problem the only way she knew how. Norah reached into the fridge and grabbed a beer before heading back to bed.

The clock on the stove read 11:37 p.m.

# CHAPTER 9

# *Celeste*

FOLLOWING SOMEONE WAS A TERRIBLY AWKWARD business, but Celeste didn't trust herself around Norah. If only her gifts worked for spying as well, Norah would be close enough to see and hear while Celeste kept far enough a distance to go unnoticed at all times. Unfortunately, it didn't work that way.

So there she stood, across the street from Norah's apartment, tucked as much as she could be behind a maple tree, watching, and desperately missing her perch from above.

She watched through the new, but unfortunately sparse, leaves of the maple tree as Norah stumbled her way into her apartment. Dread filled her stomach. Celeste's mind went instantly to thoughts of Chris. He tried his hardest to be there for Norah, and she refused to see how much he cared for her. She worried it was only a matter of time before he had enough; that he was going to hit his limit soon.

Celeste also tried her best to get Norah to stop drinking. It was hard enough to get a Soul to pick up on signs, and even harder if they lacked a clear head most of the time, but when Norah's ultimate goal was to punish herself, no amount of unsavory outcome was too much.

Right after Sam died, Norah spiraled. Benny sat with Celeste for hours as they watched over her together. She trusted

Benny as her Mentor, and all the ways he showed her how to help, but Celeste couldn't accept that their role of Guardianship meant there were limits to what they could do. It never felt like enough; it always felt as if there was more she could have been doing.

Celeste pushed out her chest to stretch her upper back and wrapped herself tightly in the puffy pink jacket she wore. She was continuously surprised by how cold it got once the sun went down. A sensation her body had long forgotten and one she did not wish to become accustomed to. She rather liked the sun and the warmth and the continuous, perfect weather back home.

She let out a long yawn and leaned her right shoulder into the maple tree. Celeste had been there for all the other lives that made this Life Lesson all that much more difficult for Norah. There was Thomas, August, Eugène–Oh, Eugène. Celeste knew that Norah's soul hadn't quite healed from the pain of Eugène's life—such an unimaginable circumstance—and when Sam died, Celeste knew it was going to be that much harder for Norah, given the way Eugène's had ended. Sam's death felt like a cruel joke from the fates.

She listened to Benny's way of doing things for a while. She understood heartache after all, the pain of losing someone, and she tried to give Norah time to heal. Sympathy and empathy could be great tools for Guardians, or an even greater distraction than colorful decor. Three years really wasn't much time to allow someone to adjust to the type of loss Norah had endured, after all, but too much was at stake. Celeste couldn't risk Norah not healing.

A woman walked by with a waddling beagle at her ankles, and Celeste couldn't help but squeal. She stuck her hand out for the pup to sniff so quickly that both the woman and the dog jumped back a bit.

She bent down a little more slowly, and the beagle approached, lifting Celeste's spirits and restoring a bit of energy.

She returned to her spy post and mentally ran through all the ways she and Benny had tried previously to guide Norah.

She and Benny sent Norah dreams of a happy Sam; they placed grief counselors in her path via pamphlets and patients at the Greenville Diagnostics Center that barely received acknowledgement; they sent her Barb, a force of nature they thought for sure would help break her out of her self-made cage. They didn't bring her Chris; Celeste had a sneaking suspicion that Norah was a Lesson for poor Chris in his journey. Regardless, and as much as Celeste was rooting for him, Guardians couldn't force love. That one was up to Norah and Chris. They did try movie previews, books, social media posts, anything they could think of they put in front of her, but Norah was stubborn in her resistance.

Movement caught Celeste's eye and, sure enough, Chris came storming out of the apartment moments after, anger on his face, sadness in his shoulders. Celeste's heart broke as she watched him walk down the sidewalk away from her. Celeste thought of following him, but he was too far gone by the time she pulled herself together. She had to stop from storming into Norah's apartment and either shaking her madly or hugging her tightly. If she knew Norah, which, of course, she did, Norah was playing it cool and distant like she didn't give two hoots about Chris. But if she allowed a shred of honesty into her heart, she'd be able to admit to herself she gave a whole lot more than two hoots.

Celeste desperately wanted to talk to Norah.

There was only one way she was going to be able to fix things from down here. She was just going to have to be very careful.

# CHAPTER 10

## Norah

T HE NEXT DAY, NORAH WOKE WITH A CRUSHING HEAD-ache and a pit in her stomach that she was all too familiar with. Normally, she would have to piece the prior evening together, snippet of memory by snippet of memory, but this time she knew instantly the cause.

She had been terrible to Chris and knew she was going to have some serious work to do if she was going to make it right.

She groaned and gripped her head as she rolled over in bed. Maybe it was better this way. It was probably easier for Norah. No one to worry about. No one to hurt. No one's needs or expectations to not live up to.

She met Chris six months after the one-year mark of Sam's death.

The first anniversary snuck up on her, quick and fierce. She left Pittsburgh for Greenville shortly after Sam died, telling herself she just needed a change. But truthfully, it was a way to prolong having to face the fact that he was gone. Everyone told her it was okay to cry, but she was too numb to actually do so. Everyone assured her that it was okay to need time and space. Her boss, co-workers, the handful of people she considered friends from medical school.

It's okay to slow down and take a step back.

Until it's not okay.

The reality of Sam being gone hit her months later, and she cried too much, isolating herself, refusing to move on.

And then, before she knew it, her mind and her life were out of control. The one-year anniversary passed while she was already under the wave of grief, while she tried her best to keep her head above the water just to breathe.

She met Chris downtown one night when he was out celebrating his best friend's bachelor party. She thought he was just like every other guy. He didn't care to see the red flag–that she was out on a Saturday night getting drunk alone because what would it matter when Sunday morning rolled around?

She was surprised the next day when he called her for lunch, then invited her for dinner, and he continued to surprise her when he kept showing up.

It was nice at first, having someone to do things with again. The first time he asked her to go for a run with him, she almost said no because running was a joy she had left behind after Sam. It was an old release that she didn't deserve to have anymore. It was after a particularly bad night she spent drinking that he asked her, and he told her it would make her feel better to be up and moving. To feel her heart pumping.

He was right.

He brought that side of her back to life after that, even though she often let it slip again.

The second year mark came up more slowly than the first. She began to get a little of her life back. Some of those Valleys snuck in, but for the most part, she and Chris had gotten to a good place. But the irritation crept in, the itch for a drink, the need for isolation all came slowly at first, barely noticeable... then all at once she fell. Hard. And she didn't stop falling for some time.

He was patient and tried to be supportive in the way he thought she needed. It wasn't his fault he handled things the way he would have wanted and not how she would have wanted; he had to guess. But it wasn't her fault either.

She didn't know what she needed.

She wanted someone there with her, but was miserable and pushed him away when he tried to be. She cried constantly and wanted to be told that everything was going to be okay, but when Chris did tell her that, she screamed that he didn't know what he was talking about. Worst of all, she felt herself doing it but didn't know how to stop it.

The first time she and Chris fought over her drinking, she woke up the next morning having accepted the fact that he had left for good. Another person she pushed away. Another person she lost due to her own actions.

But he showed up first thing that morning with a coffee and told her that whatever she was battling, he was there to help her, but she had to be willing to talk to him for him to be able to.

She tried to cut back on the drinking; there were times she did a good job of it, too, but every time she felt as if things were going well with Chris, the cravings got stronger, not lighter.

And now Sam's three-year anniversary was right around the corner, and she was doing it all again. She got drunk, pissed Chris off, and this time it felt as if she pushed him away for good.

Sam would have loved Chris, but they'd never get the chance to know each other. Sam would never get to make fun of Chris's awful fashion sense, or how he laughed at the dumbest jokes, or that he constantly quoted awful movies. Sam would never get to tell Norah how much she didn't deserve Chris.

Chris would have loved Sam, too. He would have adored him as a brother, just like Norah did. He would have seen through all those jokes and known Sam as the sensitive kid Norah met all those years ago, and Chris would have been there for him when he needed him most, just like he had been with Norah. And if Sam would never get the comfort, assurance, and happiness that Chris gave to everyone he knew, why should Norah ever deserve those things?

It was hard to stop the thoughts and the memories of Sam when everything she did was a constant reminder of where Sam should be, too. How could Norah find love when Sam never could? How could Norah build a career when Sam would never get to?

Norah forced herself up out of bed, head throbbing as the blood rushed upwards, and made her way into her living room. Her eyes wandered to the little blue sofa she had since she moved in, the stain on the right arm still visible from when Chris, always so graceful, dropped a fork full of pasta. She spun slowly and wandered into the kitchen, then filled a cup with water and took one big gulp. She opened each cabinet, the fridge, and gazed around the countertops. She stared mindlessly at the bag of cheese puffs she kept stocked for Chris, the bag still unopened weeks later.

She slunk aimlessly back to her room and caught a glimpse of the old framed photo sitting on her bedside table. It was of her and Sam on her graduation day from the University of Pittsburgh. She imagined where she might be now–almost done with her residency perhaps, a different kind of tired, she thought–and allowed herself a small laugh. The thought came just quickly enough for her to swat it away. She looked around the rest of the room and mentally scanned her apartment. The walls, end tables, hallway, scraps of paper on the fridge.

She thought back to Chris's apartment and all his photos throughout. Norah didn't have a single picture of her and Chris, and yet, placed on her bedside table was a picture of her and Sam.

This was for the better. She didn't deserve Chris, just like she hadn't deserved Sam.

She took another big gulp of her water and thought seriously about crawling back into bed to sleep off the hangover. A day wrapped in her blanket, not talking to anyone, seemed like the perfect thing to do. Out of the corner of her eye, she caught her green running shoes sticking out from under the bed. Her eyes traced back to the picture of her and Sam.

Norah closed her eyes and took a deep breath. She grabbed her running shoes and a sweater and headed out the door.

IT TOOK HER ABOUT HALF A MILE TO FIND HER STRIDE. She walked at first before steadily increasing her pace. Getting her blood moving felt good, the cool air in her lungs as she picked up her pace felt good, the sensation of her feet hitting the pavement felt good. Each step was more encouraging than the last to move faster, pick up the pace.

Norah made her way down the city street, jogging along the crowded sidewalks, and navigated her way across the main road to the calmer side of town. She entered the side streets and left the feel of the city behind as buildings faded into the background, apartments became homes, and sidewalks began to fill in with trees instead of trash cans.

Her body carried her left instinctively, her mind blank for the first time in forever. She made her way to the running trail along the river and entered the public park. She always loved running here. Full of families playing and running around, dogs chasing frisbees, people walking and running along the trail, and yet calm enough to free herself from herself. To run just to run.

This was the escape she needed.

# CHAPTER 11

# Celeste

AFTER CHRIS STORMED OUT OF THE APARTMENT THE evening before, Celeste was prepared for Norah to do one of two things: spiral into a bottle or chase the runner's high. Given the last few months, she was praying for the latter but expected the former.

And so, when Norah came out of her apartment in full running gear, Celeste's heart filled with excitement to see the old Norah again, to know she was picking the right path.

Celeste squealed as she bounced on the tips of her toes. She knew exactly where Norah was going.

Celeste was standing in the same spot she had been the night before, across from Norah's apartment. The sun was nice and warm on her shoulders, a magenta puffer coat tied tightly around the waist of her canary blue fleece sweatpants. Not the best outfit to run in. She looked around the busy Saturday morning city street and noticed an alleyway just down the block behind the Main Street Diner. Celeste turned the corner to a conveniently placed porta-potty, with a conveniently placed orchid colored backpack leaning on the wall beside it. Celeste didn't need to look inside, she grabbed the backpack and entered the porta-potty to change.

She sported the absolute best pair of bright green leg warmers, a look she had been obsessed with since Suzanne Somers made it popular, a pair of black leggings with matching green hearts, and a matching oversized t-shirt that read *"One run can change your day, many runs can change your life."*

Celeste ran full speed after Norah...for about a minute. Then her chest began to burn, and her heart felt as if it was about to explode. Exercise was not a necessity in the afterlife.

At that moment, Celeste had never been more grateful for the wonderful and relatively new invention of ride sharing.

Once she arrived at the park, she made her way over to a bench tucked along the river to wait for Norah. The bench faced the trail, and if Celeste was patient enough, Norah would have no choice but to pass by her spot.

She knew from all the times she saw Norah here how packed the trail became with walkers, runners, and bikers. People walking aimlessly with friends, with their dogs, children running ahead of parents, or couples slowly strolling hand in hand. This could either be used to her advantage, or she could get too lost in the shuffle. Sitting and waiting for Norah to lap in front of this bench was Celeste's best bet at spotting her.

Celeste inhaled deeply, her heart rate calming instantly despite the intensity of the morning being far from over. She looked up at the open sky, the sun's angry glare contradicting its soft, warm hug along her skin. Still, she couldn't bring herself to look away. The clouds billowed above, soft and delicate, moving across the sky ever so slightly. She closed her eyes to take in the rest of her senses. The rushing water around her brought Celeste even more calmness. The cool spring air grazed her arms, mixing with the warmth from the sun, and she was reminded of the cold from the previous night, grateful now not to be back there. The smells once again hit her with great intensity. Nature filled her nose, strong and comforting, the sweet aroma of wild flowers enhanced by the musty smell of earth.

She searched for Norah once again, and her gaze landed on the people walking along the trail. Two friends laughed at something one of them said. A dad bent down and scooped up his son with practiced ease, placing him gently on his shoulders. An older couple strolled silently side by side, both with a sense of serenity surrounding them.

She was here, on Earth. Feet on the ground, wind in her hair. This was it, this was why the world was worth all its heartache, all the pain and struggle, this view, this feeling. These people.

She inhaled deeply once more and caught sight of Norah running around the bend. Her stride steady, her face set. Celeste's heart quickened as Norah approached, but she allowed her to run past her. For now. Celeste knew Norah needed this; she needed the time to clear her head, to feel the burn in her chest, to allow herself back to this place.

It also gave Celeste the time to sit and think of some sort of plan of how to get in front of Norah again, hopefully without having to spill another coffee on her.

What felt like forever and no time at all, Celeste watched as Norah veered off the trail and into the sandwich shop that sat along the riverbank. Celeste picked absentmindedly at the mauve nails on her left hand before taking a deep breath, peeling herself away from the bench, and making her way into the sandwich shop.

Celeste followed two women up the path to the front door, both talking animatedly about a third named Sarah who had the absolute audacity to cheat on Michael, a very good guy. One woman barely finished her sentence before the other jumped in. Celeste, now invested in if Sarah did in fact cheat, stepped into the line behind them. Celeste was debating reporting Sarah's behavior to her Guardian—if she could track them down—when she caught sight of Norah. The women were the only barrier between them.

*Oh well*, Celeste thought to herself. *I can't exactly find a way to talk with Norah* through *these two*. She did her best impression of casual and looked around the room. *Not many open tables side by side...guess I'd better go.*

"Katie," came a voice from the left, and the two women looked in answer. "We ordered, just come sit." Celeste watched them both walk over, curious if one of the women at the table was Sarah, before realizing their departure cleared the distance between her and Norah.

Celeste's stomach. "Now what?" she said, a little too loudly.

Norah turned to face her and gave a small smile.

Celeste jumped at her chance. "Hey," she exclaimed, watching as Norah's eyes transitioned from vacant friendliness to wariness. "I think I might owe you a white shirt?"

Celeste instantly regretted the goofy lead-in.

Norah's smile brightened as recognition set in. She pointed at Celeste and said, "Oh wow, yes, from the coffee shop! No worries, I actually threw away any clothing lighter than the color dove gray." She teased, gesturing to her all black leggings, black tank top, and gray sweater tied around her waist. "So now it doesn't matter."

Celeste felt her cheeks flush and managed a giggle that she prayed was not as awkward as it sounded to her.

"How are you?" Norah asked.

"I'm–I'm good," Celeste said and glanced anxiously around the restaurant. She should have spent more time planning exactly what she was going to say while waiting on that bench instead of smelling nature. "I'm guessing you live around here?" she asked, just as Norah was about to turn away, desperate to keep their interaction going.

Norah nodded.

"Same," Celeste said as Norah took a step forward in line, her body remaining half turned forward and half toward Celeste.

"Are you from here? I noticed a lot more transplants than locals," Celeste said, mimicking a phrase she'd heard a million times since Norah had arrived in Greenville. She felt as if she had been dropped into the middle of a television series. A complete outsider to the characters who knew everything about them.

Grateful for all the years of watching. The difficult part would be not to mix up the seasons.

Television. That was a neat little invention Celeste got to see develop from afar, but was envious of it not being around in her time. Although one could argue that she watched live TV daily.

Norah raised her hand and shrugged her shoulders. "Guilty transplant. I am originally from Pittsburgh, but moved to Greenville about," Norah appeared to be doing the math in her head, "two and a half years ago."

Celeste knew that Norah knew all too well how long it had been. Every moment before and after Sam's death was continuously calculated.

"That's great. Do you love it? I just arrived here, so I'm hoping for some good news." Celeste was proud of herself for how well she was doing as she started to get into the groove of this conversation; it was even becoming a bit fun to make up who she was. "It's so nice to see everyone enjoying the outdoors, spending time together. What a beautiful thing to witness."

"It is." Norah's eyes looked thoughtful as she nodded. "And I do. Love it here. You're right, it is a beautiful city." She checked that the line had moved, and she was up next. Norah turned back to face Celeste. "I'm sure you'll love it," she said, reassuringly.

Norah stepped up to the counter to order, which gave Celeste a moment to collect her thoughts. Norah looked tired, Celeste noted, and she was sure she could detect a hint of alcohol lingering on Norah's breath. Celeste chose not to focus on the negative. Norah was out of her apartment, on a run, and engaging with her.

The whole I'm-new-here thing could be good. Everyone wanted to meet people when they were new somewhere. She needed to be careful, not be too pushy.

Norah stepped aside and waited for her sandwich to be made while Celeste ordered.

*Gosh, Norah had made it look so easy to order.*

Standing there, the gentleman at the counter stared at her, waiting for her to choose. There were way too many options, and such tiny print. How was she supposed to decide in the two seconds she had with a line behind her and the guy waiting and–

"I'll take the number three, please," she blurted out, with no idea what exactly a number three was.

Once done, Celeste met Norah where she stood. "It's busy in here," she said, as if noticing it for the first time.

"Yeah," Norah agreed. "A lot of people are on the trail on the weekends, so this place gets pretty packed. They need to either expand or open new places."

Celeste fiddled with her receipt. She knew it was a bad idea to ask to sit together. The better idea would have been to sit on her own and stage another bump-in a few days later.

But instead, she asked, "Would you like to share a table?" When Norah didn't respond right away, she added, "Not to intrude." Celeste could see Norah's hesitation—she didn't exactly have an open arm policy for new friends, even when Sam was alive, even more so after.

Norah shook her head and said, "No, no, of course not. Yes, let's sh–share a table."

They both retrieved their lunches and walked over to one of the few empty spots. Celeste overheard a woman who could only be *the* Sarah complaining that Michael had the most obnoxious habit of drumming his index fingers on every surface he encountered. Celeste clicked her tongue disapprovingly.

"What?" asked Norah, freezing mid-sit.

"Oh, not you, sorry." Celeste nudged her chin in the direction where the other women were sitting and lowered her voice. "Sarah over there is allegedly cheating on her boyfriend." A small ping of guilt entered the pit of her stomach, but wasn't gossip how women bonded?

Norah's mouth fell open. "How do you know that?"

Celeste took a peek underneath the top layer of her rye bread. Tuna with cheese. Could have been worse. "I overheard them talking as I walked in." She shook her head, eyes wide. "She's going to have some explaining to do, that's for sure."

"Hey, now, her boyfriend could be a real asshole, we don't know."

"Butthole or not, Sarah's clearly no saint."

Norah giggled as she bit into her turkey bacon melt.

Celeste said, "That looks delicious. You must be like, the best sandwich picker of all time." And Norah covered her mouth with her hand to stifle another laugh.

Celeste felt that same sense of coming home that she had in the coffee shop. Strange to have watched someone for so long, day in and day out, a strong sense of responsibility, yes...but sitting there with Norah, it was more than that.

Celeste couldn't quite put her finger on it, but she knew what she had to do to get Norah back on track. Her new point of view into Norah's life was going to be front and center. If there was anything she knew about Norah, it was her need for a friend, whether or not Norah understood that herself, and the new girl in town seemed like the perfect fit at the perfect time.

Thoughts of Benny were far from her mind.

# CHAPTER 12

## Norah

IT TOOK CHRIS A WHOLE WEEK–SIX AND A HALF DAYS TO be exact–to reach out to Norah. She did think about picking up the phone to call him often, but it never felt right. If he wanted to, he'd call her. If he didn't call, she knew she pushed too far and that was that.

She hesitated for a moment, staring at the name on the screen as she placed her finger over the green answer button, then away, then over, until finally it went to voicemail. She'd listen to what he had to say and go from there.

> "Hey, Norah. Sorry, I haven't been in touch. I just needed some time, you know, to myself. Not that you've reached out to me... sorry, that was...passive-aggressive. Anyway, I promise we'll talk, I'm just asking for some time."

He called her Norah and not Babe or Baby. Terms of endearment that Norah felt he'd started to use far too early in their relationship. She eventually got used to it, but on some level, it always secretly made her cringe.

But in this voicemail, he called her Norah, and the lack of the nickname hurt her more than she expected.

Norah's cheeks burned red as she replayed the voicemail. He didn't ask to see her. He didn't reassure her that things were good. He called her to tell her he didn't want to talk. Wonderful.

He had a way of breaking through her moods. She may not have been open to admitting what was causing them—some memory of Sam, some good thing that happened that day that she didn't feel she deserved, a bad thing that happened that she *did* feel she deserved—but Chris would take whatever attitude or snubbed shoulder she threw at him and turn her mood around. She would grumble and push back, then he'd smile and find a way to make her laugh.

The emptiness of the room sat heavily on her chest, and she regretted every grumble, every push over the last year and a half she and Chris had been together.

The storm from Sam's two-year anniversary, a storm Norah looked back on with regret, while never settling, eventually calmed. Chris tried his best to build something with her, and while she was good at the date nights out or evenings in, anything that began to feel deeper made her freeze.

He surprised her four months ago with a weekend at a mountain cabin about two hours away. It was two nights just for them. He planned a three-mile hike the first morning that led to the most stunning sunrise. The cold of the mountain air added to the adventure. He cooked seafood pasta for dinner, and they laughed about the rickety two-burner stove being used for such a fancy meal. He made it a point not to bring any alcohol, a detail he later let slip in one of their fights, but to Norah's surprise, she didn't miss it. The weekend was an escape from everything, feelings of grief and guilt included.

Until they returned home, and Norah shut down. She fell right back into her old ways. She knew then that she was doing it. She scolded herself for the tone she used with him, told herself not to blow him off as she hit send on the text to

cancel their plans. He pulled back a bit, and she breathed easier, as she cheerfully greeted him the next time they met for a
drink. Norah was well aware of the rollercoaster she'd put him
through. Chris was a good guy, and he didn't deserve the way
she treated him, but the problem was she didn't deserve the
way he treated her, either.

With the evening a few weeks ago, to the one that tipped the
scale the week before, one would think three years meant Norah
should recognize the spiral sooner.

Norah pursed her lips and slapped her palm to her forehead.
Sam's three-year anniversary date was just a few days away, a fact
she'd let slip from her mind this past week and a half, something
she would have previously thought to have been impossible.
How could she be so selfish?

She ran her hands through her hair, trying to focus. Only
one guilt trip at a time was allowed.

She knew it wasn't fair to be upset at Chris when she,
too, hadn't reached out–like he started to say in his voicemail–but she just hadn't learned how to stop herself from
lashing out, and now, it seemed, it was too late. She wanted
to tell him how good she'd been that week. She'd gone on
runs, hadn't been drinking, she'd done well at work, she even
made a new friend, sorta. Chris was always telling her she
needed to make some friends. You'd think with the two people in her life, Barb and Chris, always telling her, she'd have
listened to one of them sooner.

They were right: meeting Celeste turned out to be a
happy accident. She was nice. A little odd, but nice. They
exchanged numbers after they had lunch together, and just
that morning, she received a text with a gif of a dog with a
cup of coffee, barking, "You Got This!" Norah's instinct was
to roll her eyes, yet she couldn't stop herself from smiling.
She needed that silly image of the dog, and she had no idea
how Celeste knew it.

Celeste reached out a few times that week. A call to ask her who her "favorite local dentist" was. "Um, my dentist is good, I guess. I can give you their number," she'd offered. Which turned into a twenty-minute conversation on the importance of hygiene.

"Trust me," Celeste said. "I've seen some bad teeth through the years. It's crazy to witness all the advancements in dental care." There was a slight pause on the other end. "Read, I mean, crazy to *read* about it all."

She sent a text with the most random list of movies Norah should watch. *It's a Wonderful Life, Good Will Hunting, The Secret Life of Walter Mitty*. And once she FaceTimed to ask for Norah's opinion on her outfit for the day. The choices were white jean overalls covered in floral print, or an oversized long-sleeve T-shirt with a rooster on the front, tucked into a long red tulle skirt. Neither was Norah's style, but Celeste's excitement was infectious. Norah chose the overalls.

No matter the conversation, Celeste found a way to throw an uplifting compliment to Norah. Celeste couldn't stop telling her how endlessly grateful she was for the dentist's number, that Norah was a hero for getting it to her. And she had no idea what she would have done without Norah's help with her outfit that day.

Celeste was Norah's total opposite, and yet Norah felt as if she had known Celeste for years. Her friendship was the first thing Norah felt excited about in a long time. And for once, Norah wished she could call Chris, not Sam, to tell him all about Celeste.

Norah groaned and tossed her phone aside. She needed to do something to get her mind off everything. She may have felt as if she'd known Celeste for a while, but calling her and asking her to hang out seemed too forward still. Maybe she'd call her another day.

Chris's voicemail played once more in her mind, and the

urge to have a drink itched somewhere deep within her. If his promise to talk was ever going to stand a chance, she needed to make better choices. She decided to bake some brownies instead.

# CHAPTER 13

# *Celeste*

CELESTE SAT ON THE FLOOR CAREFULLY STOCKING CANS of cat food and humming quietly to herself as Dylan, her not-so-motivated young co-worker, stood at the checkout paying far too close attention to his phone. A phone was one thing Celeste had been excited to get her hands on when she arrived, but she quickly lost the excitement. Why on Earth do people want to stick their noses in them all day, every day, when there is so much else to see here?

Celeste had panicked when Norah asked her what she did for work. She told her she had recently accepted a job offer, then panicked even more when Norah asked her where. "Puppy store" was the first thing that came to mind. Celeste loved dogs, but the division she worked in never allowed much interaction. Dog Guardians come from a very special department, Elite, and Guardians were too busy to foster them. But she always loved watching them from above.

She couldn't wait to report all the things she was discovering back to Benny. It was one thing to watch it all happen and quite another to live it. For now, though, she was more than happy to focus on stocking products and cleaning out cages. She'd learn the technology only when she absolutely had to.

As if the thought conjured him, Benny appeared in front of her so suddenly, it made her jump and drop the cans she was holding. She was used to everyone popping in and out of view in the Guardian afterlife, not so much down on Earth.

Gravity. That was another thing she was less impressed with than she thought she would have been.

Thankfully, sitting on the floor meant not too far a drop, and the boy up front didn't flinch a bit.

"So sorry," Benny grimaced. "Didn't mean to startle you. Just wanted to see how things were going."

Celeste's pulse quickened as she picked up the fallen cans and placed them slowly on the shelf, steadying her shaking hands. Technically, she knew he could pop in on her whenever he liked—he was the key to her getting back and forth after all—but she was struck with the realization that Benny could unexpectedly pop in when she was with Norah. Terrifying. Chances were slim, Celeste told herself; she wasn't his only Trainee, and mentoring wasn't his only job. He was probably just there because this was all still new.

She tried to push down the uneasy feeling. What was she even worried about? Interacting with Norah was a part of the deal; she hadn't done anything wrong.

She busied herself arranging the shelves, too nervous to look him in the face. "It's okay," she murmured.

"Really love where you've picked to live. Excellent choice."

Celeste couldn't help but laugh. "I'm working here, not living here." Her eyes finally focused on Benny, and her giggle turned into a boisterous one.

Benny looked around him, eyebrows pinched tight, at what Celeste could possibly be laughing at.

She inhaled deeply to settle herself. "I'm sorry," she said. "It's just, without your glow, the way you are dressed–"

Benny placed his hands firmly on his hips. "What?" he demanded. "What's wrong with the way I am dressed? We always dress like this."

On one hand, his lack of glow made him look *normal*, and therefore hilariously unsettling, but on the other hand, Benny's typical dress, which did not fit in well with, shall we say, the locals, made him look vastly out of place. Benny, with his white linen pants and white linen top, looked like someone who'd just walked off a beach photoshoot and into a pet shop.

Thank the heavens they didn't wear those ridiculous wings humans always depicted them with; he'd be knocking everything off the shelves.

Celeste explained as best she could. "You look a bit out of place. We're in a small city at the start of spring, and you look as if you are on the cover of a beach read. You don't exactly match the vibe here."

Benny's eyes light up with understanding. "Ah, well, don't you know I can pull off anything?" He winked.

After a quick look around to ensure no one was watching, Benny changed instantly to a pair of jeans and a nice flannel, and since he hadn't shown up angry, Celeste was feeling relatively confident that he wasn't there to reprimand her for interacting with Norah. They were able to chat a bit about how the mission was going.

Celeste expertly steered clear of revealing too much as she explained how great it was to be there. She decided not to tell him that she and Norah officially met. She wasn't sure she was ready to.

Where was the line between bystanders and getting too close?

"How's the Council doing?" she asked.

He waved off the question. "Ah, you know them. Every day a new crisis, every day something more critical to focus on. Old Reggy is ever the giant pain in the ass he strives to be," he said with a wide grin.

"And the other Trainees?" Celeste continued shuffling around the cans of cat food as they talked, despite the very low chance Dylan was going to come looking for her.

"They're all good. Silas asked about you a few times. We should have guessed he'd notice your absence." Celeste raised her eyebrows. "Don't worry, I've covered for you. I have you doing something or another for me. We'll have to figure out those details later; although, I think telling him that you're doing something special for me only fueled his fire. He is a persistent fellow, I'll give him that."

"Why does Silas care where I am or what I'm doing?"

"I think it's more about me than you. I gave him poor marks on his latest test. I was the only member of The Council who did, and he took it personally."

Admittedly, Celeste hated the tests the Council put them through. It was incredibly nerve-wracking to be watched by the Council members. Although the ultimate test was if a Soul learned all seven of their Lessons, the tests that the Council ran aided in their final vote when the time came. Celeste shuddered at the thought and almost felt bad for Silas.

"Can I ask which part he did badly in?" Celeste guessed it was *Planting Subtle Thoughts*. Those whispers people get somewhere deep within them. Silas was never good at being subtle.

"No, you know tests from The Council are confidential. Anyway, he knows Reggie and I don't necessarily see eye to eye on most things, and he thinks I judged him unfairly. He's done a few things since then to try and butter me up. I think he is afraid I won't vote for him to pass his training. I don't *not* like Silas; he's a passionate Guardian and I think he'll do well. He's just being overly worried."

"What does that have to do with me?"

"Maybe he thinks if he can catch you in something, it's a way to get to me?" Benny said, shrugging it off as if he wasn't an accomplice to a situation that Silas would love to expose them for.

Celeste groaned. It was one thing to worry about the Council finding out where she was, it was another to worry about Benny checking in, and it was a whole other level to worry about Silas. The thought stupidly hadn't crossed her mind.

"He's constantly telling everyone how his Soul only has two more Lessons left and how close he is to graduating. It's obnoxious. How can someone be so high-and-mighty, so much of a know-it-all, so selfish, and become a Guardian, let alone someday get anointed as a member of the Council?"

"Now, Celeste, you know not everything is so black and white. Humans are not all or nothing, and neither are we. Silas is a good Trainee who lets his insecurities about not succeeding get in the way. I might not like the stiffness with which Reggie does things, but that doesn't mean I don't respect him as a Guardian."

Boy, did she know it.

"The point of the Lessons is to become one's best self, but best does not mean perfect. It's how we try and how we manage that matters. Silas will get there and will do very well once he is able to take on more responsibility."

Celeste stopped her busy work to focus on Benny, doing what he did best, teaching.

"No need to worry about Silas. He's not selfish, despite what you say. He's ambitious. I don't think Silas would go out of his way to take you down. Keep doing what you are doing. I'm sure you'll have to interact with Norah at some point, but be careful and don't get too close," he said, tilting his head and raising his eyebrows. "Keep dropping hints and putting up signs. She'll get the Lesson in no time, and you can come right back home before anyone ever notices a thing."

Celeste had to stifle a very heavy eye roll, turning back to the shelves to hide her reaction from him. Signs. Benny knew they were well beyond signs. If not, she wouldn't have had a reason to come here in the first place. Humans loved to believe in them, but simply refused to listen to ones that were actually useful.

No. Signs were not good enough. There was only so much time, especially with Silas poking around. Straight to the source was the only way.

She turned back to Benny, who thankfully was facing her and not the doorway, just in time to see Norah walk through the door. Norah locked eyes with Celeste and waved, and Celeste smiled as casually as her nerves would allow. Benny turned to look, but Celeste grabbed tightly to his shoulders, forcing his focus onto her.

Celeste said, "Well, I really should get back to work. That kid up there might not look like it, but man, is he gruesome if I take too long a break."

Benny furrowed his eyebrows and peered around the aisle to peek at Dylan still standing aimlessly at the register with his phone resting lightly in his hand. Celeste pulled Benny into a hug before he could notice Norah.

"Let's walk into another aisle so he doesn't see you pop away, shall we?" Celeste said, smiling. She placed her hands firmly on his back and pushed him into the next row.

"Oh, wait," he said, craning his neck to look behind him at Celeste while she continued to nudge him along. "I wanted to give this to you."

They were out of sight of the front of the store, and Celeste relaxed cautiously before reaching out and grabbing the little gold pendant that rested on Benny's outstretched palm. The pendant was a flat circular object, the size of a quarter, with a series of numbers on one side.

"It's a way to call me. We did this so quickly, I forgot to give it to you. Remember, you can't come back to our afterlife without me, and this is a way for you to get in touch with me. I have this one's partner," he said, pointing to the digits engraved on the pendant. "When I leave you a message, it will warm up. All you need to do is press down with your thumb and forefinger to listen. You do the same to record a message, and I'll be notified."

Almost like the old pager system people used to have. Celeste never had a need for such a device and would have been more intrigued with the pendant if she wasn't concerned that Norah may be approaching. She smiled sweetly before placing it in her pocket. "Thank you," she said. "Now go. I need to get back to work." Benny vanished with a smile and a wave.

Celeste let loose a sigh of relief and walked out of the aisle, while Norah made her way towards her.

"Hey!" Celeste exclaimed, waving enthusiastically. "How are you doing?"

"Hey, I'm good. How are you?"

Celeste beamed. "It's so good to see you. Surprised to run into you. What a funny world it is down here, I mean here, that we live in," she fumbled, her nerves not quite settled from the close encounter with Benny.

Norah laughed. "Well, it helps that we live so close."

"Yes, of course. So what are you doing here? You don't have any pets. I mean," Celeste fumbled over her words, "you didn't mention any."

"I have to grab cat food for my friend, Barb, from work. She was panicking about not having time to get some, and I start work later than her today."

Celeste guided Norah to the aisle she'd been in with Benny only moments before, and helped Norah gather cans of cat food.

"Oh, funny," Norah exclaimed. "You went right for what Barb uses. A natural here already."

"Yes, lucky guess." Celeste laughed, as if she hadn't heard Barb talk nonstop about her cats for a few years now. Always riveting tales involving those three.

*Be more careful, Celeste.*

The conversation lulled as they made their way up to the front of the store.

Norah broke the silence. "Let me know if you ever need any more recommendations in the area, and um, if you ever want to grab lunch again or something, give me a call."

There was *something* about the look on Norah's face that made Celeste think of Luisa, from all those lifetimes ago; she just couldn't quite put her finger on it. They looked nothing alike, except for maybe the dark hair. Still, the young Portuguese woman was there in that face all the same. It had to have been the eyes; the Soul can always be seen in the eyes.

"I will," Celeste said. "I'd love to grab lunch again." Celeste kept her voice level while she internally jumped for joy. Celeste reached over and squeezed Norah's hand in goodbye as Norah turned to the register.

They both startled in surprise and pulled their hands apart. "We shocked each other," Norah laughed while Celeste looked on in horror. "It's okay, really," she said, brushing it off. "Thanks for the help."

Celeste watched as Dylan greeted her with as much enthusiasm as a sloth, and Celeste didn't allow herself to breathe until Norah was well out of the door.

# CHAPTER 14

## Norah

NORAH TUCKED HERSELF INTO BED EARLY FOR THE FIRST time in a long time. The combined stress over Sam's three-year anniversary and the constant thought of Chris was exhausting. She thought drunk sleep and hangovers caused the worst exhaustion, but there was something to be said about emotional strain. She crawled into bed with a half-drank camomile tea, different from stumbling in with a whiskey nightcap, and let herself sink deep into her pillows.

Thoughts of her day swirled through her groggy mind. Mr. Stagger, an older gentleman who came in frequently for blood-work, was one for whom she saved the crossword puzzles from all of the magazines that most people ignored. He told her that day, with a heavy sadness, all about his wife's cancer diagnosis. Norah made a vow to bring him something special at his next visit—a card and flowers, perhaps.

Her mind drifted to Celeste and how nice it was to run into her, always so warm and welcoming. Norah was happy that the comfortable feeling she had around Celeste remained. Perhaps it was her awkwardness that helped put Norah at ease. Norah couldn't remember a time she pursued a friendship. She hoped her mentioning lunch wasn't too forward, but she also couldn't help but feel a bit proud of herself for asking Celeste. Norah was drifting and felt sleep overcome her.

NORAH DREAMT ON AS GREAT PLAINS, MOUNTAINS, AND river valleys rolled in and out of view. A sudden spin of the air and she was standing on a small farm. She felt like herself, but watched as another woman's hands, tanned and rough, scooped grain from a tin to spread out in front of a field of chickens. She righted herself and looked out along the remainder of the farm, and a warm feeling washed over her. She watched as the goats and the cows grazed in the field together, and could hear the chickens clucking at her feet. All was well.

The image spun, and a man stood before her, tall and handsome, and her heart was instantly full. He spoke in perfect Spanish, yet somehow Norah understood every word.

"Luisa, my love, we will marry and have our own land, our own farm. I will provide for you and give you all of your heart's desires."

Luisa and the man, Alvaro, were happy.

Norah watched as Luisa and Alvaro fell madly in love, and felt Luisa's parents' joy of knowing their daughter was going to be taken care of.

A feeling of unease took over her while her mother and her father began to discuss her dowry. She had a sudden urge to warn them, but try as she might, when Luisa opened her mouth to scream, nothing would come out. Her voice wouldn't work. They began to add more and more to her dowry, as Alvaro loomed over them, growing bigger and bigger, his shape engulfing them. Norah reached for him, trying to get him to stop, but her hands slipped right through as if she were a ghost.

Her eyes remained frozen on the scene: Alvaro laughing behind her parents while telling them over and over that he and Luisa just needed one more livestock, more bags of grain. Terror seized her as a scroll fell from his hands and rolled all the way across the floor. The list of demands she knew her parents couldn't afford, but they would do anything to make their daughter happy and Alvaro promised he'd take care of her–promised he'd take care of them. Whatever they gave him he would double, no, triple. His promises rolled off his tongue, black block letters spewed from his mouth and filled the room, burying her parents in deceit.

The image spun once more, and it was just the three of them, Luisa and her parents. This time Norah looked on, removed from frame completely, as if watching a movie. Not only could Norah see the pain in all of them, their shoulders hung low, eyes full of tears, but she could *feel* everything Luisa was feeling.

She was angry at Alvaro for being a liar and a thief; she no longer felt the love she once did for him and did not mourn the loss of him. What she did feel, however, was the pain of hurting her parents. The shame of being tricked by Alvaro. The guilt at causing such a great loss to their family.

The dream itself was new to Norah, yet somehow she knew how the story would end. Luisa's–no, *her*–parents, would never recover the farm from all of its loss. They'd have to sell off land to build back up the livestock, but less land meant less space—causing a vicious cycle, and the family's downfall only got worse. Not only did Luisa no longer have a dowry, big or small, to offer a suitor, but she no longer had room in her heart to trust another.

Least of all, herself.

NORAH WOKE WITH A START. HEART RACING, LEGS STICK-ing to the sheets with sweat. It took a moment for the fog to lift. She looked over to the side table with the picture of her and Sam, scanned left to see her navy blue curtains drawn tight. She was home in her bed. Relief washed over her. She could not think of a single time a dream felt so real.

She had the idea to run to the bathroom and examine herself in the mirror before deciding how silly that sounded. Instead, she sat up and made her way into the kitchen to grab a drink of water. The heavy feeling of guilt slowly slipped away as reality came back into focus. Norah's apartment, Norah's kitchen, Norah's hands reaching for the glass.

It was just a dream.

# CHAPTER 15

## Celeste

Norah called her to get together! She couldn't believe it. Celeste squealed when she hung up the phone. She was fully aware Norah had no one else to call, but it didn't matter. Norah still chose to call Celeste.

*Am I excited because that shows she understands the need for the support of others, or because she wants to be my friend? Doesn't matter. It's progress.*

She hesitated for only a moment. An image of Benny showing up and furiously pulling her back home, never allowing her to come back, swirled around in her head.

Only for a moment.

Norah *called* her, actively sought her out to get together. That was huge, and Celeste wasn't about to pass it up.

She quickly changed into her favorite cloth overalls, the ones with the strawberries printed all over them, both comfortable and adorable, and left to go meet Norah.

Twenty minutes later, they stood in line at the very same coffee shop where they first met. Celeste wasn't very fond of coffee. She had heard of the drink while she was alive, but it was still so rare she'd never had the opportunity to try it. The bitter taste was made worse by adding overly sweet caramels and the creams and the fancy things that the people on Earth seemed to love. She also found caffeine to be stronger than she had imagined. How do people walk around feeling so jittery all the time?

"Can you make mine decaf?" she asked the barista.

"That's actually probably smart at this hour, but unfortunately, I don't even think the caffeine affects me anymore," Norah said, shrugging her shoulders. "But I do love my coffee."

"Oh yeah," Celeste said, shaking her head enthusiastically. "I love coffee."

When she first called, Norah suggested that she and Celeste go grab a drink. Celeste rambled off a long-winded story about her great-grandfather being an alcoholic and how his years of irresponsible behavior wreaked havoc on their family, tore relationships apart, and ultimately killed him through a brutal and lonely death. So, she really didn't drink.

"Oh, wow," said Norah, her shock radiating from the phone. "That's, um, that's... sorry to hear."

*Okay, maybe that was a little too much.*

Celeste suggested coffee instead, and now she was stuck having to force down the stuff.

She was a good friend.

Given the early evening hour, the space was fairly open, but Celeste, hopeful to begin making progress with Norah, led the way to a table tucked away in the far right corner for privacy.

They sat and chatted for a bit, but Celeste learned quickly that she hated small talk. It was difficult to fake questions she already knew the answers to, and she constantly panicked when trying to answer things Norah asked her on the spot. The last time that had happened, Celeste found herself needing to find a job.

So far, she'd told Norah both of her parents died when she was eighteen in a house fire, that she lived off of an inheritance from a rich uncle (work was just to stave off the boredom, of course), and that she didn't really have a favorite color. Celeste was disappointed in herself for the last one. She loved purple; who doesn't love purple!

"Your life sounds like something out of a book," Norah commented as Celeste explained the years she'd spent in Tokyo.

"Oh, it's not really all that exciting." Celeste waved her off. She made a mental note to write down everything she'd said when she got home so she wouldn't forget. The conversation stalled a bit, and Celeste noticed Norah gnawing at her bottom lip.

It's funny how little people know of themselves. Habits such as lip biting, hair twirling, nervous eye contact, or lack thereof, a specific finger tapping rhythm, aren't only passed down from generation to generation, but from Soul to Soul. And Celeste knew all of Norah's tells.

For instance, Norah, although she may not have realized it, gnawed relentlessly at her bottom lip whenever she wanted to talk but was stopping herself from doing so. The same way Thomas did all those years ago.

"So, exciting about the new job, are you loving it?" Norah asked, creating what one would call 'small talk'.

Celeste nodded her head excitedly, "Yes, I can't believe they let me work there. I am so lucky."

Norah laughed. "Well, that's the spirit. Happy you like it already."

"I love it. Who wouldn't want to play with dogs all day? Their owners bring them in to pick out toys and treats and get groomed. It's fantastic," she exclaimed. "And I got to see you yesterday. I guess it's true what they say, everywhere is like a big city, never know who you are going to run into."

Norah pulled her eyebrows together. "Oh, I think you mean 'be careful of small towns, you never know who you are going to run into'."

"You say that like it's a bad thing."

Celeste watched as a little girl, folded up in her chair so as to be hidden by its back, poked her head around playfully. She wiggled her fingers in hello and the girl's eyes showed bright before she tucked herself back behind the chair. Her mother told the girl to turn around and sit forward, and Celeste focused back on Norah. "How's work for you? You said you work as a lab tech, right?" Her eyes fell to her hands, toying with her napkin. Work was a sore subject for Norah.

Norah groaned and shifted awkwardly in her seat. "Yeah," she answered. "It's okay."

Celeste's eyes met Norah's questioningly, as if she didn't know the source of that groan. *I should have been an actress in one of my lives.*

Norah waved her off. "It's fine, just not what I really wanted to do."

Celeste allowed a pause as she choked down a sip of her drink.

Yeah, no, she still hated the taste of coffee.

"I wanted to be a doctor actually." Norah grimaced.

Celeste feigned surprise. "What? That's great! I'm sure you'd be an amazing doctor." Norah smiled as Celeste asked, "What stopped you?"

Norah picked at something on the table in front of her and worried her bottom lip in between her teeth.

*Come on, Norah,* Celeste thought.

"Life, I guess. I was pre-med undergrad, made it to medical school, and was preparing to apply for residencies, but then some things shifted around a bit, and I ended up doing this."

Celeste studied Norah's face as she cupped her coffee tightly and faked a sip.

"Ever think of getting back to it?" She wished she could silence the noises of the coffee shop around them, make everything still for just a moment. Celeste couldn't risk a fork dropping and shaking Norah out of this. Might seem like casual conversation to a passerby, but Norah was *willingly sharing.*

Celeste needed to be careful not to cross the line from gentle nudges to outright interfering, but the conversation was going smoother than she anticipated.

"Oh, I don't know. Not sure it's really for me anymore."

Celeste had the sudden urge to shake her. Of course it was still for her, it was everything Norah ever wanted and Celeste knew she still did. But she needed to let Norah come to certain realizations on her own.

Norah looked down and continued to pick at that same spot on the table. "Actually, I had a friend pass away, and it sorta didn't feel right continuing without him."

*Wait, what? Did she just bring up Sam?*

Celeste sat up and leaned closer to the table.

"I am so sorry to hear that," she said. She wanted to reach across the table and hug her. She had wanted to do that for years, lifetimes actually, and now she was close enough. She couldn't, though—that would be weird. *Right, that'd be weird? Yeah.*

"It's okay. It'll be three years," she sighed. "I should really be over it by now." Celeste opened her mouth to protest, but thought better of it. Would that be crossing the line? Besides, Norah was on a roll.

"It's just, he was more than a best friend; he was my brother. Sam and I knew each other forever. He was the only person who ever really got me, and I know he felt that way about me, too."

Celeste sat quietly, allowing Norah the space she needed to talk.

"We never had anything but friendship. I always knew who Sam was, no confusion there, and so there was never an awkward teenage crush phase between us. We just got to be us, always, together. I miss him every minute of every day."

Celeste was waiting for the real confession, the one she knew Norah felt, and the reason she couldn't move on.

"It's my fault he's not here," Norah continued. Celeste began to shake her head no but Norah put her hand up. "No, it is. And every day I live is a day he didn't get to. And I haven't talked to his parents, his amazing, sweet parents who practically raised me, since it's happened. I can't bring myself to. I ignored them at his funeral," she said, her voice began to rise as she threw her hands up in frustration. "I walked in, cried when I saw his casket, and walked out. No one would go near me, and honestly, that was the only thing I appreciated about the whole thing." Norah sighed and placed her head in her hands, elbows resting on the table in front of her.

"So, not only did I lose Sam, but I lost the only family I ever had, and I can't bring myself to reach out to them. They moved after Sam died, anyway. I'm sure they don't need me stirring up old memories." There was a long quiet between them, as Celeste let the words settle.

Norah shook her head as if coming to. "I am so sorry. I genuinely do not know where this is all coming from. I'm typically being lectured for not talking about it."

Celeste knew she meant Chris. He tried so hard to be there for her, and she would never allow it.

"No, really," Celeste protested. "I promise it's fine. Sometimes people find strangers, or near strangers, easier to talk to."

Norah gave Celeste a look she couldn't quite read.

"Yeah, I guess,"she agreed. "Still, that was a bit much. I'm sorry."

"So, you've never really talked to anyone about all this? Don't they have," she paused, snapping her fingers lightly, "what's the word, people here to talk to? Don't they have those here?"

Norah laughed. "You mean do we have therapists here? Yes, I believe we do have therapists here."

Celeste felt her cheeks grow warm, but was happy it made Norah laugh a moment.

"I've thought about it. It's just not really for me, I think." She shook her head once more.

"Sounds like it may be good for you, though. Probably wouldn't hurt to try it." *Guiding. Gentle nudges.*

Norah pressed her lips together in a tight smile. "Anyway, yeah, enough about that." She went to take another sip of her coffee and noticed it was empty. "I think I am going to grab another. Would you like one?"

Celeste had her fears about getting too close, and she still needed to be careful not to say or do too much, but a bystander would have never been able to get Norah to open up like that.

"Yes, definitely. I would love another."

# CHAPTER 16

# Norah

Y OU SURE I CAN'T TALK YOU INTO COMING?" BARB asked Norah, for the third time that day.

Norah reached for her bag and did her best to look sympathetic. "I'm sorry. I just have too much going on tonight."

Barb rolled her eyes. "You always say that, but I'm telling you it's a fun group of ladies, and I promise they're not all old like me. There are some women your age. You need some girlfriends, Norah. I've been telling you since you moved here, you gotta put yourself out there."

That was true; she had been telling Norah to just get out there. Finding friends as an adult was a little like dating, Barb told her–it's awkward and you'll catch more weirdos than good ones, but the one or two good ones you find will make it worth it. Norah never told her she had already lost the only real good one she'd ever needed.

"I have actually made a friend, thank you."

Barb dropped her jaw in mock shock as she reached for her purse. "Who is the alien you speak of that has infiltrated your mind?"

Norah laughed and waved her off.

"We just started hanging out, and you were right, it's a little awkward like dating. It was so much better in college when you were basically forced into the same social circles. She's nice though, I'm sure we'll be great friends," she added with a wink to Barb.

"Okay, smartass, but one day you'll thank me for looking out for you."

Norah didn't tell Barb how Celeste felt like someone she'd known for years instead of weeks, and how she'd already opened up to her more than she had with anyone in a very long time. She was still trying to process what that was all about. She left their coffee date the other day slightly mortified that she had so drastically overshared, but it was as if she couldn't stop talking once she started. Thankfully, Celeste hadn't seemed put off by it.

"Well, as proud of you as I am you can still come hang out, ya know. There isn't a friendship limit." Barb had far more of a social battery than Norah could ever keep up with. Norah loved to come into work and hear all about whatever shenanigans she had gotten into that evening or weekend, but Barb's best stories by far were the ones involving her three cats Whitney, Janet, and Mariah.

"Besides," Barb added. "It'll take your mind off Chris a bit."

Norah shifted her weight from left to right, pulling herself towards the door, and narrowed her eyes at Barb. "I told you, I am fine without Chris. And I am terrible at trivia, especially trivia about books."

*Unless it's a book explaining how to perform an emergency tracheotomy or how to stabilize a punctured lung.*

Norah reached for the old spark, some feeling of excitement at the thought of studying medicine. Nothing.

Barb countered, "That's why you join the book club."

Norah shook her head and reached for the door. "Have fun tonight, be careful, win a round for me."

"Yeah, yeah," Barb called after her as Norah walked out the door.

Norah stepped out onto the busy sidewalk, and her mind wandered to her dream about Luisa and Alvero yet again. It was still weighing on her, the realness of it. The feeling as if she were Luisa and all the emotions that came with that, still rang through her. She'd had vivid dreams before, colors vibrant, whole conversations still there in the morning, but nothing like that. She carried the weight of Luisa as if she were the one who lost her family for something as foolish as love. She laughed at her own cynicism, especially given her current circumstances.

She asked Barb earlier that day if she ever had a dream that felt as real, but she couldn't relate. "Never could remember my dreams," she'd said, and that was that.

She was sure she was being overly sensitive. The memory of the dream will fade eventually, just like they all did.

Norah continued down the sidewalk, dodging people absentmindedly as she walked, barely noticing as she brushed through the 5:00 p.m. foot traffic.

She had to laugh at herself for the college social circle comment, like she knew anything about that. Norah and Sam had their acquaintances they would go out with, but for the most part, they stuck to each other. She didn't branch out from Sam until medical school. A bond is certainly formed there amongst the shared exhaustion, stress, and pressure, but she didn't exactly have the time to socialize outside of the occasional get-togethers, especially in the earlier years of school. Ultimately, she never really felt as if she fit in with anyone other than Sam, and he her. He needed her, a part of her always knew that, and she needed him too.

But Celeste was a start. The opposite of Norah with her blonde curly hair, big blue eyes, and bubbly personality. Sam was probably rolling over in his grave with laughter.

Maybe Celeste was a gift from Sam? Maybe he wasn't mad at her, and he wanted her to make a new friend? Norah laughed at the thought. If only that were the way it worked.

She was certain of one thing–if Chris knew how easily she had opened up to Celeste, he'd be hurt.

"Norah!" exclaimed a familiar voice from behind her. Almost as if she thought him into existence, she turned around to see Chris walking towards her.

Norah felt a rush of heat from the pit of her stomach as he approached. He was clearly coming from work. Out of his typical joggers and T-shirt, and wearing cool blue slacks and a charcoal gray long sleeve button down shirt. His long hair combed back, tucked behind his ears. She tucked her own dark hair to help tame it from the wind coming off the cars along the road and braced herself as best she could.

"Sorry, I, ah, I know you walk this way after work," he said. Norah tensed as he leaned in for a half-hug. "I wasn't thinking about how crowded it'd be at this time." He shoved his hands as deep as he could into the front pockets of his pants as he looked around at all the people. "Can we maybe go down to the park and grab a bench?"

Norah waited a moment before she nodded. She'd thought to reach out a few times over the past few weeks, but now that he stood before her, immediate dread filled her. It would crush her if he didn't want to work on things, but she knew she would give him what he needed if that was the case.

Chris led the way through the crowd and off the sidewalk to the small park off Main Street. It was a small garden, one with memorial plaques from a time long before the city built its giant cement buildings around it. It was full of people here, too, but at least they could sit without being bumped around.

Norah sat several inches to the left of Chris, her hands tucked between her knees, feeling colder than the weather called for.

"I'm not really sure how to say this, so I am just going to go ahead and be really honest with you, Norah," he began, and Norah's stomach felt like a fist had gone through it.

Anytime she pissed Chris off, he'd come right back around and tell her it was okay; he'd say he knew she'd been through a lot and that she still needed time. He knew he didn't always understand, and he certainly got it wrong sometimes, but he said he'd always be there to work through it with her.

Something in the way he looked at her told her this time was going to be different, and her heart sank.

"I've really tried to be patient. I've tried to understand where you are and what you've gone through, but every time I feel like we're headed in a good direction, we end up right back here."

There it was. She'd finally done enough to push him away.

Norah heard her voice come out forcibly. "You know it's Sam's anniversary soon. You know it's a hard time for me." Why couldn't she be softer with him? She talked to Celeste about things, and she barely knew her. Why couldn't she open her heart to Chris despite how much she wanted to?

"Norah, I know it's hard for you because I am a fucking human being who can understand what it might be like to lose a best friend. But I can't fully understand because you won't let me in."

"I *do* let you in," she said, moving forward on the bench. She felt as if she wanted to jump from her skin.

*Norah, calm down.*

She didn't deserve him.

Chris shook his head. "I'm not here to have this argument with you again. I'm sorry, but I'm not." He sighed and grabbed at his knees. "I just thought it would be good to see you in person, and I didn't want to have this conversation over the phone. Norah, if you aren't going to do the bare minimum and try, then I can't do this anymore."

Norah felt her whole body flush. "So you're going to tell me to just get over it? You can't just toss away grief, Chris, it doesn't work like that."

"No, it doesn't, I know that. But you have to let yourself live your life. You have to at least take the steps to let yourself move on."

Norah shot up from the bench, tears burning her eyes. She'd never move on. She'd never allow herself the happiness Sam could never have.

"Please, Norah, I am asking you to help me help you."

She glanced at him long enough to see the anguish deep in his face. "I don't deserve your help," she said, leaving Chris and disappearing back into the crowded sidewalk.

# CHAPTER 17

# *Celeste*

CELESTE FOUND HERSELF, AT LAST, IN THE GRANDEST OF grand places. She felt, well, as much as she could imagine this feeling to be, like someone walking onto their very favorite set from their very favorite television show. It was even better than if she were seeing the many different shades of blues and the different shapes and textures of the clouds for the first time. For every life she'd watched, for every generation she'd been a part of, this was the greatest invention of them all—the library.

One building, no matter how large or small, that housed so many different stories, so many different lives. True or imagined, all magical. Celeste was in awe of humans' ability with the written word, to string the most perfect sentence together, to form vivid scenes with just a few simple characters, to create worlds they didn't need to see to dream up. A book was the greatest magic ever created, and the library its wand, the magic's vessel to get it to as many readers as possible.

Celeste looked longingly at the corner chair, green fabric plump with stuffing that looked as if it would form perfectly to her body, and the beautiful display of "Librarian Picks" that surrounded it. No, her mission today was not to cuddle up with a good book. She was at the library for a very different purpose.

Worry settled deep in her stomach as Celeste briefly thought she might be overstepping a boundary with Norah. But, if she wasn't here to push those boundaries a little, what was all this for? Celeste wasn't overstepping a Guardianship boundary—well, aside from the whole *sneaking down here against the Council's orders and then interacting directly with her Soul* thing, but whatever. Peanuts. What Celeste was doing in the library wasn't going to *directly* point Norah to the final Lesson.

Maybe the pit in her stomach had to do with Benny. She hadn't quite figured out what to do about him yet. She had no way to prevent him from popping in on her again, or checking in on her and Norah from above. She would figure that out if the time came, and continued to hope Benny trusted her enough not to surprise her with an unwelcome visit. She was making far too much progress to stop now.

Norah reached out to Celeste the day before, asking if she could stop over to Celeste's apartment. Celeste could tell quickly she was agitated, but did her best not to push.

"Would you like some tea?" Celeste had asked.

"Actually," Norah countered, "do you have anything a little stronger than tea?"

"Ah, sorry," Celeste said, snapping her fingers. "Fresh out. I polished off the last two bottles of wine last evening." Norah had worn a look of confusion, and Celeste remembered her story regarding her great-grandfather and his alcohol abuse. "You know how it goes, on-the-wagon, off-the-wagon."

Thankfully, Norah looked at her with all too knowing eyes.

The tea helped. Celeste could see Norah start to calm as she walked her around her little apartment. "Wow, those are some bright colors. It's—it's great."

Norah absolutely loved her fluffy purple chair, teal couch, and pink walls, just like Celeste knew she would. Celeste never understood why Norah surrounded herself with such dullness, her apartment being decorated in almost all grays and black.

It didn't take long for Norah to open up to Celeste about Chris and their talk in the park. She explained a lot about their relationship that Celeste already knew, of course, but Celeste did a great job of acting as if it was new information, asking questions and appearing surprised at all the right moments.

However, Celeste had been surprised that Chris all but gave Norah an ultimatum. She'd guessed it may happen at some point—Norah's insistence on pushing him away was one of the driving factors that made Celeste feel she needed to come down here in the first place, but admittedly, she didn't expect Chris to leave Norah so soon after she arrived on Earth. Norah may not have been willing to see it, but Chris was the one person since Sam who Norah could rely on.

Norah tried to remain nonchalant as she described her conversation with Chris to Celeste, but Celeste could see the tension in the way she held herself.

"It's fine, really. We've only been together a year and a half. We haven't even talked about living together or anything," she said. "I get it, though. I can be a lot to deal with." Celeste could practically see the cold lettering of Ha-Ha leave her mouth as she tried to fake the laughter.

The only time Norah couldn't maintain her nonchalant facade was when she talked about why Chris was so upset with her.

"I don't know why I have to share all my deepest thoughts and feelings with him," she said, shoulders tense once more. "Aren't people allowed to keep things to themselves? Why can't we just enjoy each other's company?" She paced about Celeste's living room, arms flailing. "And I am not the only person who likes to have a drink every once in a while. Why am I the one with the problem?" Norah scowled, then winced. "Sorry, I hope that's not too insensitive to say."

"Maybe Chris is just worried about you," Celeste said. "And he wants to see you be your best self."

This had earned Celeste a severe side-eye.

"And I do get what you are saying about not needing to share everything with everyone, but maybe he's being genuine when he says he wants to help you. Maybe he wants to know what your triggers are so he can avoid making them worse next time or anticipate your needs sooner. It seems like he just wants to be there for you."

"I don't need him to be here for me."

If only that were true. Celeste knew without a doubt that Norah wanted Chris in her life. The anger was a mask she wore, her aloofness her suit of armor.

Celeste had watched Norah force everyone else out of her life, but Chris refused to go. Celeste empathized with Chris; a person can only take so much, but her heart was loyal to Norah.

Which is why Celeste found herself at the library. The fear of what the breakup might do to Norah called for some extreme actions.

And while Celeste loved being surrounded by thousands of books, she wasn't going to find what she needed in them. She needed to finally learn how to use a computer. Apparently, there were two things her abilities didn't allow for: She couldn't force free will, the whole debacle with Chris would have been a whole lot easier, nor could she make technology do whatever she wanted without understanding exactly how it all worked. Weird.

Lucky for her, librarians knew everything.

She scanned the room. Walls lined with towering bookshelves, rows spilled out into the center of the room, a section of tables with computers along one side of the back half, another comfy sofa area along the other. A walled-off corner filled with overstuffed bean bags, a table with a rather beat-up-looking train display, and large wooden puzzle pieces scattered about.

Celeste looked towards the front desk, noticing it was vacant. In the librarian's place was a black and white printed sign that read "Off helping a fellow reader, BRB."

Celeste tried to figure out what BRB meant. *Bees Read Better*, she thought, laughing to herself.

She continued to scan the room and noticed the librarian talking to a young man who looked rather frazzled as she placed a number of books in his outstretched hands.

Out of the corner of her eye, she caught a teenage girl curled up in one of the reading chairs, a large book open on her lap while she stared with great concentration at the cell phone in her hand.

Celeste scoffed and had half a mind to tell the girl to put down the phone and read the book. Didn't she know how badly those things were rotting her brain?

Technology. Youth. Who better to teach her about technology than a youth?!

Twenty minutes–and twenty bucks–later, the girl loudly sighed—not for the first time— as she walked Celeste through signing up for a social media account on one of the computers in the back of the room.

"Do they ask for any identification?" Celeste asked.

The girl stared blankly, waiting for Celeste to explain what she meant.

"Like a certificate to prove I was born here on Earth?" she asked the girl.

The girl sighed heavily yet again. How she had that much air just stored in her lungs baffled Celeste.

"Just click there," she said, pointing at the screen.

Celeste moved the mouse over to where the girl pointed, squinted her eyes closed tightly, and clicked Submit. Just ten minutes later, Celeste had her very own profile picture on her very own account.

Another two hours later, after an hour and a half hole where Celeste found herself watching countless videos of big dogs being terrified by tiny kittens, she located a Mr. and Mrs. John and Maureen Bryers.

She whooped in excitement to the absolute horror of the librarian, who scolded her through squinted eyes, which only made Celeste more giddy at having a true, authentic library experience.

Finding the Bryers wasn't direct meddling, and it wouldn't exactly lead to the true Lesson in question, more like nudging Norah in the right direction. She was guiding her. Wasn't this what Benny was referring to when he first came to visit her here? It is very similar to what the Guardians do from up there, really. Signs.

She couldn't exactly go to either of Maureen's or John's Guardians and tell them what she was doing to get information on them, but Celeste doing the physical research and handing Norah the exact information was nothing more than a guardian angel sending a sign to her person.

The Bryers may not be the answer, but seeing them and talking to them might be just what Norah needed.

# CHAPTER 18

# Norah

ON THE MORNING OF THE THIRD ANNIVERSARY OF Sam's death, Norah watched *The Goonies*, Sam's all-time favorite movie, wrapped in her favorite blanket. *The Goonies* wasn't Norah's favorite movie, she found it a tad bit obnoxious, but it had become tradition to watch it after Sam died. When they were young, she grumbled every time Sam suggested watching it and nudged him when he'd quote the movie as it played. A band of outsiders, yearning to find their place to feel as if they belonged. All along, they were enough as themselves. Fitting for Sam.

She watched intently for the most part, giving it the attention Sam begged her to give it when he was alive, but she found herself sifting aimlessly through old pictures on social media, too. Something she hadn't allowed herself to do much. She felt grateful for the first time that she grew up in the generation that shared too much.

She came across a picture from undergrad. It was a selfie of the two of them sitting on some disgusting couch in the basement of the Alpha Phi Alpha house; she could actually see the couch stains in the picture, which made her stomach turn a bit. But the memory of the night made her smile.

Frat parties were far from their scene, but Sam had been in a mood over Bob Ingles.

*"Do you really want to date a guy named Bob?" Norah grimaced. "Imagine trying to be sexy while whispering the name Bob."*

*Sam pushed her playfully. "Stop. Let me sulk. I need to feel my self-pity for a bit."*

*"How about we go out tonight? Try and meet some people?"*

*"Ew, no. You and I do not meet people."*

*Norah pulled him up off her dorm room bed. "Maybe that is part of the problem. Go get dressed."*

*They arrived at the party that evening and made one round through the three story house. Through a crowded living room that smelled like stale beer and piss. Up a creaky, and honestly not very solid, set of stairs where they ran into Kelsey Harris throwing up in the bathroom. Norah got her a cold washcloth and rubbed her back for a minute, before they proceeded back downstairs, all the way to the basement.*

*It was a Pittsburgh basement at its finest, which meant dirty floors, old cement block walls, a random sink and toilet set up in a corner, and terrible overhead lighting. They had a loud and heated game of beer pong going along the back wall and the couch was set up for an audience.*

*Norah and Sam sat for a moment, snuck in a quick selfie, and left to get pizza.*

Per what was sadly becoming a tradition, her day was focused completely on Sam, but every once in a while she would think about Chris. Not for the first time, she wondered if her finding a friend and opening up a bit to her would prove to Chris that she was trying. A possible happy byproduct, not a premeditated intention.

She thought back to her conversation with Celeste the other day, her face flushed with embarrassment, as if she were perpetually stuck in the moment as punishment. She didn't go to her to complain about Chris or to play the victim. Hell, she didn't even think she felt most, if not all, of those things she said. Norah knew relationships were built on letting the other person in, on communication and trust. Holding such a big part of her life from Chris didn't exactly show him she trusted him. Knowing and being able to do it were two different things.

And the drinking. She could admit now that Chris was right. There was a difference between having a good time with friends and, well, whatever it was she kept dragging herself back to. She didn't need a fight with Chris to know she needed to fix it.

One silver lining to her current disaster of a situation was that she was at least letting herself overshare to *someone*. Celeste. Norah found an ease and a comfort with Celeste. Such a natural pull, that felt anything but normal to Norah.

She looked around her and found a mess. Balled up tissues covered the bed, snack bags scattered around her, Sam's favorite movie played on her television and pictures of Sam lit up on her phone.

Norah was certain that, although finding a friend in Celeste was a good step, her situation proved she wasn't moving on from Sam the way Chris needed her to.

She spent the remainder of the day alternating between crying over Sam and angry at Chris, to crying over Chris and angry at herself. It had been exhausting. By about 7:00 p.m., her eyes felt raw as if she had them open in a pool filled with chlorine all day, and her head throbbed.

She flopped back hard on her bed, wrapped herself even tighter in the blanket, and thought about a nice whiskey. She grumbled to herself, Chris clearly wasn't coming back, who was she trying to be good for?

Her phone chimed the sound of a text message. She let out a guttural groan and shoved it under her pillows without looking. When it chimed a second time, she let out a full body sigh and pulled it out to look. Her pulse increased as she contemplated whose name she would see.

"Hi!!!! This is Celeste."

Her heart dropped, but Norah couldn't help but giggle. The excessive use of exclamation points. The need to give her name. The many oddities of Celeste that Norah found surprisingly endearing.

"I was wondering if you were free tomorrow after work? I have some fun (!!) news I'd like to share with you."

Well, at least Celeste didn't seem too upset with the way she behaved the other day.

Norah tapped her fingers along the edges of her phone, moving to type a response, then pulling her fingers away. It was great to know that Norah didn't run her off too, but the thought of functioning, of pretending to have fun, seemed like too much right now.

Norah grumbled once more and rolled over, abandoning her phone, text message unanswered.

Still, she felt a slight smile cross her lips as she closed her eyes. It was nice to have a friend.

# CHAPTER 19

# *Celeste*

Celeste sat comfortably in her chair, fireplace crackling beside her. A book laid open on her lap. All she was missing was a good dog curled up at her feet. She did think of adopting one–How amazing would it be to own one of her very own?—but she had to admit, it would be cruel to give the dog a home, then need to leave him or her behind.

She considered trying to get together with Norah but thought better of it. Sam's anniversary day was always very tough on her. She could justify trying to be a friend supporting her, but even Celeste knew that, to Norah, their friendship wasn't quite there yet. She sent her a quick text letting her know she had news to tell her, the Bryers information burning an imaginary hole in her imaginary pocket, and hoped that the message was enough to let her at least feel thought of today.

And so, with no real job or fake job to attend to at the moment, Celeste found herself actually cuddled up with a real book. She couldn't think of the last time she had been able to take her mind completely off work.

The story was about a soldier who became a prisoner of war in World War I, whose love joins the U.S. Army Nurse Corps in hopes of finding him and bringing him home. A captivating story Celeste was instantly sucked into, yet she couldn't help her mind from wandering to the days she first became a Trainee all those lifetimes ago.

It was an easy choice to become a Guardian. She entered her afterlife in the form she died in: an Irishman in his late thirties, not so old in comparison to these days. Good looking, intelligent, and kind, she liked his form, but when given the option to choose, she chose the form of Celeste. A fun loving, free spirit who was a caretaker in her lifetime. Her Lesson of Empathy was strong, but so was Kindness.

When the option of becoming a Guardian was presented to her, she didn't hesitate to accept. The role was to help guide Souls through one or more of their lives, and to help give them the opportunity to achieve the ultimate goal: to make it across to their afterlife. What greater honor could there be?

When she first met the Mentors, Benny, Reginald, two other members of the Council and a handful of non-Council members, she was disappointed when she was assigned to Benny. Initially, she'd hoped for Reginald.

Celeste shuddered at the memory.

He had such a strong presence, spoke of Guardianship as being the ultimate role, one to be proud of and one to take seriously. Benny seemed too laid back. Celeste *needed* to know she was going to succeed with this Soul, and wanted to be trained by the best.

Once she got to know Benny, and Reginald for that matter, her mind was changed and she couldn't imagine being trained by another. Benny knew how to be lighthearted and playful, and serious and stern.

Turned out they were the perfect match.

Just like Silas and Reginald were.

"Just know, we don't always end up with likable Souls," Benny had explained to her. "Sometimes Trainees get a little overly excited and then quickly disappointed when they learn even arseholes have Guardian Angels. We don't get to choose who we watch over, but we still have to look out for their best interest."

Celeste promptly corrected his language, then told him he was wrong. She was going to love and support whomever she was assigned.

When she was given Norah's Soul–at the time it was Thomas–and the excitement of the Mentor assignments settled, there was an instant connection, an instant feeling of ease. Celeste knew right away they were a perfect match. She meant what she said to Benny, that no matter who it would have been, she would have cared for them to the fullest extent, but never expected to feel the pull she felt with her first Soul. She knew their connection was special. She promised herself then and there that she would do everything in her power to make sure that Soul made it through.

Benny told her she got the perfect first Soul because they were on their last Life Lesson; they already accomplished so much, so how hard could it be? Apparently, very hard!

Celeste shook her head and tried to focus on the book in front of her, re-reading the last sentence on the page for the third time. She was just about to turn the page when she felt a spot along her right wrist grow warmer. It took a moment to realize what it was. She took to wearing the pendant that Benny gave her as a bracelet so that it was never far from sight. She had grown accustomed to wearing it as a nice piece of jewelry, but he had yet to message her through it. Celeste felt her stomach turn as she played the message Benny left her.

"I am coming to see you right now."

Benny's voice practically boomed from the device.

Celeste stood instantly from her chair, taking deep breaths in through her nose and out through her mouth. Maybe this is an exciting message and he missed her terribly and just needed to come say hello.

"Right, Rover?" she said out loud to the imaginary dog pacing the floor beside her. "He has no idea, just like when he came to the pet store. This is purely a check-in visit." The tone of his voice certainly lent to the forced optimism.

She was doing her best to convince herself she and Norah hadn't gotten too close. There was no real risk of Norah finding anything out, or of Celeste letting too much slip. Getting the Bryers' information for Norah wasn't exactly directly interfering... She had just enough time to pace the length of her floor one more time before a red-faced Benny stood before her.

He hadn't bothered to change his clothes. The red face added to the image of a vacationing beachgoer, but somehow, this time it wasn't quite as funny.

This was not a friendly check-in.

# CHAPTER 20

## *Celeste*

"CELESTE, WHAT DID YOU PROMISE ME YOU WOULDN'T do?"

She looked at him sheepishly without replying and placed her book gently down on her purple reading chair, afraid to break eye contact with him.

He clenched his fists at his side as redness spread from his cheeks to his ears. "You promised me you would not get too close. That you would never directly intervene."

"But you let me come down here. How else do I help from here if I don't get close to her?"

"I told you nosy neighbor, not best friend. You are getting *too* close. Too close means slip ups. You'll start to share too much information."

"I am sorry," she pleaded. "I didn't realize how much of the visual advantage I would be losing by coming here. I *had* to get closer to Norah, more so than you or I realized initially. I wasn't doing it to go against your orders, and I swear I'd never do anything to directly jeopardize your position—or Norah's chances, for that matter."

"And you don't think digging into Sam's parents' address and then handing it to her isn't getting a little too close to interfering?"

*Shoot.*

Celeste felt her cheeks grow red as she looked away from Benny. "I didn't give it to her yet," she murmured.

"I know you made plans to, Celeste. You know I can check on you, too, right? It doesn't matter that I got to you before you actually could."

The weight of his words landed heavily on Celeste's chest. So stupid. *How could she have been so stupid?* Of course Benny was watching her. She thought he'd be preoccupied with his other Trainees and his own Souls to look after. She thought he trusted her and wouldn't bother. She tried to come up with more reasons to need to get close to Norah, but each one seemed more ridiculous than the last. The truth of it was, she couldn't stop herself from becoming friends with Norah. From the moment she saw her she felt a pull too strong to trust, and she went against her better judgement anyway.

"You are lucky the Council rarely pokes their heads around. That is what we are for," he said, pointing his index finger at his chest. "Mentors are supposed to be keeping a close eye on you Trainees, and we are most definitely not allowed to provide passage from there to here. Do you know what that means?"

Celeste could do nothing but shake her head slowly.

"That means I will lose my position for this, me." He jammed his finger into his chest again.

"I promise I didn't consider the address direct interference, I am sorry. Going to see them isn't something Norah has to do. It was meant to be a nudge."

"Handing her the information and saying 'go here' is a little too on the nose, regardless if she does or doesn't get the right Lesson from them. I should take you back right now. You've only been here a month. You can explain to Norah that you need to move away, that happens all the time. You would be a blip of a person in her lifetime. She'd forget all about you in no time, no harm done."

That hurt more than Benny could have realized.

"Benny, let me stay. I only have two months left. I'll step back a bit."

Benny gave her a warning look.

"A lot. I'll pull back a lot."

Benny settled down on her couch, and Celeste followed his lead. He inhaled deeply through his nose and exhaled slowly through his mouth. "I can see where losing your view would make things more difficult. I thought a more casual interaction with Norah would be enough to help her. I didn't think through the logistics of it all before."

Celeste, encouraged by his calmer demeanor, said, "I will keep finding ways to discourage her from drinking. I'll also do what you said to do in the first place. I'll find ways to drop hints to Chris to not give up on her, ways to push Barb into helping her more. I couldn't reach them from the afterlife since I'm not their Guardian, but down here I can."

"At this point, I'm not sure getting more people involved is the answer, but you have the right idea. Guiding should still be nudging and directing, even from here."

Celeste smiled. "I won't draw attention to myself, and I won't become friends with anyone."

Benny said, "You have to remember that it will do more harm than good."

"I will not suggest to Norah that she go see John and Maureen." She could no longer swoop in and be the hero who already found them, but it was the right thing *not* to do.

She and Norah had plans to go for a walk, and she would begin to distance herself from there. She would be *just* an acquaintance.

# CHAPTER 21

## *Norah*

NORAH LEFT WORK IN A RUSH, WORRIED SHE WOULD BE late to meet Celeste. It was nice to be excited for something; it was nice to have a friend. Norah hadn't felt this way since she lost Sam.

Her curiosity pulled at her all day, wondering what it was that Celeste was excited to tell her about. She anxiously counted down the very slow minutes of the first seven-and-a-half hours of her day, until the very last half hour when she was slammed with questions and tasks from patients and her coworkers.

Norah and Celeste decided to go for a walk on the trail. She was relieved when Celeste suggested it. Walking with someone was almost like going to the movies. She didn't have to carry on a conversation when she was focused on putting one foot in front of the other. The sounds of nature played all around her, filling the silence and the need to talk. She didn't want to repeat her last couple of conversations with Celeste and overshare, anyway, but she was never good at small talk either. She needed to strike a balance.

She watched as Celeste trudged down the trail towards her, her shoulders dropped low.

"Hi," Norah said smiling, her own brightness surprising her.

Celeste's hand came up in salute, accompanied by a tight smile.

Lines formed between Norah's brows as she frowned in concern. "You okay?" she asked as Celeste stopped to stand next to her. She lacked her usual bubbly energy.

Celeste nodded and said, "Yeah, sorry. Just a long day."

They started down the trail in silence. Norah was unsure of how to jump in; perhaps her theory about a walk date was wrong. "How have you been? How's work going?" she ventured.

"It's good. Nothing too exciting; just work." Celeste crossed one arm about her stomach, gripping her opposite arm and leaving it to hang freely as she moved.

Norah nodded with a sideways glance. She wondered if perhaps she had read the tone of her text wrong, but that didn't seem to add up. Why ask to meet with her if she didn't want to, and what could the exciting news be?

"I think this is the first time I've seen you not wearing bright and colorful clothes," Norah said, gesturing with her chin towards Celeste's black leggings and a pale blue T-shirt.

Norah's attempt at lightening the mood received a small laugh from Celeste. "Yeah, just something I threw on to walk in." The conversation stalled once again.

Norah walked beside her in silence. The trail was surprisingly sparse today. The usual whorl of bike wheels and pitter-patter of joggers was replaced with the burble of the stream beside her and birds chirping above in the purple Crape Myrtle trees. The thought crossed her mind to make up some excuse to leave. Celeste was clearly not in the mood, and Norah couldn't tell if asking her about her big news would help or hurt the situation. She thought of apologizing for her outburst about Chris the other day, but thought better of it.

She was just about to fake feeling her phone vibrate, planning to step away and give herself the chance to think of a clever excuse to leave, but Celeste spoke up before she had the chance.

"I'm sorry, I promise to try and shake this funk. Just one of those days. How was work for you today?"

A heavy fog of guilt washed over Norah. "No need to apologize. It's fine, really," she insisted, kicking herself for almost leaving. "Anything you need?"

Celeste shook her head. "Really, it's okay. Tell me about your day."

They chatted about their days as they walked, and Norah noticed Celeste's mood improved. She wasn't completely back to her normal self, still seeming a bit guarded, but Norah chalked it up to a bad day, something she knew all too well about.

During the next lull in the conversation, Norah brought up Celeste's news. "So," she started, feeling braver to ask in the midst of the more casual conversation, "what was the super fun news you had to tell me?"

"Oh, yeah, right," Celeste said, continuing to walk while looking down at her feet. She shook her head as if to clear it. "Why I texted you last night." She looked around her while keeping her pace. "That's an odd smell, huh? Do you smell that?"

Norah eyed Celeste. If she knew Celeste better, she'd say she seemed nervous to tell her something.

Celeste made eye contact with Norah and quickly looked away. "I shouldn't have even texted you yesterday of all days," she added. "I'm sorry about that. I wasn't thinking."

Norah scrunched her eyebrows. "What do you mean?"

Celeste wrung her hands together. "You know," she stammered. "Sam's anniversary and everything."

Norah stopped walking and turned towards Celeste, who noticed a few steps too late and had to turn back. Norah eyed Celeste while she ran through the last few conversations they had. "I never told you yesterday was Sam's anniversary."

Norah watched as Celeste's whole body tensed. "Yes, you did. I mean, you had to have. How else would I have known?"

People shuffled around them, doing their best to keep moving. Norah stepped back off the trail and motioned for Celeste to follow her. Celeste stepped off to the side, keeping a small distance between them.

"No, Celeste," Norah said, shaking her head. "I told you about Sam, but I never told you the exact date of his anniversary. I know I didn't. What is going on?"

Celeste looked utterly speechless. Norah knew she hadn't mentioned the anniversary to Celeste, and she could see Celeste knew she hadn't either by the way she stood there fidgeting. How did Celeste know the date?

Norah's heart began to race. "Celeste," she said through clenched teeth. "You need to explain."

"I can," she said. "I can explain." She closed the distance Norah had put between them and reached for Norah. Celeste's fingers wrapped around Norah's forearm, and in an instant, Norah was gone. She wasn't standing beside the trail with Celeste.

Instead, similar to her dream as Luisa, Norah found herself not only in someone else's mind and body, but in another time altogether.

THE WORLD WOULD NOT SEE HIS STORY AS TRAGIC; he knew that. If he were a woman, things would be different. They all embraced Thérèse and wept for her for years after it happened. How could a mother ever survive such a loss? But no, they didn't see a need to weep for Eugène. He learned quickly that you didn't need sympathy from others to know that your pain was real.

All in all, if he looked at the span of a life that lasted seventy-eight years, it wasn't all tragic. He lived through both wars, but married the love of his life, Thérèse, and the years he had with Serge were happy ones.

In a lot of ways, having lived through those made Serge's death stand out even more.

He set his success on hard work and honor. In the end, it will be a heart attack. A fairly quick and painless way for him to go, at least by comparison to some of his fellow soldiers from the second war. He will rest easy with who he was in that life. It was one split second in that span of seventy-eight years that was enough to mark the whole damn thing as tragic, but again, only to him.

Eugène overheard Thérèse and Serge discussing the issue a few weeks before. They sometimes forgot how thin the walls were, how quiet the countryside could be at night.

"No, Maman, I am not going to do it. He doesn't want me to do it." He heard his son say.

He could picture the soft look on his wife's face, the way she placed her hand on their son's shoulder when she wanted to be comforting. Was she always better at dealing with people than he, or was it the war that took that piece of him away, too?

"Your papa loves the lake. I know he would want you to ask him to go fishing with him."

Eugène did love the lake; besides his garden, it was his favorite thing about the five acres of land they lived on. The lake itself took up nearly an acre, and he loved the solitude of being on the water.

An audible sigh left Serge. "I don't know how to fish. He will only get frustrated with me when I can't do it."

Thérèse's response held more caution than Eugène liked. "That is absurd, Serge," she said. "He would love to teach you."

Eugène got up from his paper and quietly made his way to the kitchen door. He could go in pretending he wanted a second glass of wine, even though this would surely give things away to Thérèse. He paused for a moment, feeling the sweat build on his palms. He thought he must be getting sick, a small fever perhaps, as he lifted his hand to push at the door.

His wife said, with a gentle shake to her voice, "It was the War," and Eugène stopped dead in his tracks. "He wasn't always like this," she continued softly. "So distant. I knew who he was before the War, and even before you were born," she teased, and Eugène heard the popping sound she made, indicating she popped Serge playfully on the nose. Eugène could feel her pause, always so cautious with her words, especially with their son. "I know my Eugène is still in there, and I know how much he loves you. He just has a hard time showing that sometimes, my love."

Eugène removed his hand from the door with care, ensuring they wouldn't hear him retreat to his favorite chair. He turned the page of his newspaper. "The Algerian drama intensifies," it read. The year was August 1955.

It was true. He was different before the War. But weren't they all? Even the women. Leaving Thérèse at home as a young, quiet girl who looked forward to laundry drying on the line and children at her feet, and returning to a strong, assertive woman he didn't quite recognize. He understood the women took on a great deal of responsibility while the men were away, but it certainly took some getting used to.

But the men. They saw and did things their women and children would never understand. Why should he have to explain himself? The War was behind them all now, and that was precisely where he would keep it.

He continued to grumble his unwarranted defenses to himself until bed.

Over the coming days, Eugène noticed Serge walking along the lake alone, a solemn look on his face, and he would think back to the conversation he overheard between his wife and son.

*Soon,* he would think to himself. *Tomorrow.* But soon and tomorrow came and went, and Eugène found other things to do. First he'd read his paper, first he'd tend to his garden, first he'd clean out the shed.

One morning, after bearing a particularly long, knowing glare from Thérèse, he went searching for the boy outside, where Serge spent most of his time. He'd rehearsed the conversation in his head. Not because he was nervous, but sometimes, ever since the War, he found it difficult to gather the right words.

"Serge," he called out to his son. No reply. "Serge," he called, with more growl in his voice. Still no answer. Eugène first walked, then jogged, then ran to every area of land he could think of. The grouping of trees that Serge liked to climb, the chicken coop where Serge sometimes collected the eggs on Thérèse's orders, the stone wall he sometimes pretended was a fort, launching rocks at pretended enemies.

Nothing.

Eugène spotted a bare foot lying among the vegetables in the garden. He ran over at full speed, flung open the wire fence leading in, practically tearing it from its hinges, and all but dove on top of the boy.

Serge startled awake. Eugène jolted upright, blood boiling beneath his skin, and scanned the boy's body for injuries.

Upon seeing none, he shouted, "What are you doing? I have been calling your name. Why did you not answer me?"

Serge stammered a reply that he must have fallen asleep, but stopped when his eyes darted down at Eugène's hands, balled tightly into fists.

"You ate half of the green beans and half of the beets!" he roared. "What were you thinking? What is your mother going to cook for supper, Serge, if you keep eating the vegetables straight from the garden?"

Eugène gripped him by his shoulders and dragged him back to the house. Thoughts of fishing lessons far from his mind.

Weeks later, on the day the *incident* happened, it was just like any other ordinary day. He didn't wake up with a gut feeling that his life was about to change. Thérèse would talk for years about how she knew something was wrong, a gnawing deep in her gut, but not Eugène.

He sat in his favorite chair, reading a long-forgotten book, when Thérèse screamed. He ran out back to see what was wrong.

"He is gone, Eugène. Serge is gone!" she cried.

Anger, not panic, seized Eugène as he walked amongst the green beans and the beats with the last instance fresh in his mind, but no Serge.

Eugène walked his land a hundred times, inch by inch. "Serge!" he shouted until his voice was raw. The sun began to settle, sweat drying thick on his skin, with no sign of the boy. "Serge!" he forced through the ache in his throat. He looked once more behind the log that sat rotting at the edge of his land, the view now so familiar he could count the tree's rings in his sleep.

A heavy fog settled around him as he came to grips that the boy was nowhere to be found. Distant sounds of birds calling, mixed with the shouts and cries of Thérèse, were warped as if he had shields over his ears. He would hear her shouting Serge's name in his sleep for years to come.

Hours later, they found the boat flipped, a fishing rod lodged underneath its bench. It would be years later, when Eugène would need to replace their fridge, that he would find a note that had fallen underneath.

The note read:

Gone to teach myself to fish.
— Serge

NORAH FELT THE THROBBING IN HER PALMS BEFORE SHE felt the solid cement below them. Celeste crouched beside her. "It's okay, it's okay..." Celeste repeated over and over, voice shaking slightly.

Norah's head began to clear as she looked around her. She must have fallen, her top half landing back onto the trail path, feet in the space she last remembered standing. Celeste reassured the strangers who stopped to check on Norah and sent them on their way.

Norah brushed off her hands, then gently lifted herself up from the trail. "What the hell happened?"

Celeste hovered over Norah as she stood, as if she wanted to help her but was afraid to touch her.

"I'm not sure. I touched you and you just sort of zoned out, froze, and then you dropped," she said, panic rising in her voice with every word.

Norah tried to shake the remaining fog from her head, the weight of Eugène from her heart.

"Eugène," she murmured to herself, trying to make sense of it. "Serge."

Celeste gasped and clasped her hands over her mouth.

"What?" Norah asked. "What does that mean?" And just like that, the moments prior came rushing back. Celeste knew the date of Sam's anniversary.

"Celeste, what the fuck is going on?"

Celeste looked around as if she was expecting someone to be there, watching them.

"I swear I can explain," she said, the fear in her eyes causing Norah's heart to race.

She didn't know what was going on or who Celeste really was. Norah's only thought was that she needed to get away from there and fast.

Without letting Celeste say another word, Norah turned and ran.

# CHAPTER 22

## Norah

THIS WAS NOT A THING A RUN WAS GOING TO FIX. THIS was a thing that called for a drink. And a lot of them.

Billy greeted her cheerfully. "Long time no see," he shouted as she sat down at the far end of the bar.

This was not a social visit—she wanted to drown in a drink and be left alone. Norah grumbled in response, and, thankfully, Billy took the hint. He handed her the beer and whiskey she signaled for and left her to it.

The bar was nearly full that evening, and she hoped the noise of people talking and the sound of the music would help her clear her head, but it was to no avail. Her mind wandered to Eugène, and to Serge, over and over. She had never been to France, and yet in the dream they spoke fluent French. The place felt like home. She could feel the soil of the garden between her toes, could smell the lake where—

Her heart ached when she thought of Serge. Ached was too soft a word for the loss of a child. How Norah could feel a loss so strong was beyond comprehension. Serge was not her son, yet the pain of her world shattering was all too real. The guilt and the shame from letting Serge down. If she had just gone with him, been the father he needed. A father is supposed to protect, more so even than a best friend.

Her head spun with anger at Celeste, fear and confusion

from what she could only describe as a hallucination, and the pain of Eugène. It couldn't have been real. This thought. This memory. No, not a memory, a hallucination. How did she do it? How did one touch from Celeste send her into this hallucination? No, not a hallucination–a memory.

Celeste wasn't with her when she dreamt of Luisa, but there had to be a connection between Luisa and Eugène. The memories and the feelings from both were all too real. She should have paid closer attention to the signs from the Luisa dream, the intensity of the emotions of guilt and shame, and how clearly she saw Luisa's parents and Alvaro. How much she felt as if she *were* Lusia. All her other dreams, she woke up foggy, never once questioning if one was real. Luisa was all too real.

After drink number three, it became easier to convince herself it wasn't real. She had been under a lot of stress lately with Chris and Sam's anniversary. These odd experiences were self-projections. That's all they were.

A fresh round of guilt crept over her at the thought of the way she exploded at Celeste. She must have thought Norah was a crazy person. There was no way Celeste could have understood what Norah saw.

She signaled for another round, and Billy popped the top of a beer. "A whiskey, too, please." He raised his eyebrows but reached for a fresh glass.

But *was* Norah the crazy one? Celeste's eyes were full of horror as she stared at her, yes, but as Norah thought back, it was a *knowing* horror. Celeste kept saying she could explain. She kept apologizing. And that she knew Sam's anniversary still chewed at the pit of Norah's stomach. How did she know that?

Norah tried to recall if she'd met Celeste before. Was it possible Celeste knew Sam? She wondered if Celeste was a girlfriend of Sam's she didn't know, but the fact that Sam would have kept a secret from her was even more unbelievable than it being a woman.

None of it added up. None of it made sense.

Billy's voice was muffled as he said, "How about I get you water." It wasn't a question. Norah lifted her chin from her chest and pried her eyes open. She looked around. The bar was nearly empty. She accepted the water and drank half the glass before stopping.

Billy asked if she needed some assistance getting home, and Norah shook her head no.

"Chris will help me," she slurred, before remembering Chris was no longer there.

NORAH SAT THE NEXT DAY, ONCE AGAIN, MASSAGING HER temples; the Tylenol just was not cutting it.

She'd rolled out of bed that morning, twenty minutes past the time she was supposed to be at work, and grabbed the closest clothes she could reach. A pair of black slacks and a maroon blouse, wrinkled and stained with God knows what. Norah always appreciated that Dr. Ross didn't make reception wear scrubs, but at that moment, she wished she didn't need to think about what to wear.

Barb covered for her but Dr. Ross, made a comment about how well she'd been doing lately with a long up-and-down look. As if Norah hadn't been feeling bad enough already.

Someone tapped twice on the plexiglass behind her, where Barb typically sat. "Excuse me?" *Tap, tap.*

Barb was on break, and Norah sat at her own desk facing her own customer window, which was unoccupied. Norah stifled a groan as she turned to face Barb's empty desk and the patient at the window.

"Excuse me," the woman said once again. "My appointment was fifteen minutes ago, and I need to be somewhere in an hour. How much longer?"

Norah put on her best customer service voice she could muster.

"I apologize, ma'am, but we are running just a little behind schedule. The doctor will be ready for you soon, I'm sure." She forced a smile. The lady began to protest, but Norah ignored her and turned back to her window.

Norah jumped and placed her hand to her chest, surprised to find someone standing in front of her. No, not just someone.

"Shit, Celeste, you scared me." Her racing heart was quickly replaced by a surge of annoyance at Celeste having shown up at her work.

"I'm sorry," Celeste said, fidgeting with her purse straps. "It's just, I think we need to talk. I shouldn't have come to your work, but I've tried calling and texting. I didn't know what else to do."

Norah groaned and gestured to the desk. "I'm busy. I can't talk right now." She shook the mouse on her computer, bringing the screen back to life.

"Twenty minutes," Celeste bargained.

"I can't." The last thing Norah wanted to do was talk with Celeste. She convinced herself the hallucination was the product of stress, her imagination running wild. She also told herself it was even possible Norah *did* mention Sam's anniversary date to Celeste before. Who knows.

But the situation still left a residue of unease she couldn't scrape off. She needed time to process, and having this conversation through a hangover seemed like a terrible idea.

She glared at Celeste.

"Ten?" Celeste begged, eyes pleading. She stood, now pulling at the sleeve of her top. A sherbert orange sweater adorned with yellow smiley faces, with heart shaped eyes.

There was no getting out of this. "Let me see if I can get Barb back from her break," Norah said. "I'll meet you outside."

Three minutes later, Norah walked out to talk with Celeste, her palms sweating. She inhaled deeply and scolded herself for her nerves. Celeste was odd, yes, but nothing more. She had nothing to do with the hallucination.

The door chimed as she opened it, and as soon as she was outside, Celeste turned to her. "I really can explain everything."

Norah crossed her arms as she let the door close behind her.

"Look, I don't remember telling you the date of Sam's death, but maybe I did. Let's just forget it. My reaction was out of line, and I'm sorry," she said, doing her best to ignore the anxiety building in her gut.

Celeste shook her head and said, "No, you weren't out of line. I can only imagine how scary that was for you. It's never happened before, at least not to my knowledge. This is not something they teach in our training. I'm not even supposed to be—" Celeste cut herself off, and took a deep breath. "I just don't know how or why it happened."

"Wait, what are you talking about?" Norah asked. They were clearly not talking about the same thing. A chill ran through her spine as images of Serge played in her mind.

Celeste stepped closer and leaned in.

"I know you saw it all," she whispered, as if she was afraid of being heard.

Norah stepped away from Celeste's reach. "I really don't know what you mean. I fainted; it happens to people all the time. I worked myself up. I've already been stressed with Chris and Sam and everything. It's fine. I gotta get back inside." Norah gestured towards the door.

"I know you saw Eugène. You said his and Serge's names when you came to. I was thinking of them, I touched you, you fainted, and then you said their names when you woke up."

Celeste took a deep breath while Norah couldn't find a breath to take. "I made it happen—I must have. I didn't mean to, and I was definitely not supposed to. I am sure I'll get in trouble." Norah began to ask what she meant by *get in trouble*, but Celeste wouldn't slow enough to let her. "The problem is, since I don't know why it happened, I can't be sure it won't happen again. I'm not supposed to be telling you any of this, Norah, but I think the line has already been crossed, and I just don't know what to do." The panic was vibrant on Celeste's face. Norah almost felt sorry for her.

"Celeste, you're all over the place. What the hell are you talking about?"

"It was a past life. Your past life."

Norah shook her head. "What? No," she laughed. "That's insane. I'm

going back to work."

"No, please!" Celeste called out as Norah turned for the door. "I know it sounds crazy to you, but it's true. Eugène–that was you. You died in 1987. The life right before this one."

"Celeste, stop," Norah said, throwing her left hand up as she reached for the door with her other. "This *is* crazy." She pushed open the office door and paused a moment. "I think maybe we just need to stop hanging out for a bit," she said before stepping back inside.

This was what she got for trying to make a friend.

# CHAPTER 23

## Celeste

No, no, no.

Celeste paced the floor of her apartment and resisted the urge to tear her hair out. She should have canceled the walk with Norah after her visit from Benny. She convinced herself it was wrong to simply disappear on Norah in her fragile state, for her to lose yet another friend—especially when she was opening up to her. Instead, Celeste feared she made matters much, much worse.

Celeste thought back to the moment she grabbed Norah's arm. She knew why the memory happened, even if she didn't know how. She was thinking about Eugène and Serge, the terrible heartache he felt at the death of his son, and all the years he carried that pain with him. It was so similar to what was happening to Norah and Sam. Celeste felt the connection the moment she touched Norah, a surge of energy she had never felt before. It was almost as if she was sending Norah the memories.

Norah's reaction to seeing Eugène was understandable, not that there would be a known level of expectation, but a near panic attack, pure terror. She wasn't surprised that Norah ran away from her, either.

But today. The look on Norah's face after she told her Eugène was a past life replayed in Celeste's mind. Pure confusion and disbelief gave way to a look that wrecked Celeste: Norah's eyes screamed *This woman is crazy.* It hurt Celeste the most. Celeste couldn't blame her; she was certain that if the tables were turned, she would have reacted the same way.

Celeste tried to collect herself. She needed to leave for work in a few short minutes if she was going to make it on time. She nearly laughed at the thought. Of course, she didn't *need* to get to work. Her own life here wasn't real. She could leave right now and be done with it.

But no, figuring out what caused Norah to see Eugène was far too important. Celeste had no idea what the consequences were, how many more Norah might see, and surely her seeing her past lives would be direct interference with the Lesson she needed to learn. There had to be a way to not only fix Norah seeing these memories, but to solve why it happened in the first place. It did put a wrench in the chance of pulling back and focusing on casual acquaintances...

She'd just need to fix things before the next time Benny came poking around.

# CHAPTER 24

# *Celeste*

I F ONLY SHE WERE ABLE TO CHANGE HER FACE AS EASILY as she was able to change her clothing. She didn't know who made up these stupid rules, but she absolutely did not like them. It should be that once someone moves on to the ultimate afterlife, they are free and clear to do whatever they want, but nope. The form that's chosen for the afterlife is the one you're stuck with. Stupid rules everywhere she looked.

Celeste stood at the front of the store, absentmindedly arranging and rearranging the counter. She was placed on cash register duty today while Dylan did the stocking. How he got any stocking done with his face glued to his phone was beyond her.

The last couple of days were never-ending. Norah wouldn't respond to Celeste's texts or calls. She tried once to track down Norah, disguising herself with big sunglasses, a big hat, and all-black clothing. Celeste couldn't believe it. *All black.* She was mortified enough to have worn black leggings and a solid blue shirt on the trail, but not to have *any* color. Appalling.

But alas, trying to disguise herself was far too stressful. She spent so much time hiding behind things that she missed every opportunity of actually seeing Norah. On top of that, she was so paranoid about Benny watching her that every noise or slight activity around her caused her to freeze or jump. It was exhausting.

She couldn't talk to Benny about what was happening with Norah, and she only had so much time here on Earth to figure it all out. There was the Archives–a place where all the Guardian records were stored–that may possibly hold some information on Souls seeing past lives, but asking Benny to bring her back and forth would surely cause suspicion.

If she didn't mend things with Norah, if she couldn't get through to her, then there really was no guarantee she'd make it through this life, and then what was it all for?

The smart thing to do would be to cut her losses. Leave now, return to her home, and hope that Norah learned the Lesson with help from Celeste the good old-fashioned way.

"What's got you all down in the dumps today?"

Celeste turned to see Dylan walking towards her. She looked around to see if there was anyone else he could be addressing, but the store was completely empty except for the two of them. She pointed at her chest. "Me?"

"Yes, you," he snorted. He made his way to her and leaned his elbows on the counter, customer side. "Normally you're so cheerful and excited to be here. I thought we were on an episode of Undercover Bosses when you first started."

*What? Undercover Bosses?* Celeste made a mental note to search for this reference when she was at the library next.

"But today I haven't heard a word from you. You didn't try to play with the beagle that came in earlier. You didn't even say hello to white bunny and gray bunny."

*Casey and Gigi.*

"Or to the goldfish dude over there."

*Lilly.*

"And you've rearranged those dog treats like nineteen times since you've been here."

Celeste's heart warmed at the thought of Dylan noticing all of that. If you asked her a minute ago, she would have said he didn't even know her name. She felt a ping of guilt over being so judgy about his cellphone. Only a little. He really was on that thing far too much.

"Oh, it's nothing." She sighed, and he raised his eyebrows skeptically.

She tried to quickly think of the best way to explain the situation.

"I'm fighting with a friend of mine. I *kinda* withheld some information from her; she found out and I tried to explain but now she doesn't believe me and things are a mess."

There was also the bit that Celeste forced a past life on her and completely freaked her out, but that was not something Celeste could explain to him.

Dylan nodded his head in understanding. Across the store, the pair of blue parakeets chirped.

Celeste picked up the jug of dog treats for the twentieth time, apparently, and just as she was slamming it down, admittedly a little too hard, a spider crept along the counter. *Too late.* Her arm was already in motion and unable to stop. "Oh no!" she shouted, lifting the container to evaluate the damage. She'd done it. She'd killed the poor little thing. She tried to hide her eyes from Dylan, but a tear escaped and made its way down her cheek.

Dylan stood, eyes wide, mouth open, arms thrown up. "You are not crying over a spider." His display of exasperation was so huge, it almost made Celeste laugh.

She wiped at both cheeks and said, "It's been a long day."

"Girls are weird," Dylan said, shaking his head. He bent low to reposition his forearms back atop the counter in front of him.

Celeste tried to pull herself together. "Anyway, I'm thinking about just moving home. Starting over."

He shot straight up to standing, his full height once again taking Celeste by surprise. All elbows and knees that one. "Over one little fight?"

"Well," Celeste shrank into her shoulders. "It was kind of a big deal. I want her to understand not only am I sorry, but why I didn't tell her in the first place. And that it really was all for her own good. But I just don't know what to do. I am afraid I messed it up for good." Her eyes scanned the counter beside her, landing on the spider. Scooping it up in a napkin to then throw it in the trash didn't feel right.

"This girl's your friend, right?"

Celeste turned back to Dylan and smiled ear to ear. "Yes, I'd even say she's my best friend."

"Seems crazy to leave town over one fight. Sounds like you guys just need to talk it out."

"What if she won't talk?"

Dylan shrugged. "Would you want her to give up on you?"

Celeste pressed her lips tightly together and shook her head.

Dylan gave a quick nod of his head as if to say 'and that's that,' and turned to go back to stocking the store.

"Thank you," Celeste called after him.

He shouted over his shoulder without looking back at her, "There's literally nothing to do today."

# CHAPTER 25

# Norah

A FEW DAYS HAD PASSED SINCE NORAH LAST SAW Celeste. The memory—feeling—of Eugène and Serge faded away more and more each day. She no longer needed to tell herself that it was some crazy invention of anxiety. She was officially and completely convinced.

It was probably what drew her and Celeste together in the first place. Two crazies finding each other so randomly. Like attracts like. She shuddered at the image of Celeste, wide-eyed and pleading, telling her that it was a past life she saw. Acting as if she knew something about it.

*Celeste did confirm the names Eugène and Serge.*

*No.*

It was for the best that she found out that Celeste was crazy early in their friendship. Norah's first red flag should have been that she was able to make a friend in the first place.

It didn't take a near-mental breakdown to know that when Norah drank less, her life was better. If she didn't get her habits right, she was going to have some serious consequences. The problem was, she once again found herself alone in her apartment, with her own thoughts, which never led to much good.

One can only run so many miles a day and bake so many brownies. She needed something to occupy her mind.

Which was how she found herself on a park bench, knitting, of all things.

If Sam could see her now.

She had gotten the idea from one of those long-forgotten magazines tossed on the side table in the waiting room at work—it boasted *"Fun and easy knitting patterns for beginners!"* She figured if she could focus her mind on her hands, she wouldn't think so much. A day or so of YouTube videos later, and she could at least do a few decent lines of a garter stitch. She was well on her way to making a blanket, or a scarf, or maybe just a lopsided dishcloth. Norah didn't care, it was just nice to have her mind focused on something productive.

Norah gazed at the field across from her, her eyes landing on a father playing catch with his son. Nearby, a golden retriever jumped up to catch the frisbee his owner tossed. The craziness of the last few days seemed more and more outlandish in the calmness that was surrounding her.

She watched the needles slowly work the bold pinks and purples of the yarn into progressively smoother knots. Celeste's voice rang in her head, squealing over Norah's color choices. She clenched her jaw and narrowed her eyes, forcing herself to focus on her knots. There was no way Norah was going to admit to missing Celeste's bubbly optimism, not even to herself.

Norah's shoulders relaxed while she worked, making steady progress. She listened to the clinking of her needles, the birds chirping in the distance, and the gentle rustling of leaves in the tree above her. She felt the warmth of the sun on her cheeks and the cool of the wind on her hands. Knot after knot.

"No, not like that." The girl beside her giggled. The girl waved her hands in front of Norah's face. "Peggy, you there?" She giggled again.

Norah shook her head and looked at the girl. Dark brown ringlets hung over both shoulders, and her big blue eyes stared at her, sparkling with amusement. Norah scanned the girl. Her baby blue dress, long and full with puffy sleeves and outlined in lace, looked like something out of *Gone with the Wind*. Norah looked down at her dress, drabbier compared to the girls in cloth and color, definitely not the jeans and long-sleeve T-shirt she had been wearing. And her hands, instead of holding knitting needles and yarn, held a small needle in one and a cream cloth in the other.

The park she had been sitting in transformed into a beautiful garden full of pristine marble statues of what Norah assumed to be gods and goddesses scattered amongst roses, hydrangeas, and ivy. Gone were the dad and son, the dog and his owner.

"You need to undo your last few rows of stitching. That will be an awful mess if you keep stitching like that. At this rate, it will take me years to teach you."

Norah's cheeks grew warm with embarrassment, and her heart filled with an overwhelming sense of gratitude for this young girl. She loved her dearly; she could feel it.

The scene shifted quickly, and Norah now walked down the corridors of a grand house. Portraits hung high on the walls, sconces lit in between each one, and she passed door after door, room after room. She felt at ease here; this was a place she knew well, but it was not home.

She entered a door to her right. "Finally, Peggy," said the same girl—only now she was a teenager. As she stood eagerly waiting, she said, "I need you to help me get ready for tonight."

Norah turned instinctively to the wardrobe and opened it knowingly. "How about the yellow?" she heard herself say with a voice that was not her own.

"Oh, I don't know." The girl shifted. "It doesn't feel right for such a big night. Why don't you fetch one of Anna's dresses? I am sure she will understand just this once. She knows how much this means to me. Oh, Peggy, I wish you could be there with me. I am so nervous," she squealed.

Norah's excitement rose as she went straight to Anna's room. Anna was Amelia's sister. *Amelia.* She made her way back down the same hall, walking as fast as her legs could carry her. Walking. Running would be undignified.

The scene shifted once again. They were back in the same garden they had been cross-stitching in as young girls. Flowers in full bloom around them. Norah sat on a white sheet across from an even older Amelia. She handed Norah a little navy box, a smile strung from ear to ear.

Norah shook her head no as Amelia pushed the box further into her hands.

"Peggy, you've been a true friend to me. I know I could never do enough to show you all my gratitude, and I know it's silly of me to think that if you didn't work for my family, we'd still be friends, but I'd like to. I'd like to think we found each other in this life for a reason. Happy Birthday."

Norah knew Peggy had never felt happier.

Peggy now found herself in a very dark library with mahogany wood shelves lining the walls, standing across from a stern-looking woman sitting, clenched hands resting on the mahogany desk in front of her. Peggy picked at her fingernails with her hands hidden behind her so that the lady of the house could not see. She felt true fear rise within her.

The woman spoke low and slow, in the way she talked to all the help, as if they needed it in order to understand her.

"Now, Peggy, I know you and Amelia have become...close," she said, pausing as if the word itself tasted sour, "over the years you've worked here. But, might I remind you, I hired you as her handmaid as a reward to your mother, who herself has worked for this family for many years. If I find that you have lied for Amelia, I assure you–you and your mother will never work for another family in this town again. Do you understand me?"

Peggy gnawed relentlessly at her bottom lip as she thought of her mother and what would become of them if she lost both their jobs. She tried to speak, but her throat and mouth had been robbed of all their moisture. She slowly nodded instead. She stared down at the floor, unable to look Amelia's mother in her eyes as she prepared to betray her only true friend.

Dread filled every crevice as Peggy collected herself enough to speak. "The rumors are true. Ms. Amelia has been meeting with James Mason without a chaperone."

NORAH TOOK A GULP OF AIR AS IF COMING UP FROM water. She looked down at her hands–for sure her hands this time–holding the pink and purple yarn and knitting needles. She surveyed her surroundings in search of any clue that something had changed. The same father and son tossed a ball in the field across from her, the same golden retriever ran back to his owner with the frisbee gripped tightly in his mouth. It was as if time stopped.

And yet it felt like she had lived a different lifetime.

The ache in her heart over the betrayal of the one true friend she ever had was all too real. For the girl who treated her not as a maid but as an equal, who taught her to read and write, to cross-stitch, and all about boys. The girl who told her everything, all of her secrets.

Norah felt tears burn hot down her cheeks as she recalled the last moments of Peggy's life, lying in her bed full of pain and guilt over how much Amelia hadn't deserved what she did to her.

If only she could apologize. If only she could take it all back.

Norah shook her head and wiped her cheeks as the visions and the feelings of Peggy's life faded. Her surroundings came back to her. The birds still chirped, the leaves still rustled, the sun still hit her cheeks.

What the fuck was happening?

There was no denying it that time. She needed to talk to Celeste.

# CHAPTER 26

# *Celeste*

Celeste knocked lightly on the door, her stomach clenched in anticipation. Arriving at Norah's unannounced was either going to be a very good idea or a massively terrible one. She shifted the weight of the basket onto her right arm and knocked once more.

The apartment door opened, and Celeste braced herself for a...surprisingly welcoming Norah?

"What's up?" asked Norah after an initial look of surprise, a sharp intake of breath, and what Celeste knew to be a look of forced indifference.

Okay, so not *welcoming* exactly, but certainly not the wrath she had been expecting.

"Hi, mind if I come in for a minute?"

Norah's eyes fell on the basket Celeste held before stepping aside and waving her in.

"I won't stay long," Celeste continued, filling the dead space between them as she walked through the door. "I know you don't want to talk to me."

Norah bit at her lower lip and dropped her gaze.

Celeste waited for Norah to speak, but when she didn't, she said, "I needed to tell you again how sorry I am, and I also thought it would be helpful if I could show you that I was telling the truth."

Celeste settled herself on the couch and scanned the room. Being in this apartment was as surreal to her as it was the first time she saw Norah in person. She'd seen this apartment so many times these last few years, but now she was there. It was a real space.

A deep crease formed along Norah's brow. "What do you mean, show me?"

"Well," Celeste started, handing Norah the basket she brought. "I know that I am late on this, but I also know that on Sam's anniversary, you watch *The Goonies* every year because it was his favorite movie."

Norah paused, opening the basket to look up at Celeste, a look of confusion on her face.

"And I know that you do that because you two spent years having Friday movie nights. At first, it was in homemade sheet tents in Sam's bedroom, which turned into giant pillow beds on Sam's bedroom floor, which then moved to dorm rooms and your shared apartment on Greystone Avenue."

Norah's dark eyes lightened as she shifted her weight continuously, unable to keep her body still. The brim of her eyes began to glisten with tears, and Celeste continued to talk.

"You took turns picking movies, rotating each Friday, and you both always picked the same snacks." Celeste nudged her nose towards the basket, breaking the spell from Norah. Norah continued opening the basket.

Hands shaking slightly, Norah pulled each bag out one by one, laying them on the coffee table in front of them. Twizzlers, Mike and Ikes, and a bag of Doritos for her. Milk Duds, Peanut Butter M&Ms, and cheddar popcorn for Sam. By the time she pulled out the final bag, pearl-sized tears streamed down her cheeks.

Celeste watched Norah take a moment, staring down at the snacks on the table.

"I don't understand what is going on here," she whispered softly.

Celeste threw her arms up and gave her best jazz hands. "Norah, meet your Guardian Angel."

It was a bold move, telling Norah who she really was. More to keep from Benny. But if she was going to get to the bottom of what was happening and stop it from directly interfering with the Lesson Norah needed to learn, she needed to be able to talk to her about it.

Norah scoffed. "Come on, be serious," she said, a little shake to her voice. "How do you know all this?"

"I am being serious. I've been with you your whole life. It's how I knew Sam's anniversary and why it would be a hard day for you. Beyond that, actually. It's how I knew about Luisa and Eugène."

Norah sat down on the couch next to Celeste, ran her hands through her hair, then promptly stood again. She walked around the coffee table, sat down on the couch, then stood once more.

"I don't think I can process this right now."

"Okay, okay." Celeste nodded as Norah made her way to her kitchen.

Moments later, Norah came back out holding a bottle of whiskey, two small glasses, and a smile.

"If there was ever a time I was in need of one of these..." She stopped dead in her tracks. "Oh, I'm sorry, you're trying to stop drinking," Norah said, realization crawling across her face. "Wait a minute. You weren't really trying to stop drinking, were you? There was no horrible grandfather who ruined your family." She stood there, the hand that clasped the bottle rested firmly on her hip, while the other, gripping the glasses, finger pointing at Celeste.

Celeste stood up from the couch, as tall and menacing as she could muster. "No," she said, tone authoritative. "Those were strategically manipulative stories provided for a reason. Norah, you should not be drinking." She pointed her finger right back.

"Celeste, I'm serious. Given the information you just gave, if there was ever a time–"

Celeste puffed out her chest, hands gripping her hips. "No," she said. "Give me the bottle." She stretched out her arm, palm up, and folded her fingers in a 'give-it-here' motion.

Norah looked down at the bottle, up at Celeste, back down at the bottle, and grunted. She sulked over to where Celeste was standing and shoved the bottle at her.

Celeste took the bottle back into Norah's kitchen, dumped the contents down the drain, and true to her abilities, conveniently found her favorite tea tucked in the back corner of one of Norah's cupboards. She met her back on the couch minutes later, with two steaming cups of tea.

"You know that drinking is not the way to solve problems," she said, handing a mug over to Norah, "but a good cup of tea can solve most of them."

Norah took the tea, hunched and brooding. Better than the yelling and freaking out as Celeste had expected.

"Now what?" Norah asked.

"Well, you can ask me anything."

"Something happened yesterday...but, no. I really don't think I want to talk about all this right now."

Curiosity bit at Celeste, but she didn't feel it was the time to push. Norah did have a lot to process.

She didn't want to leave her just yet. She may have dumped the whiskey, but it wouldn't be hard for Norah to go out and get more. "Why don't we set all that aside for now and just hang out?"

"Hang out?"

"Yeah, you know, do something together. We don't have to talk about anything you don't want to. But now that you know who I am, we can just, you know, be friends."

"You want me to act like everything is not fucking insane right now and just hang out and be friends with my Guardian Angel."

Celeste raised her shoulders and offered a tight-lipped smile.

After a moment of silence, Norah finally said, "What the hell. Let's just hang out. This can't get any weirder."

Ignoring Norah's word choice, she had been scolded enough already, Celeste said, "We could watch a mov–"

"No, not that."

"Too much, got it."

Norah went to sit down, but paused to glance sideways at Celeste before allowing herself to finally settle.

"Oh," Celeste exclaimed, practically jumping from her seat. "Would you teach me how to bake something? When I was alive, we made everything from scratch like you do, of course, but it wasn't exactly fun the way it seems to be now, and my guess is it all tastes a gazillion times better."

Norah hesitated, causing Celeste to slump back into her seat, worried it was a silly attempt. Eventually, Norah nodded and stood from the couch. "Sure," she said. "I've got enough ingredients for *something*."

Norah offered Celeste several options before she sheepishly requested an apple pie. She could practically smell the apples, butter, and spices. Norah wrinkled her nose and said, "I don't have any apples, but I did just buy a bunch of strawberries and blueberries. We can bake, like, a mixed berry pie?"

Celeste squealed and followed Norah into her kitchen, tight on her heels.

Norah worked her way around her kitchen, gathering all the ingredients while Celeste filled the space with chatter.

"I miss pies. We typically filled them with meat, but every once in a while we'd have fruit to fill them with. It was always such a treat."

"And when exactly was this?"

"Oh, sometime in the 1600s."

Norah dropped the spoons and spatulas she was gathering. Without so much as a glance at Celeste, she scooped them up and made her way over to the sink to wash them up. "Was that when you, I guess, what, like, died?" she asked, keeping her focus on the washing.

"Yes, officially, I guess you could say. I lived many lives before that."

Norah faced Celeste, lips pinched tight.

"Norah, we can talk about Eugène if you'd like?" Norah's shoulders tensed, and Celeste instantly regretted bringing him up. Focused on Norah's profile, Celeste could see her mind spinning.

"You know what I miss? Barb and those darn cats." Norah let out a laugh, body relaxing as she turned to look at Celeste full on. "How the heck is good 'ol Barb doing?"

"Barb is Barb," Norah beamed. "Always miserable, always worried about me, always the best."

Celeste kept the conversation as light as she could from there, getting a lot of practice in small talk, which still wasn't getting easier. A few times here and there, she noticed Norah pause, biting at her lower lip, lost in thought, then she'd cling onto whatever distraction she could pull from. Celeste didn't push.

If Norah decided she didn't want to know anything else about Celeste's identity or her past lives, and if she decided she never wanted to see Celeste again, Celeste would have to come to terms with that.

Celeste didn't stay long after they'd finished baking, wanting to give Norah her space to process. After she polished off a slice, Norah sent her home with the rest of the pie. Truthfully, the pie was too sweet for Celeste's liking, but she thought Norah had enough truth for the evening. This little white lie wouldn't hurt.

The next morning, Celeste awoke to a text from Norah asking if they could talk. The thought of Benny, yet again, tickled at the back of her mind for just a second. But her response was cool, calm, and collected—well, for Celeste, at least. She typed *"Of course"* with five exclamation points, then deleted a few, and finally settled on two.

From now on, Celeste promised herself she would only share the most necessary information with Norah. She vowed to stop making things worse.

# CHAPTER 27

NORAH SAT WITH A STEAMING CUP OF TEA CLENCHED between her hands. She tucked herself into the corner of the couch, knees close to her chest. The evening prior was overwhelming, to say the least. Norah wanted to talk about Eugène, Luisa, and Peggy, but once Celeste explained who, or rather what, she was, her Shit I Need Explained list grew exponentially to a jumbled mess of too much. She needed the time to process.

After Celeste left the night before, she spent her evening trying to make sense of things. She hardly slept, thinking about not only how the visions worked, but the meaning behind them. Why her, why now? Even with Celeste showing up in her life, Celeste herself didn't know the answers to these questions. She woke, or whatever waking was from a night of restless sleep, and immediately texted Celeste to come over.

It was late afternoon when Celeste arrived, and it took them a minute to get settled. Celeste dropped her tea within minutes of Norah handing it to her.

Celeste laughed as she used a napkin to dab at her pants. "Gravity can be very tricky. I didn't realize how hard of a time I would have adjusting."

Norah smiled as if that was at all relatable. "I can look and see if I have something you can change into."

"There will be something there if I look, but no need. I'm fine."

Celeste may know everything about her as her *Guardian Angel*, but there's no way she knew the size of everything she had in her dresser. "What do you mean there *will* be?"

"Guardian Angels have the power of...convenience. If I needed you to have clothes for me to change into, they would be there when I looked."

Norah raised a single eyebrow. "Your magic?"

"Not magic. I can't just wave my hand and clean up this spill."

"Right, to call you magical would be weird." Norah laughed.

It felt good to be with her friend again, even with how batshit crazy it all was.

Once settled, Norah explained her recent vision of Peggy. Despite what Celeste had already explained, her knowing nod and sympathetic smile were unnerving. Not only was it starting to feel as if Celeste knew Norah better than she knew herself, but she knew her past lives.

"You know the story of Peggy and Amelia?" Norah asked. She pulled her knees even tighter into her chest before wrapping an arm around her shins, the other gripping her tea. A piece of her expected to wake up from the life of Norah as if *this* life was a dream.

Celeste explained that Peggy was born in England in 1773. It was just her and her mother, as her father passed away shortly after her birth. Her mother, Mary, procured a job as a housemaid for the Westchesters, a very wealthy family, who, for the most part, treated Mary well. Peggy grew up on the estate and became close with Amelia, the younger of the two daughters. When Peggy turned twelve, she began working as Amelia's handmaid. Despite their roles and the power dynamics that came with them, the girls were very close, practically sisters.

Until one day, when Mrs. Westchester threatened Peggy. If Peggy refused to reveal a secret she was keeping for Amelia,

Mrs. Westchester would relieve both her and her mother of their positions.

The pieces of the dream connected for Norah as Celeste described it all. The fear and the nerves that Peggy felt then crept into every crevice of Norah's being, as if she were reliving it all again.

"Peggy knew Amelia had been seeing the Mason boy, someone whose station Mrs. Westchester found completely unacceptable," Celeste said, a slight tone of gossip to her voice. "It was also a very big deal in society back then to court in secret, to be without a chaperone." Celeste twirled her finger in front of her, a physical cue of et. cetera. "This was the secret Mrs. Westchester forced out of Peggy. Well, you. The secret destroyed your friendship. Amelia lost the love of her life, and she never forgave you for it. As it turns out, she never did get over him. As time went on, you continued to work in the house, but were moved to the kitchens, and a new handmaid was hired for Amelia."

Norah took a big sip of her tea, trying to process the way Celeste was referencing Peggy as if she *were* Peggy.

Conversation wandered to Eugène, and Norah found it hurt to talk about him. The pain of the loss of Serge still felt so raw. "He was your most recent life," Celeste explained. "It makes sense that his story would feel the most intense—I'm guessing, anyway." Celeste lounged on the couch, tucked cozily into the corner, leg propped up on the coffee table. "Not to mention the loss of a child. Unimaginable."

"This is all way too much." Norah ran her hand along her face.

"I'm sorry. I really am. Like I tried to explain, I'm new to this. You're actually the first Soul I've ever guided," she said.

Celeste explained the training process to Norah, such a funny concept, and that she will get to watch over more than one Soul once she is done.

"And does a Soul have the same Guardian for all of their lives?"

"Sometimes reassignments happen. It could be due to a number of things: a Guardian retires, a Guardian whose workload is too full can request that one of their Souls gets transferred to another Guardian, or the Guardian doesn't feel connected enough to the Soul and the Council feels the Soul would be better off with another Guardian."

Norah's head was beginning to throb. "You're making enlightenment sound like nothing more than an eternal job. Sounds awful."

Celeste laughed. "You don't have to be a Guardian; you can choose to do whatever you want in your afterlife. Being a Guardian is very high up in the ranks, though, and it is a rather rewarding position." She sat up taller on the couch and took a sip of her tea, lost in thought.

"I made you see Eugène's life, *your* life, when I grabbed your arm the other day. I think it's because it was the one I was thinking of at that moment, and when I grabbed you, I sorta sent it to you. I really don't know, though. I've never heard of this happening before. But then for you to be able to see Peggy, and I wasn't even around you...." Celeste sighed and tapped at her teacup. "I have never heard of this happening before."

"What about a woman named Luisa?" Norah asked cautiously.

Celeste's foot dropped heavily from the coffee table as she leaned forward toward Norah. "You know about Luisa?"

Norah nodded, eyes wide at Celeste's reaction. "I dreamt of Luisa, and Alvaro, and her–my–parents. It felt so real. I remember every detail." Norah shook to clear a bit of fog. It was going to take this lifetime just to process all this.

"Luisa was born in Portugal in 1723. You fell in love with a horrible man named Alvaro, who used you and stole everything from you and your parents." Celeste scowled.

Norah hung her head, unable to look Celeste directly in the eyes. She knew what she saw and, more importantly, *felt*, with all of them, but– "This is unreal," she finally managed to mutter. "I'm trying, but it's just all so hard to believe." If her tea hadn't cooled to room temperature, she would have been tempted to spill a little to test if she felt the burn.

Celeste smiled and rested her hand gently on Norah's arm. "I've been here with you through it all. Well, since becoming your Guardian. Eugène, Peggy, Thomas, I could name them all. Different lives, yes, but they're all *you*. It's *your* soul that carries through. I've watched you achieve every milestone of every life, witnessed you fall in love countless times, mourn your heartache and loss. As a woman, a man, a child. Doesn't matter, at the real heart of it, you're all one."

Tears welled in Celeste's eyes, the color bluer than usual, as she described her the way a mother would proudly reflect on the accomplishments of her daughter. Norah felt a pull so strong she had to stop herself from reaching toward Celeste for a hug.

She looked away and cleared her throat, saying, "So there's one of you for every one of us? That seems a bit crazy. Half of the human population is really just angels watching over us? Aren't you supposed to be up there?" She pointed up towards the ceiling of her apartment.

*Heavens*. Whatever. Norah didn't even think she believed in God and Heaven and Hell and all that stuff, but angels sitting on clouds out of sight seemed far more believable than them living on Earth.

Celeste laughed. "Oh no, that *would* be crazy. We aren't allowed to be here at all." She grinned. "I'm not actually supposed to be talking to you, let alone revealing who I am—and who you are." She extended her hands wide and nearly spilled her tea once again. Her pink cheeks oddly comforted Norah. If this were all true, Celeste being embarrassed over her clumsiness made things less scary.

"Why are you here if you aren't allowed to be, then?"

"Weeellll," Celeste dragged out the word, shifting in her seat. "You needed a little extra help."

Norah's instinct was to scoff, but looking back at the last several years of her life, she couldn't exactly deny it.

"Will this get you in trouble?"

Celeste picked a very small piece of something off her fuchsia T-shirt and said, "Don't you worry about that. We just need to get you through this Lesson."

"Lesson?" Norah asked.

"There are seven major Lessons involved. The Lessons are far more complicated than simple words and definitions, but at their core, the Lessons are Kindness, Humility, Empathy, Generosity, Temperance, Honesty, and...the last I can't reveal. That's the Lesson you are on now. For me to just tell you would be detrimental to you. You wouldn't be able to learn it on your own fully.

"Each of a Soul's lives are meant to teach a lesson. Not in any specific order, as long as the Soul Learns them all. Sometimes it only takes one life for a Soul to learn a Lesson, sometimes a Soul can learn multiple Lessons in one life, and sometimes it takes many lives to learn a single Lesson. Regardless, each one sets a Soul on the proper path to the afterlife."

Norah nodded. "Enlightenment."

"If you need to put a word to it, that seems to be the most popular one these days," said Celeste.

"Okay, and what happens if I don't learn all the lessons? I just keep going on forever? That sounds exhausting."

Celeste suddenly found another very small something on her shirt, only this time it took several attempts to remove it.

"Celeste," Norah said, her voice cautious. "What happens?"

Celeste cleared her throat. "Well, each Soul gets twenty-five lives to accomplish all Lessons."

Norah laughed. "I only have one Lesson left? That's ridiculous. Like you said, I am a total mess. That would point to some sort of perfect person."

Celeste rolled her eyes. "I never called you a mess, and no one will ever be perfect, and the Council, they are the Guardians who determine if a Soul learns all their Lessons, doesn't expect perfection. But you are all of those things and more, Norah. You may slip up from time to time, but you can choose to do the right thing, to correct your own behavior, to be there for others: the *good* in you all adds up."

Celeste continued to explain how each of the Lessons carries over from life to life. "Babies, especially old soul babies who have lived multiple lives already, are the wisest. The problem is that people mistake wisdom for intelligence. Ever have a baby stare into your soul? They know things. But then their current life takes over, and their old memories fade to make room for what they are learning in their current life. But those true Lessons stay. Not always granted, some people have to take a few steps back, repeat a Lesson. We all know how brutal life can be."

It was odd hearing the Celeste she had come to know—silly, goofy, childlike Celeste–talk with such clarity, such wisdom herself.

Norah furrowed her eyebrows. "Speaking of babies. I hate to say this, but not everyone could possibly live long enough to learn a Lesson. How does that work with only twenty-five chances?"

Celeste smiled knowingly and said, "If you do sadly pass before the age of five, then it doesn't count towards your twenty-five lives; that's the general rule. Souls do need the chance to learn the Lesson, of course."

Norah's eyes grew big. "Five doesn't seem fair, either."

"Remember, children are the wisest," Celeste said, sipping at her tea. "You'd be surprised. You passed away at four in 1608, and it didn't count, but in 1623, you were twelve. That did count. In that life, you learned Temperance. You were the caretaker of your younger siblings, and..."

"Okay, if I am on my last Lesson," started Norah. Maybe someday she'd be able to sip tea and comfortably talk about the life of assumed suffering where she died at the ripe old age of twelve, but she needed to refocus the conversation. "And if what you say is true, and I have already successfully learned six of the seven Lessons—but also know that learning a Lesson can take multiple lives—how many lives have I lived?"

Celeste paused, biting at her lip. Norah could tell that she desperately wanted to look down at her shirt, but she wasn't going to allow Celeste to avoid the hard answers when she'd already told her so much.

"This is your twenty-fifth Life."

"Holy shit, no wonder I'm so fucking tired." She laughed before registering what the number meant. "Wait, you said only twenty-five lives. What happens if I don't complete this Lesson?" Norah untucked her feet from the couch and planted them firmly on the ground. "Please don't tell me I have to start all over. I'm too fucking tired for that."

Celeste shot Norah a disapproving look over her choice of language, and Norah fought the urge to shrink into herself. The shift from the typical, corky Celeste to a more serious, parental role was jarring, and Norah nearly laughed at the absurdity of it all.

"It's taken you a while for you to catch on to this particular Lesson. It's okay," Celeste said, assuringly. "Five of your lives, not including this one, have been dedicated to this Lesson in particular. It really is the hardest one. Almost *every* Soul has a difficult time with this one. And that's why I wanted to come down to earth and guide you." Celeste's smile shone brightly, but her eyes said otherwise.

"Celeste," Norah pushed, scooting a little closer to her on the couch. "What happens if I don't complete the Lesson?"

Celeste stared down into her teacup.

"Your Soul isn't reborn."

# CHAPTER 28

# *Celeste*

S HE TOLD HER WAY TOO MUCH. STUPID.

Get a good cup of tea in her hands and she's too darn comfy to keep her mouth shut.

Celeste walked the main street through town to get home. It was a long walk. She hoped it would clear her head. She needed to find a way to dig herself out of the hole she was in. A hole she created. A hole she kept digging deeper.

She had just under two months until Benny brought her home, and if he found out she told Norah who she was, she'd be pulled back in an instant. Would Benny remove her from her training? Surely he couldn't tell the Council he let her go to Earth, but would he find his own way to punish her?

At least she kept their conversations strictly to what was going on directly with Norah, and didn't hint at what her Lesson was. That was still fully in Norah's hands to learn.

Norah had no idea of the trouble Celeste could be in, and she intended to keep it that way. Norah didn't need the added stress, not that Celeste fully comprehended what might happen herself. Celeste needed her own Guardian. No, she needed a Mentor. She needed Benny. She wished she could go to him for help, ask him why Norah was seeing her past lives and what it meant for her.

She was at a loss, and clearly, the more she did, the more she messed things up. She shouldn't have listened to Dylan's advice to talk it out with Norah. She should have gone home and continued her Guardianship the way it was supposed to be. After all, Norah was still young in this life. She had plenty of time to sort it all out. That is, if she didn't fall ill or get hit by a bus while running.

Sometimes it really was terrible to have seen so much.

Life was so unpredictable that even a Guardian couldn't stop fate.

Celeste needed Norah to get through this life, and Celeste needed to help Norah succeed. The thought of Norah not making it to her afterlife brought an ache to Celeste she couldn't quite explain. Through all her training, each Guardian she knew who watched their Soul fail their own Lessons, no one ever talked of the heartbreak that came with it.

The sidewalk was fairly empty given the early evening hour. Celeste absentmindedly looked in each shop's window as she passed. She came across the cutest bookstore/teashop called NovelTea, and practically gasped at how perfect and cozy it looked. A little tea bar was tucked into the corner, rows of glass jars showing a variety of loose-leaf teas were displayed along the back wall. Bookshelves surrounded the bar, bursting with books begging to be read. Couches of different sizes and colors were arranged throughout. People slumped into the cushions, so relaxed they practically melted into the furniture, sipping tea and reading books. Celeste thought it looked heavenly, and she sighed deeply.

Typically, people watching was her favorite thing to do, especially from this vantage point, but too much was on her mind.

This was beyond her now. Celeste had no clue what Norah's past lives meant, why she could see them, and the real impact it could have on Norah, or her and Benny, for that matter. It went deeper than Celeste's involvement potentially, and inadvertently, ruining Norah's chances at learning her final Lesson. If only she could dig around in the Guardian Archives without drawing too much attention.

"Could it have anything to do with..." Celeste thought out loud, stopping mid-stride to pinch her nose in frustration. A young kid behind her was forced to swerve around her to avoid colliding.

"Sorry," they both said in unison as he kept walking.

"No," she said to herself as she continued along the sidewalk. "That can't be it."

Why did she have to be such a workaholic in the afterlife? She should have been taking all these centuries to relax, make friends, and read good books.

She felt Benny's pendant grow warm where it rested on her wrist, and a mixture of emotions swirled about her stomach.

His voice sounded frantic.

"Celeste, I have to get you back here. Now. I'll
be pulling you back in a few. Be prepared."

She scurried onto a side street, away from any possible eyes. "Now what?" She groaned, afraid of what waited for her. Did Benny know already? She felt the pull deep in her gut, as if a rope was pulling her from the inside, and the street around her disappeared as everything went black.

A few seconds later, Benny stood before her, surrounded by the gardens tucked between the Great Hall and Guardian Tower. If anything, he looked more frazzled than angry. Relief washed over Celeste.

"I'm sorry to pull you back without much warning, but Silas is looking for you."

She huffed in response. "For what?"

"I don't know exactly, but he's been asking more and more questions lately. You need to show your face around here and to him."

"I thought you said you weren't worried and that you told him I was working on something for you?"

"I did," he said, arms flailing. "But he's getting nosier and nosier, and I think it would be best if you go see him. He just asked me again where you were. I panicked and told him you were going to take a walk in the garden, and for him to see if he could catch you." Celeste couldn't help but grumble. "I have to run to a Council meeting. Just go talk to him, Celeste. I'll send you back to Norah when you are done."

Benny sprinted toward the Great Hall, and just as she was about to shout to ask where she was to meet Silas, the know-it-all himself walked around the bend.

"Hello, Celeste, good to see you around. I was beginning to think something happened to you." His beady eyes crinkled at their edges.

Celeste flashed her teeth, doing her best not to show her annoyance. "Hello to you, Silas." He stopped in front of her. Celeste said, "How are you doing?"

"Oh, you know. Same old, same old. Hard at training alongside Reginald. My Soul only has two more Lessons to learn, and at the speed they've learned the others, I should be set to graduate soon." Celeste clenched her jaw to stop from speaking. If she needed to be seen by him to stop his suspicions, she needed to play nice, too. "Speaking of." Silas steepled his fingers under his chin and feigned a thoughtful expression. "How is your Soul doing, Celeste?"

"She's great. We're almost all set, too." Silas squinted his eyes and rested his chin deeper atop finger tips. "In fact, she's on her last Lesson—just one more to go! Yep, we are all good over here." She fidgeted while she peered around the gardens, as if entranced with the view. She didn't want to look at Silas and his prying eyes.

"Celeste," he said in a sing-song voice.

"Yes?" Heat rushed up her body and warmed her cheeks.

"I've asked Benny several times where you've been lately, and he just sort of waves me off, tells me you're doing this and that for him. I was beginning to think it strange that there was always some sort of errand or something keeping you busy."

"Oh. Ha ha. Yeah, you know Benny. Always has his Trainees going above and bey—"

"But, you know," he said, wagging his pointer finger in front of him as he paced a few steps in front of her. "Reginald did tell me how you went in front of the Council to request going down to see your Soul."

At that, Celeste's face burned with anger. The nerve. How dare Reggie say something? "That's really none of your business."

Silas turned, stopping once more to face her, and *tsked* his tongue.

"Now, now," he pandered. "No need to get upset. Reginald was just letting out some of his frustrations with Benjamin. He let it slip that he was actually on your side. I personally found it quite funny." He laughed. "To think, you actually thought the Council would send you down." He pouted and said, "I am sorry to hear you are having such a difficult time."

Celeste stepped closer to him, hands balled together at her side. Before she could speak, Silas said, "But don't you find it odd that after the Council denied you, you all of a sudden disappear? Going on all these *important tasks* from your Mentor? The Mentor who supported you going down to Earth for your Soul in the first place?"

It was as if the wind was knocked out of Celeste. She stepped back from Silas, nearly bumping into a Guardian walking along the garden path behind her. The ground below her felt wobbly, and it took everything in her not to buckle at the knees. Silas's face beamed with triumph.

"I don't know what you are talking about," she said, cursing herself for sounding breathless and weak.

"I believe that you do. And I am going to do everything I can to prove it."

"There is nothing for you to prove," she said.

"I think there is. I sincerely hope that whatever it is you and Benny are wrapped up in, you only end up with a slap on the wrist. We don't want you to get kicked out of the Guardian training or for Benny to lose his seat on the Council."

Celeste thought of Benny helping her go against the Council and what that might mean for him. *Would* he get kicked off the Council?

"Silas, it's...it's nothing."

Silas's eyes glistened.

"I can explain." She tried to think on her feet, to make up a lie, but his discovery hit her too hard, too quickly. How foolish of her to think that no one would notice her absence. She needed to think of something, and fast.

"There is nothing to explain, Celeste. If you broke the rules—and make no mistake, I will find out if you did—it is my duty to report you to the Council. It will hurt me as much as it hurts you, but I couldn't let this go unreported; that would reflect poorly on me." His eyes practically glistened in the sunlight.

"Silas, you're wrong."

"Or," he purred, "you could talk to Benny about how great a Guardian I would be, make sure he votes for me to graduate with good—no great—reviews. I could turn a blind eye to whatever all this is that you two have going on."

Furry bubbled up in Celeste. "That's what this is about?"

"He's already given me a bad mark on my *Planting Subtle Thoughts* test; I just know he has it out for me."

*I knew it,* thought Celeste.

"If you talked to him for me, explain how good I am."

A cool breeze made its way through the garden in juxtaposition to the heat rising within her. "This isn't very *Guardian Angel* of you, Silas."

"And whatever you're doing is, I'm sure. I want to be the best of the best. One day, I'll sit on the Council. Do you know how much good I could do in that position? How many Souls I could help?"

Celeste shuddered at the thought of Silas on The Council. Two Reginalds? No way.

"From the moment I got here, I knew that was what I wanted to do. If Benny prevents me from passing to be a Guardian, or worse, getting on the Council in the future, I don't know what I would do."

*Well, that tugged at the heartstrings a bit.*

A lightbulb lit up in Celeste's mind. She could stop Silas from tattling by giving him what he wanted, and prevent Benny from checking in on her. She may even be able to get help with figuring out why Norah was seeing her past lives.

It was either a genius idea or the stupidest thing she'd ever done.

She pulled him further into an alcove of the garden, took the deepest breath she had ever taken, and then told Silas everything.

He laughed harder than she'd ever seen him laugh before.

"Let me get this straight," he started, back to the Silas she knew and disliked. "You not only went against the Council and went down to be with your Soul, but you then went against Benny, the one member of the Council who supported you, and you have directly interfered."

Celeste had to stop herself from actually biting her tongue. She began to say yes, and to explain, again, the situation, but Silas had more to throw at her.

"And *then*," he continued, at least with enough self-awareness to keep his voice low, "and then, you went as far as to show your Soul their past lives?" He threw his head back in quiet laughter and exaggeratedly wiped fake tears from his eyes. "This is definitely a new square on the Bingo card."

"I didn't mean to do that. I don't know how it's happening," she said, teeth clenched.

She allowed him to carry on with his theatrics for a moment more.

"Silas, this is serious," she hissed and looked around to check for prying eyes and ears. "I need your help."

A Guardian named Anya walked by, her big warm smile always at the ready, and Celeste threw up her hand in a quick hello.

She looked back at Silas and whispered, "It started to happen when I touched her. At the time, I was full of emotion, and I think that brought on that specific life—but actually there was a time before—"

The memory of the pet store, when Norah came in and Benny was there, she and Norah bumped hands and shocked each other. That was right before she dreamt of Luisa.

"She's seen others, too. I just...I don't know the consequences, which is why I need you. Have you ever heard of this happening before?"

He made a big show of trying to calm himself down, quaffing the sides of his chestnut hair, and fanning his hand in front of his face. He began to shake his head. "No, I haven't. Admittedly, you've even stumped me."

"This could be dangerous, right? I need to stop this and just come home, right?"

Silas's dark eyes grew to the size of small plates. "No, no. You need to see this through. You need to see what happens. This is her last life, and she has to learn this Lesson, right?" Celeste nodded her head. "Then you need to keep going. And, um, what exactly does this have to do with me and Benny?"

Oh, right. Celeste was so wrapped up in finally being able to talk to someone about what was going on, she forgot about the more threatening issues of Silas telling the Council and how to stop him from doing so. "Well..." She leaned toward Silas once more and whispered, "If you help me figure out what's going on with Norah, I'll convince Benny to let you help him keep an eye on me. You'll get to work closely with him and get on his good side, but you cannot tell him about all of this. Just tell him enough to keep him convinced you're watching over me, so he doesn't have to."

Silas stepped back, deep in thought and consideration. "All you did was touch her, right?"

"The first time I touched her, there was a shock between us, and I believe that is what led to Norah dreaming about her life as Luisa. Then, when we were walking, I was already emotional over Benny and distracted by trying not to give Norah the address for the Bryers. My mind drifted to Eugène and how the guilt of the loss was similar to the way Norah was feeling about Sam. I made a very stupid mistake mentioning something I shouldn't have known, and I panicked. When I touched her, I think I gave her the memories of Eugène."

Celeste hadn't figured out Peggy yet, but it was as if the jolt opened up a window into Norah's past lives for her to see.

Silas listened quietly, now taking the information seriously with his newfound role in the matter. Other Guardians continued to pass by, strolling among the gardens, barely noticed by Celeste as she kept her focus tightly on Silas. So much now weighed on what he said next.

Silas said, "I can find a way to get information out of Reginald, I am sure. This can't possibly be the first time this has ever happened." The mention of Reginald carved a pit in her stomach. Of course, Silas would think to go to him for answers. "Okay, I'll help. I'll play along and be your babysitter for Benny. But," he said, pointing a finger so sharply at Celeste she took a step back, "this better get me on Benny's good side."

The *or else* was implied. Celeste felt her whole body shudder.

# CHAPTER 29

## Celeste

After Silas left the gardens, Celeste sat for a while collecting her thoughts. Eventually, she'd go find Benny so she could return to Earth, but already she regretted her decision to include Silas.

True, he would have kept digging, more than likely discovered that she was on Earth with her Soul, and he would have told the Council, ensuring the end to her–and Benny's–Guardian status. Also true that she needed help figuring out why Norah was seeing past lives. If seeing her past lives caused any damage to her ability to learn her final Lesson, Celeste had to be able to stop and correct said damage.

But *why* did her *only* solution have to be working with Silas to trick Benny?

How could she make sure Silas stayed satisfied enough not to go looking beyond what he needed, and keep Benny from checking in on her?

By the time she arrived at Benny's office, Celeste had the details of her plan flushed out.

Benny's ears grew red as she relayed parts of her conversation with Silas. "He was going to keep poking around. I knew if I didn't tell him something, he was going to discover what we were doing on his own and tell the Council."

"How could you have told him?" he shouted.

Benny's office sat along the outer wall of the top floor in the Great Hall. It was always piled high with old cardboard filing boxes. He liked to use the records from the Souls he helped pass over to their afterlife in his training. Celeste hoped the boxes would help to insulate the walls of his office.

"You told Silas, of all beings, that we went against the Council's orders, and I allowed you to go down to Earth to intervene with your Soul. Do you have any idea what might happen?"

"He cornered me, Benny. I panicked," she said, backing into a stack of boxes.

"You could have denied it, Celeste, then came and talked to me. We could have thought of something."

If only it were that simple. If only things hadn't gotten so complicated.

"You told me he was harmless," she said, reminding him of the conversation they had in the pet store. She expected his angry reaction, but she needed him to know about Silas for her plan to work, and playing dumb was essential.

"That was before you went waving a white flag in front of him, when I thought there wasn't any real chance of him finding out."

*Fair point.*

"Not to mention," he continued, "I was trying to prevent you from worrying. Silas is training to be a Guardian. I do believe he's a good Soul and I don't think he'd go so far as to lie or cheat, but he is ambitious." Benny leaned his backside on his desk, both hands gripping the top. "I know he's worried about my vote to pass him. I know his dream is to have a seat on the Council. You just gave him everything he would need without him having to lie or cheat. He could go right now, directly to the Council, tell them everything he knows, and get me kicked off without barely needing to lift a finger."

Celeste lifted a stack of papers from his desk chair and placed them on his desk, next to his mini Rock 'em Sock 'em robots. "You were right about him worrying you weren't going to pass him. I think we can use this to our advantage."

Benny ignored her and said, "At least you aren't directly interfering with Norah. We'll just bring you home now, and with no damage done, maybe we'll both just get a slap on the wrist." As he spoke, his tone turned from anger to fear. He plopped himself down heavily in his chair.

A fearful Benny was far more terrifying than an angry Benny.

There was a brief moment in which she questioned her plan. "I'm sorry," she said, unable to look him in the eyes. She had been blinded by her mission to help Norah and had no idea just how impactful her adventure could be on Benny. She shouldn't have allowed him to support her going, and so blatantly breaking the rules. She was putting his position on the Council at risk for her own selfish reasons.

But her concerns subsided quickly. There was no way she was giving up and going home. "Please let me go back down to Earth. I can't give up on Norah. You're right. Knowing Silas, he won't keep our secret unless he's getting something out of it, but there has to be something we can do."

She faked a sudden flash of genius perfectly, further pushing away her guilt over Benny's position. "What does Silas want the most?"

Benny, still leaning on his desk, crossed his feet about the ankles and shrugged. "To pass his Guardian Training and one day be on the Council."

"Exactly!" she exclaimed. "Let him watch over me for you. I know you're busy with the Council, your Souls, and your other Trainees. I already promised you I wouldn't do anything else to make things worse. He can report on my actions to you."

"I don't think involving him more is the answer."

Celeste pushed, "It will help you two build a friendship."

Benny shook his head. "Celeste, I didn't get on the Council by passing Trainees because I have a friendship with them. I am still going to vote for him the way I see fit."

"As long as he feels as if he is getting closer to you, he won't tell the Council about us."

"I shouldn't have allowed you to go. I should have pulled you back when I first felt you were directly interfering. All of this is just as much my fault as it is yours. I thought you deserved the chance. I thought this would be a great learning opportunity. A fun exercise with one of my Trainees to see what it would be like to guide from Earth. I was wrong."

Celeste stood and forced Benny to look her in the eyes. "You weren't wrong. I was wrong for taking on too much and getting too close to Norah. I was wrong for telling Silas, but you weren't wrong for letting me go. I know I can help Norah learn her Lesson, and I know I can do it from Earth. Let Silas look after me, let him report to you as if he's involved. It will keep him occupied. I have just over a month. Please let me see this through."

Benny closed his eyes tight. "Fine," he said through clenched teeth. "But don't make me regret this."

It was risky, giving Silas more power than she was comfortable with, but ideally, the payoff would be big enough to stop him from going to the Council. She hoped that if Silas had the sense of getting on Benny's good side, it would prevent him from feeling the need to sabotage anything. She hoped this would mean she no longer needed to be worried about Benny watching over her.

She hoped.

Celeste now had two separate communication pendants to answer to. She still kept Benny's on a chain around her wrist, and he gave her a second set intended for her and Silas to stay in contact. The second, she kept tucked in her pocket. It didn't matter what Celeste wore; she *always* had pockets.

Benny threatened that if Silas reported anything that made him uncomfortable, he would pull her right back home.

If she could stop making things worse, that would really be great.

# CHAPTER 30

## Norah

A FEW DAYS HAD PASSED SINCE CELESTE WAS LAST AT Norah's. She needed a few days to process all Celeste told her, and Norah still wasn't sure how to take it all in. She had a million questions about her past lives and a million questions about her current one, especially if there was such a high chance this may be her last.

What was the Lesson she needed to learn, and how was she going to know when she learned it?

But if Norah was completely honest with herself, she simply missed her friend and was happy to have an excuse to see her.

When Norah first arrived at Celeste's that day, once Celeste grabbed some snacks and poured them each a glass of tea–iced this time–she asked a question that had been weighing on her.

"So, did you watch me all the time...or were there times you, you know, looked away?"

Celeste turned a very pretty shade of pink, one that matched the paint on her walls, before letting her know that there were rules around that sort of thing. "We don't watch every minute of every day. It's more like I check in. Full-time Guardians watch over more than one Soul at a time; it can be a lot of work. We don't watch *everything*."

"So, do you, like, just get told you're going to be a Guardian? What if you don't want to? Or is that the ultimate ending to all this? Helping the people down here not fuck up too much?"

Celeste shouted, "Language!" causing Norah to playfully toss a throw pillow at her.

Celeste caught the pillow and set it down beside her. "No, you do get to pick, but not just anyone can be a Guardian. A member of the Council approaches you when you first arrive in your afterlife. It's a weighing-of-the-soul type of thing," Celeste said, setting her glass down and gesturing with her hands, up and down like a scale. "But I could have said no and chosen any afterlife I wanted. I could've lived with any surroundings I could imagine–a cabin in the woods, a huge, old mansion, a circus, anything. I could've been surrounded by people or completely alone. I could've looked however I wanted to, could've been any form, man or woman, at whatever age, shape, or race. If a person can think of it, it can be their afterlife. That's the reward."

"And you chose to watch over people for all of eternity?" Norah asked, scooping salsa onto a chip and taking a bite.

"Well, yes."

"Why? I mean, it's honorable, sure, but the way you talk about it, it's quite the commitment."

"When I first arrived, being a Guardian just felt *right*." She explained how she learned of the many lives people led, the unknowing chances they have to get each Lesson. "It can be really beautiful to watch a Soul move through their life, learning a Lesson, watching things fall into place. To know that every Soul is on a journey to learn and grow. That everyone is human. The ability to follow and help a Soul through that process was, truly, an honor. One I couldn't pass up."

"So, what about you? What about your lives and your lessons?" Norah asked. Norah felt her eyes grow big as her next question dawned on her. "Do we get to remember everything once we get there?"

Celeste laughed. "Yes, we remember once we are there, and it's such a surreal and wonderful feeling to be able to put all the pieces together."

"Can you tell me anything about your Lives? Who you were, where you lived? How many lives did you need before you learned all your Lessons?"

"I lived twelve lives total." Whatever face Norah made had Celeste quickly saying, "It's different for everyone, and more often than not, people use all their lives to get through all the Lessons." Norah nodded and did her best to hide her reactions better as Celeste continued to explain some of her past lives.

"My lives were lived in a different world than the one you know. There was no technology, no reaching someone the instant you needed them. There was no real medical care, no running to the store for groceries, no electricity or running water. In a lot of ways, it was much more difficult, but it was also much easier. We didn't know what we didn't know, and we had what we had. My lives were centered, really centered, around the people in them. I've had husbands and wives, lives with children and lives without, lives where a single interaction I had with someone changed the entire trajectory of their life. You'll get to see the impact you had when you get to your afterlife and run through all your lives."

"If I make it to my afterlife."

Norah could see the worry in Celeste's eyes. "You will. It's what I am here for."

Norah shifted her weight on Celeste's overstuffed teal couch and changed the subject. "You mentioned looking the way you choose to. Is this how you look up there, too?" she asked.

"Yes, I could only choose once, when I first arrived, but I can't imagine myself any other way. Celeste was my favorite life. I had some good ones, but she was an inherent caregiver, always kind. Plus," Celeste nudged Norah's elbow with her own, "this was the perfect image of an angel to me."

After talking with Celeste, Norah felt a little better. She'd never know half as much about Celeste as Celeste knew about her, but, still, better.

They made their way into the kitchen from Celeste's living room to replenish the chips and salsa they had been snacking on, but before getting back to the living room–and in true Celeste fashion–she tripped and dumped the full bowl of salsa down the side of her. Norah couldn't help but laugh at her child-like excitement over getting to change her outfit. While Celeste went to get washed up, Norah tried to make herself useful by wiping up the floor and counter.

That's when she saw the piece of paper.

Norah stood staring at the piece of paper lying upright on Celeste's kitchen counter. If it wasn't right in front of her, she'd think she was imagining it, but there it was, in Celeste's curvy handwriting, in blue ink. Although it would be fair to question the things she had been seeing lately.

Looking down at the Bryers' name and address scrawled in Celeste's loopy writing reminded Nora how unsettled she felt about the situation. She was still reconciling the fact that Celeste knew everything about her. From the way she brushed her teeth to how she arranged the sweaters in her closet by thickness. But this–seeing Sam's parents' name–was almost too intimate.

She had been wrapped in the strange world of Luisa, Eugène, and Peggy, trying her best to process and tie them to her current life and what her final Lesson was, yet she simply was not prepared for the possibility of facing the Bryers.

"Phew, salsa makes quite the mess, doesn't it?" Celeste appeared from around the corner and into the kitchen, now wearing an emerald green top with a matching pair of white and emerald checkered pants. She froze when she saw what held Norah's attention.

Norah narrowed her gaze. "What are you doing with the Bryers' address and contact information?"

"I can explain," Celeste responded, cautiously stepping forward as if Norah were a snake about to strike.

Norah shook her head. "If you are about to talk me into going to see them, then no," she said. "No, I am not ready for that."

Celeste nodded slowly. "Okay, it's okay. Despite what this looks like, I actually didn't mean for you to see this. I wasn't going to give it to you."

Norah cupped her face in her hands and leaned back on the counter. "Then why do you have it?" And before Celeste could respond, she asked, "Is this what I need to do? Closure with the Bryers or something?"

Celeste scrunched her nose up tight and shrugged her shoulders.

"I can't just fly out to California to visit them. I don't have that kind of money. And what am I supposed to do, walk up to their door and say, *Hi guys! I'm sorry for being such a coward and blowing you off for the last three years despite how great you treated me while Sam and I were growing up, and I'm sorry I never apologized for Sam's death, but I am on a journey to make amends in order to move on to whatever the fuck Enlightenment is wanna grab lunch?*"

Norah crossed her arms and dropped her head back behind her. "I know you can't tell me what the Lesson is, but can you at least tell me if going to them is a part of it?"

The room fell silent, and Norah wanted to crawl out of her skin. If she had the choice between facing Serge, Luisa's parents, or Amelia, she'd take all of them over going to see the Bryers.

"I could go with you?" Celeste offered.

## CHAPTER 31

I F YOU DON'T STOP CLICKING THAT PEN, I AM GOING TO throw it into the waiting room."

Norah jumped at the sound of Barb's voice. They had been sitting together in silence for the last twenty minutes as the day wound down. "Sorry, I didn't realize I was doing it."

Barb swung her chair around to face Norah directly. "You've been distracted today. Everything alright?"

Norah nodded but didn't elaborate.

"You know," Barb continued, "I've let you stay as distant as you want to be. I'm not one to pry or force, but from the moment you started working here, I've been worried about you. You always have an air of sadness about you. I've seen you come in here morning after morning, bloodshot eyes and smelling of whatever liquor you had the night before." Norah's whole body clenched, and Barb leaned forward, managing a kindly stern look. "I've felt the distance you put between not only you and anyone else who interacted with you, but you and Chris, too. I never said anything. I've watched you find your footing and start to turn things around, only to relapse."

Barb's words sucker punched Norah hard, aimed directly at her heart. Barb may have pushed her to join her in book club and trivia nights, she had her ways of showing she cared, but she'd never been so forward with her before. The truth of her words settled deep as Norah felt the tears start to build up in her eyes.

"But despite your best efforts," Barb continued, her voice softening, "I do see you. You are the person who remembers everyone's birthday. Who checks on certain patients beyond protocol. Who runs and gets me cat food when I'm stressed, and who always makes sure I am okay if I am not feeling well. I've seen you these last few weeks, too."

Barb paused, sitting back a little in her chair. A patient came to her window, and she checked them in quickly before turning back to Norah.

"Now, I don't know what happened with you and Chris. I do know it was hard, and I know you're too stubborn to do anything about it, but I've also noticed you are drinking less. I am proud of you for that." Barb pressed her lips together tightly and reached across to give Norah's hand a squeeze. "Whatever it is you've got going on, just know you've got people who care about you, and you don't need to do it on your own."

Norah dabbed at her eyes and took a deep breath. She considered sharing with Barb, but thought better of it. Work was not the place. A piece of her was also worried she'd ruin the moment by sounding crazy.

"Thank you." She smiled. "I know I'm not the most open person, but I promise I am working on it. I really appreciate you always trying to include me, Barb. Truly." Barb returned her smile and gave an extra squeeze of her hand before she turned in her seat and addressed the patient at her window.

Norah watched quietly as Barb spoke to another patient, the cogs in her mind spinning with what she could say versus what would be too much. Once Barb was done, Norah seized the opportunity before she had time to chicken out. "What do you think of the idea of past lives?"

Barb sat back and took a hard look at Norah, clearly not the question she expected after such a heartfelt chat.

"As in reincarnation?" Norah nodded. "Well, I personally believe in God and Heaven and all that, but never really thought much of reincarnation if I am being honest. Why?"

Norah shrugged, trying to appear as nonchalant as she could. "Just thinking, I guess. Do you ever think about what the meaning of life is? What is the point in all of this?"

Barb thought about it for a moment. "I think we're all here to be as good as we can be. Treat people kindly, do what we can for our neighbors, that sort of thing." When Norah didn't respond, Barb took her silence as agreement. "Don't worry, kid. I think you are a great person, and you're going to be just fine. Even if you don't see it." She winked before turning back in her chair.

*If you only knew.* Norah sighed. The more she learned about her previous lives, the less she felt like a good person. According to Celeste, her Soul wouldn't move on if she didn't learn this last Lesson, and her chances at being reborn were done.

Before meeting Celeste and the memories, Norah would have laughed if someone told her she got to move on to an afterlife, let alone that she lived previous lives before this one, and now the very thought of this being it felt like too much to bear. It can't be enough to just be a good person, like Barb said. There had to be more to it than that.

She thought about asking Barb her thoughts on going to see the Bryers, but that age-old wall of not wanting to open up crept up strong. There was, after all, far too much to explain, far too many complications.

She decided against it.

Norah got home that night with Barb's words still ringing fresh in her mind. She was proud of herself for not drinking, and it really was great to have someone else notice it. Between the conversations she'd had with Celeste and the very touching conversation with Barb that day, she couldn't help but think of Chris.

If there was one person she wanted to talk to about going to the Bryers, it would be him. All the things she never told him weighed on her.

Without giving it another thought, she grabbed her phone and tapped his contact. Her stomach dropped at the sound of the ring, but it was too late to hang up now.

"Come on," she whispered, her knee bouncing anxiously. It was anyone's guess if she was rooting for him to answer or for his voicemail to pick up.

> "Hey, this is Chris. I'll get
> back to ya when I can."

Her heart sank, and she contemplated hanging up again, but then the beep came.

"Hi Chris," she began, clearing her throat. "It's me...Norah. I've just been thinking about you and wanted to call." She paused for a moment, unsure if she should say anything further. "I met a friend. Her name is Celeste, and she's great. I think you'd really like her. She has sorta...brought me out of my shell a bit." Norah took a long pause, unsure of how to continue, but didn't want to hang up. "She actually has me thinking of going to visit Sam's parents. I know I owe it to them, I'm just not sure I've got it in me. Anyway, all this to say that it's made me think about you a lot and—"

His phone beeped, cutting Norah's message off. She considered calling again, but thought better of it. She was certain the regret of the first message would settle in later.

She moved aimlessly from room to room before deciding to settle down with her knitting needles. She'd make something for Barb, perhaps a blanket if she could keep her sides even. If nothing else, the cats could lie on it.

She spent her evening mindlessly knitting rows of yarn, choosing a beautiful forest green and white combination. She wasn't skilled enough yet for more than two colors, but she was getting there.

It was half past ten when she picked her head up for the first time. She stretched her arms wide above her head and let out a big yawn, laughing to herself at how times had changed. She had to admit it was nice. When she was in school, there were lots of late nights studying, never a moment to herself. After Sam, it was lots of late nights drowning in her misery. This was the first time she was allowing herself to be by herself, to sit quietly, and to be the person who settles in at night at a decent time.

Her phone chimed, and she jumped in response, reaching for it quickly. A text from Chris glowed on her screen.

> Happy to hear you've met a friend. That's really cool. It sounds like she's been good for you. Going to see Sam's parents would be huge for you. I know you've got it in you. Hope you have a good night.

It wasn't a call back, he didn't say he was happy to hear from her, he didn't say he missed her, or that he'd reach out soon.

But he did respond.

# CHAPTER 32

# Celeste

From a distance, Celeste watched Silas chatting with Reginald. It was only a week or so since Silas stuck his nose in her business and caused the ridiculous plan for him to fake spy on her for Benny, but it felt like an eternity. Silas reached out via their shared pendants requesting to talk, but he wasn't a member of the Council and therefore couldn't bring her back to their afterlife himself. So she still had to stage a meeting with Benny in order to get back there.

The Council sure didn't make it easy to break all the rules.

She saw Norah a few days prior. They'd gone for a short walk together, and there was mercifully no chaotic transfer of past life memories. Norah hadn't told her yet if she wanted to go to visit Sam's parents, and Celeste didn't want to pry too much. The second time she asked, Norah simply smirked at her, and by the third time Norah told her to knock it off, she'd let her know when she decided.

Celeste hadn't meant for Norah to see the address sitting on her kitchen counter. And since she didn't outright hand it to her, could it be considered directly interfering? If there was someone who could teach Norah the Lesson she needed, Maureen would be the person. Norah saw her as a mother figure, her own mother far from present. Celeste saw this as the nudge Norah needed. Once she got her to the Bryers, Celeste could return to her own home knowing she was on the right path.

And under the three-month deadline. At least Benny would be happy about that.

Celeste really did try to give Norah the space to make her decision and not push too hard, but all the unknowns were eating at her. She had no clue what Silas was up to or what Norah was thinking. Was he going behind her back and reporting her to the Council? Was the thought of going to see the Bryers too much for Norah, and would she shut down again? Would all the progress Celeste made getting Norah to open up be wasted?

When her pendant played Silas's voice note to come meet him, she was riddled with both excitement and fear at what information he might have found.

She glared at Silas and Reginald, deep in their conversation. Silas told her to meet him there, on the second floor of the Guardian Tower, in an open communal area. She stood across from where Silas typically sat each day. If it were some sort of setup, her anger would quickly surpass her fear and excitement combined.

Celeste turned to leave, the thought of talking with Reginald was too much, when she heard her name being called. "Celeste! Woo-hoo! Over here!" She groaned before planting a smile firmly on her face and turned back.

"I didn't want to impose," she shouted back as she made her way towards Silas, frantically waving her over.

"Don't be silly. Reginald and I were just wrapping up. We meet here for our Mentor/Trainee sessions each week at this time." He gave Celeste a knowing smile.

Why exactly had she been trusting him?

*Oh, right, trying not to mess up Norah any more than she already had. Stupid.*

Celeste looked around the floor. Guardians were busy at work checking in on their Souls. It was humbling to see nothing had changed in her absence.

She continued to smile. "How are you, sir?" she asked, addressing good ol' Reggie.

Reginald stood with his hands clasped behind his back. "Well, thank you. I haven't seen you in a bit, Celeste. I hope you haven't been too discouraged by our last visit?" Celeste shook her head no, doing her best to appear convincing, while he continued. "Benjamin said you two have been working through your concerns. Good to hear he is at least trying to do his job."

Celeste inched forward as anger boiled in her stomach. The nerve of him. Reginald turned to face Silas. "It was a good meeting today, Silas. You've had some...interesting...questions lately. Keep up the good work, and both you and your Soul will be excelling soon. I will see you next week."

Once Reginald was out of eye and earshot, Celeste turned, red-faced, to hiss at Silas. "Why would you have me meet you here, now?"

He bent over in a fit of laughter. "I just thought it would be fun to see your face. And you should have seen your face."

"That was not funny," she insisted. Her voice remained low, and she looked around her to check if anyone had noticed. One or two familiar faces were looking. She raised her hand to give a quick wave before continuing. "This is not a joke."

Silas stood to look directly at Celeste. "Oh, I know this is no joke, honey. I get it."

Celeste glared at him. "What do you mean? What have you found out?"

Silas broke his eye contact and turned his head, feigning interest in something just to the left of him. "Nothing yet," he said. "Some things here and there, but I won't tell you anything until I know the full picture. I've been able to get some bits and pieces from Reginald, but without being able to ask direct questions, it's not great. I have some more digging to do in the Guardian Archives before I can be confident."

Celeste felt herself growing angrier by the second. Nothing about this felt right. "Silas, I need you to tell me everything you've found out."

"No," he said, locking eyes with her, his playful nature suddenly gone. "What you need is for me not to tell anyone else what I find. For now, I am not going to make assumptions based on a half-assed understanding. When I get what I need—what *we* need," he corrected after she gave him an even sharper look, "I will provide you with it. For now, none of it makes sense to me, and I don't want to confuse the matter."

Celeste shifted anxiously. He was smart to suggest having this meeting in an open space within the Guardian Tower. She had no room to argue with him while others were around.

"So you basically just called me here so I'd run into Reginald? To rile me up?"

Silas threw his head back and cackled. "And to let you know, I am making *some* headway. It just may not be the headway you are wanting, and I wanted you to be aware of that. If I am right, Celeste, you haven't been the honest little Guardian you're training to be. But," he said, breaking eye contact to look overly interested in his nails, "I'm not one to jump to conclusions. I just wanted you to know."

Celeste clenched her hands firmly behind her back, trying desperately to stop herself from shaking. "I don't know what you think you found. All my cards are laid out on the table. You're bluffing, Silas."

"Whatever you need to tell yourself, Celeste."

He was bluffing, she knew it. He wanted her to react in a way that made her come across as guilty for...something. She wouldn't play into his game; she wouldn't allow him to have that kind of power over her.

She took a deep breath and asked as nonchalantly as she could, "How's everything going with Benny?" If she couldn't get real answers on what was going on with Norah, at least she could leave with some comfort on where Benny stood. It had been roughly a week since she talked with him as well, which meant Silas being their go-between was working.

Silas waved her off. "Please, he's easy. I just give him the most boring details of your life, also not hard, and he's just pleased to hear you aren't interfering with your Soul. He's very easy to lie to, that one."

"And do you think it's been good for you two? Do you think bonding with Benny will help you with his final vote on whether you can be a Guardian?"

Silas stood thoughtfully for a moment before nodding his head. "I do think it might help. So, you know..." He rolled his eyes. "Thank you."

That was good news. At least she knew she could relax a little knowing that Silas playing her shield from Benny was working and that Silas was getting something out of the deal, as well.

"You didn't have to trick me into coming here to tell me nothing," she said, unable to help herself.

Silas sucked on his teeth. "Reginald saw you here. Don't you think the other Guardians will start to get suspicious if they don't see you around?"

Okay, he had a point there. "Fine, you're right."

Silas twirled his hand in an *I'm waiting* gesture. "And?"

"And, thank you," she said reluctantly.

"Also, it was really fun to see your face when you weren't expecting to see him here." He laughed.

Celeste scowled and turned away, catching sight of Anya across the room. An opportunity for an out. "I gotta go talk to Anya. I was short with her the last time I saw her, and want to go catch up."

"Thank you so much for that riveting detail into your calendar."

Celeste scoffed and turned to make her way to Anya.

Later, she thought of Silas while walking to the Great Hall to meet with Benny back in his office, a little detail gnawing away at her as she battled with what he could possibly have found.

Once she was with Benny, though, all her worries melted. While he was still not free of worry himself, he had come around to the idea of appeasing Silas. It felt as if Celeste and Benny had a fresh start, and it was good to be around someone she could be one hundred percent open and honest with. Well, okay, except for not being able to be entirely honest about Norah's past lives and Silas helping her with them. Or about just *how* close she and Norah were becoming. But still, she felt at home with Benny, and that was nice.

She told him that she was able to find ways to nudge both Chris and Barb into finding ways to help Norah. Chris and Barb's involvement was a *little* white lie to keep her own involvement out of it, but the truth was–they were making progress. For instance, Norah wasn't drinking anymore. She took up running again. She made a friend. To lay it all out for Benny was as if she were stepping back and seeing the big picture for the first time. It felt amazing.

"That's all fantastic, Celeste. Silas has kept me up to date on nearly all of this, but it's good to hear it from you." An implied *just in case* lingered in the air.

Celeste squealed on the inside. She made a mental note to thank Silas later for relaying all the information she had fed him via their voice notes. As much as it would pain her to do so.

"I knew you'd help get her on the right path."

She beamed with pride. "Yes, she's come so far. It may still take some time to get the Lesson, but I really think she's at least getting to the point of allowing herself to learn it, you know?" It helped that Norah now knew there was a Lesson to learn in the first place and the vast importance of it, but that was a minor detail Benny didn't need to know.

"Yes, that's really great. Think you'd be able to come home before the month is up? Return a little early?"

"Oh, no, no. I can't leave yet. She's got much too far to go."

# CHAPTER 33

## Norah

IT HAD BEEN A WEEK, AND NORAH STILL COULDN'T stop thinking about going to see the Bryers. Maybe it *was* time to go see Maureen and John, to talk to them and finally apologize for her part in what happened to Sam. It would never be enough, though, she knew that. It's what held her back all these years. What good were words when their son was gone? But maybe, just maybe, it was time.

Norah bonded with Sam the moment he let her ride his bike. She was the only girl in a neighborhood full of boys, and not one of them would let her play. It didn't take her long to learn they didn't let him play, either. And so, they had grown to lean on each other.

It was the summer before kindergarten. Norah remembered the date exactly because their birthdays were a day apart, his first, which meant they both missed the cutoff start day for school. They ended up in separate classes, which she knew made Sam nervous, so she made sure to pay extra attention to him at lunch and recess. He had a hard time making friends: he was quiet and not very athletic like the other boys. Norah was the opposite: loud with a big personality. When he was with her, he didn't have to do much talking, and she didn't force him to play basketball or baseball in the street. She assumed that was why they connected, not because they had so much in common, they didn't, but because they could be themselves with each other without judgment. They spent that entire summer in the woods behind his house. There, he lay and read while she climbed trees and built forts.

Norah latched onto Mr. and Mrs. Bryers the first time they had her over for dinner. She never in her whole life had two adults give her their full undivided attention, and they did it well divided between her and Sam.

Her dad traveled a lot for work then. Her mom, never maternally gifted, resented him for leaving her to do all the parenting. She joined every board, every charity imaginable, to keep herself busy and away from Norah. Norah grew up hearing about her saintly mother from others, which also made her so angry. How could her mother invest so much time in helping others, but never be there for her own daughter?

*Mrs. Ananya Bedi, who does so much for others, a wife and mother whose husband is never around. How does she do it all?!*

She doesn't, Norah always wanted to answer.

Her parents finally divorced when Norah was twelve. Her father ran off with a woman Norah met once or twice before he and the woman inevitably split a year or two later, and her mother got exactly what she wanted. The alimony, the child support, and single-mother praise, while she continued to stay as busy and as far away from Norah as possible.

The Bryers, on the other hand, asked them each in turn about their days. About what they learned in school, if they needed help with their homework, and a high and low moment for each of them. Giving them enough time to complain and a quick moment of self-pity before John would ask two important questions:

*Did anyone get hurt (physical or emotional)?*
*Will it matter a year from now?*

Sam never could understand her admiration of his parents.

*"Your parents are wonderful."*

*"They're annoying," he'd say, without looking up from what-ever book he was reading.*

*"They're perfect."*

*"They're always here."*

*"Exactly."*

It could be hard for someone to appreciate the things they had if they were given so naturally. An appreciation that is then only noticed if you are unlucky enough, or stupid enough, to lose them. Norah knew that lesson all too well.

Later, after he died, Norah replayed those after-school moments in her head more than any other memory she had of Sam and his parents. Sam never hesitated to share his parents' attention with her. John and Maureen were always so welcoming, so kind.

Her own mother did at least acknowledge Sam's death— she sent a beautiful bouquet of flowers and a card expressing her deepest sympathies—but when Norah withdrew from residency match midway through her interviews a month after Sam died, she was far from supportive. Her mother argued that Norah threw away their money, and although she wasn't wrong, Norah knew her mom was less worried about the money and more worried about the perception of others. That her daughter wouldn't be a doctor. That the perfect mother had failed. They'd spoken even less in the last few years than typical.

Reaching out to the Bryers was the right thing to do. She owed them more than a visit; she owed them an apology for running away. An apology for not being there for them when they needed her most, especially after all the years they were there for her. And most of all, she owed them an apology for her part in Sam's death.

She knew this was an apology years past due.

It was never in question that it needed to be said; it was about whether or not she had the courage to say it.

Her brain was on a constant loop, battling between visiting the Bryers and the enormous struggle it was not to call or text Chris and ask for his advice. Exhaustion was hitting Norah hard, yet she needed to get out of her apartment. While the fight not to reach for a drink was still there, she was proud that she had made better decisions lately. She was baking more, enjoying her new knitting hobby, and found her running shoes again. It was hard, but she was doing it, and it felt good to have control over at least one thing in her life.

*Although nothing made you want to find sobriety quite like having your Guardian Angel tell you you're on your last life, and you better get your shit together.*

But it still counted. Instead of releasing her anxiety in a bottle of whiskey, Norah decided to go for a run that afternoon.

For the first time since she'd started running again, the run had the opposite effect she intended. Her mind raced more and more with every strike of her foot on the pavement. Twenty-four full lives she'd lived, and if she were to believe anything Celeste said, which at this point there was little she could do to deny her, this would be her last life, and she needed to fix things quickly.

She repeated the Lessons back to herself: kindness, humility, empathy, generosity, temperance, and honesty. What was she so drastically not understanding that it had taken her six of her twenty-five lives to learn? She did her best to think back through the four lives she now knew and any common threads there.

The selfishness of a love-struck daughter. The betrayal of a friend. The neglect of a father. And the cause of the death of her best friend. In all four lives, she'd royally fucked up someone else's life. Was that it? Was accountability the final Lesson?

Norah jogged around a mother who was stopped, bent over a stroller, soothing what sounded like a distressed toddler. She locked eyes with the woman and gave an understanding smile, while continuing to run along the path.

Eugène never got the chance to make it up to Serge and never did express his true guilt and heartache to his wife Thérèse at having let Serge down, ultimately causing his death. Peggy was too ashamed to talk to Amelia about what she had done. She carried it with her, but never did what she should have to reconcile. Luisa's guilt was palpable in the dream. She knew Luisa spent her remaining days working hard to take care of her parents, but never felt as if she could ever do enough to make it up to them. All their loss was caused by her foolishness. While Celeste made it clear that she couldn't directly tell Norah what she needed to do to learn her Lesson, perhaps Celeste encouraging her to talk with the Bryers was more direct intervention than she let on.

Perhaps Norah needed to finally take accountability.

She hit a portion of the trail clear of others, wide open as far as she could see, and her lungs filled with a familiar burn as she picked up her pace, her stride getting longer, arms pumping beside her.

She wished she could talk to Chris about all this. Would he want to help her or think she had gone completely insane? Probably the latter. How could it not be the latter? Besides, it's not like he was jumping at the opportunity to talk to her anyway. He hadn't reached out to her since he texted in response to her voicemail, and she sure as hell wasn't going to be the one to reach out first again. Her chance of knowing was yet another thing she fucked up.

*One redemption story at a time, please.*

She concentrated on the way her heart pounded in her chest, the tingle in her knees as her joints worked overtime to absorb the shock of each footfall, the warmth of her heavy exhales, and the fiery-cool air entering her throat with every heavy inhale. Imagining her breath move through her lungs, life pumping through her veins. She felt Eugène's pain as he lay on his deathbed, mourning the loss of his son thirty-odd years prior. Her heart swelled with adoration as she thought of Amelia and all the practical lessons she had taught her–how to stitch, how to play cards, how to be a friend–and then felt her heart break as she imagined Amelia's pain at having Peggy betray her deepest secret. The pain of Luisa's parents at the realization that everything they had worked for was gone. She thought of Sam, minutes before his death.

She owed it to them and the lives before them and all the work that had gone into learning these Lessons, not to give up.

Humility was a Lesson she had already learned, right? It was time to set her pride aside and do what was right. She needed to talk to the Bryers.

Norah's stomach turned at the thought. Sadly, bravery wasn't on the list of Lessons. There was, however, one blonde-haired, blue-eyed angel who could guide her on the right path.

# CHAPTER 34

# *Celeste*

"H EY, LOOK WHO'S BACK TO HER OLD SELF."
Celeste sat cross-legged playing with Gigi the bunny as Dylan walked through the front door, ready to start his shift. They hadn't worked together since the spider incident.

"Yes," Celeste said, smiling, "everything is all back to normal." She was positive that to Dylan, there was nothing normal about Guardian Angels rectifying a fight they had with the Soul they were meant to guide, but no need to explain that.

If only Dylan could give her advice on what to do with Silas. She worried relentlessly about what he could have found. He had to have been bluffing. There was nothing for him to find. Nothing at all.

Besides, there were other, more exciting things to focus on.

Celeste stood, placing Gigi back in her cage, and plucked little charcoal gray hairs from her bright pink sweater. Although she had to admit that gray next to pink wasn't half bad, but only next to pink.

"You were right. I didn't give up on my friend. I went to her place to talk things through, and it's all worked out."

Dylan nodded his head in approval. "Good."

Celeste's smile reached ear to ear. "Annnnnd I'm actually going to go to California with her to visit some of her old friends. I might need you to cover a shift, if you don't mind? I'll swap with you and pick up one of yours?"

When Norah texted her that she had decided to go, Celeste danced throughout her apartment all by herself. A minute later, when Norah followed up that text asking if Celeste would like to go, she practically fainted with excitement.

After contemplating Celeste's request for a moment, Dylan said, "Don't worry about it. My mom's been on me to work more, anyway. Taking an extra shift will shut her up for a minute."

"Hey," Celeste mock-scolded, smiling. "Don't talk about your mom like that." Dylan shook his head in playful annoyance and turned to walk towards the front of the store, but she stopped him with a hand. "How does one travel to California, exactly?"

Dylan frowned and shrugged his shoulders. "Never been," he said.

Celeste did get to see air travel while checking in on Norah, but admittedly, airports weren't always the most entertaining places to watch. They had their moments, but for the most part, people either spent their time sleeping or sitting in those uncomfortable chairs for hours, or sprinting awkwardly through crowds trying to get their next flight. Typically, these were quick check-in times to make sure Norah was safe, and then she'd go about her day. Now, here she was in the flesh, preparing to take Norah across the country, and she had no idea what to expect. She lived in the sky yet was nervous about flying. Oh, the irony.

Celeste thought of the luggage people brought on trips, so much luggage, but she always had what she needed wherever she went. "What do people typically pack when they go on vacation?" she asked.

"I've taken my toothbrush and a change of clothes, my Xbox controller. That kinda thing."

Celeste nodded. "Interesting. Okay. Are the TSA people as scary as they look on television? They seem terrifying. What about the rumor that babies are planted on every flight just to annoy passengers?"

"No clue, I've never been on a plane. We've always driven on our vacations."

"Fiddlesticks. I was really hoping for the baby thing to be true," Celeste said. She loved babies.

Dylan gave a look of pure horror as he turned to finally make his way to the register.

It would all work out. She would be with Norah, and they'd figure it out together.

The remainder of her workday flew by. She went about her tasks as methodically as she always did, but she couldn't help daydreaming about all the time she and Norah would spend together. The purpose of their travels was for Norah to see the Bryers, but she couldn't help how excited she was to have Norah all to herself at times during the trip. Celeste imagined her and Norah lounging around the hotel, surrounded by loads of junk food, wearing matching bubblegum pink PJs, laughing and painting each other's nails. The idea was, of course, silly. Norah wasn't a bubblegum pink kinda gal. Still, a girl could dream.

Her day went from good to great to better. Both an English Bulldog and a Great Dane came into the store to pick out toys with their owners. Both the bestest, most loveable puppies ever. Then, as if that wasn't enough to make any day the best day ever, who else did Celeste get to meet?

None other than Barb herself.

When Celeste had gone to see Norah at work that awful day, she was too preoccupied to think about getting to meet Barb. Now was her chance. Celeste watched Barb walk through the front door and froze with excitement. It was as if she were about to meet her favorite celebrity from her favorite television show in person. She watched in horror as Dylan looked up and opened his mouth to greet her. What if Dylan got to help her first, and Celeste lost her chance to meet her? She had to do something, fast.

Practically tripping over herself, she made her way closer to the front of the store. "Hello! How can I help you?"

Barb and Dylan both startled and looked over at Celeste. Her cheeks grew warm as she raised her hand in yet another greeting. "Sorry, hi," she said at a lower volume. "How can I help you?"

"This is Barb," said Dylan, thumb pointed towards her. "She's in here all the time for cat food."

"Jesus Christ, not *all* the time." Barb laughed. "I only have the three. I am not too far gone yet."

"Three cats is the perfect number," Celeste chirped. "I bet they are all hilarious."

"Hilarious? More like pains in my ass, but loveable pains in my ass, if you know what I mean."

Celeste slapped her knee and practically rolled with laughter. "Oh, Barb," she teased. Dylan shot her a sideways glance, and Celeste realized she was coming on a bit too strong. She straightened herself and cleared her throat. "Say, Barb, don't you work at the Diagnostics Center with Norah?"

"Yeah, I work with Norah. You know her?"

"Yes! Norah and I are great friends." She beamed. She looked over at Dylan as if to say 'he knows,' but in place of the excitement and encouragement she expected, there was a look of sheer boredom on his face.

Barb paused, taking a long look at Celeste. *Good,* thought Celeste. *You don't have to trust me with her, yet.*

Barb spoke up at last. "Uh-huh, she's a good one, that girl."

"I actually helped her find your cat food once. I'll walk over with you." Celeste led the way to the cat food aisle.

Celeste helped Barb collect her cat food and bring it up to the front for Dylan to check her out. She rambled the whole time about how much she enjoyed Norah and how it'd been nice meeting someone since moving there, while Barb listened intently.

It was the perfect opportunity to talk with Barb about ways to help Norah more, just like Celeste told Benny she did. She could nudge Barb in a way that built up their friendship, and Barb could be the one to directly impact Norah. She had Silas as a buffer and didn't need to step back from Norah, but it would be the right thing to do.

She'd tell Barb that Norah needed help with Chris. Barb could encourage Norah to let him in more, that she deserved the happiness he could give her.

Just as they were approaching the checkout, Celeste's arms piled high with the cat food, Barb turned to Celeste and said, "It's good to see her with a friend."

Celeste wanted to say Norah could use another friend, someone else to show her it was all going to be okay, but there was a look in Barb's eyes that made her stop.

"I worry about her often. Do me a favor and keep an eye on her, okay?"

A chill ran down Celeste's spine as she said, "Promise." That woman was an old Soul, she knew things. Barb was just as wonderful in person as Celeste always imagined she'd be.

She watched Dylan ring her up, and they said their goodbyes. Right as Barb pushed open the door, Celeste simply couldn't help herself; she shouted, "Tell the cats I said hello!"

# CHAPTER 35

NORAH HUNG UP THE PHONE, AND THE SOUND OF IT sliding into the receiver was music to her ears. The line had been busy all day, and she'd been praying for a moment of peace. She sat back in her chair and closed her eyes when the thought occurred to her: Norah didn't pray often, but when she did, did Celeste tune in and filter them or did they go straight to the big guy? Was there even a big guy or just the council Celeste mentioned? There was no way she was ever getting used to this.

They decided to leave for California on Thursday, only three days away. Norah feared that if she waited, she'd change her mind. Once she remembered she had old travel points on a card from a few years ago that never expired, she figured that was a sign. (If she could get a sign while her Guardian Angel was here on Earth?)

Ultimately, she had run out of reasons to say no.

She recognized that if she had been honest with herself all along, she would've gone to visit the Bryers sooner. Somewhere deep down, she always knew there was no other way forward, even before Celeste came into her life. But she didn't have the courage needed to move forward. Was she more afraid they'd disown her for good or love and accept her as they once had? Did she deserve to move forward when Sam never could?

Celeste had been ecstatic when she told her.

Norah explained to Barb that she needed to take a last minute trip and asked her to help cover one of her shifts while she was gone.

She agreed without hesitation before saying, "Speaking of friends. I met your friend Celeste at the pet store yesterday." "Funny thing, huh? But she's a good one. I liked her." Norah hid a smile as she imagined how excited Celeste probably was to get to meet Barb.

And so, it was settled. She and Celeste were going.

Norah sat forward, elbows on her desk, rubbing her temples. Even if the visit with the Bryers totally bombed and they yelled at her when they saw her and never forgave her, at least she would get a mini vacation from work.

She needed one.

"Hey Barb," she called over her shoulder, "I am going to run to the bathroom while I have a second."

Barb silently waved her on as she sorted through the last patients' check-in forms.

Norah stood up quickly and felt the blood rush to her head as a dizzy spell took over. She braced herself using the back of her chair as she fought to keep the room from spinning.

"You okay?" She heard Barb's voice, faint and muffled as if she was off in the far distance instead of six feet behind her. Norah tried to shake away the confusion, but it only made things worse. She was vaguely aware of Barb standing up beside her, placing a hand on top of her shoulder, and a very strong smell that tickled a memory at the back of her mind.

She managed to release her grip on the chair and stand straight up. She tried to turn toward Barb to let her know everything was fine, not to worry, when the sharp metallic scent filled her nose and everything went black.

HE COULD STILL HEAR THE CRIES FOR HELP, SEE THE FULL body tremors, smell the mercury as it clung to his skin. But what haunted him most, up until his passing, was that if he had been more diligent in his own research, if he hadn't trusted Dr. Kohl so completely, so many lives could've been spared. Though he pledged to help people, he spent most of his career hurting them. His patients were always worse off than when they started.

August heard of the up-and-coming field of study and knew that if it had been around when his mother needed it, if he had known when he was younger what to look for and how to help her, he could have saved her. Helping people like his mother was the very reason Dr. August von Gieslingen chose the medical field in the first place. Particularly, the mental health field. It was a relatively new field of study at the time and a topic that was so rarely discussed and so very often misunderstood. In the end, he was happy she wasn't around to see what he had done to people.

He was assigned to the mental health ward in Narrenturm in Vienna, Austria, with Dr. Rudolf Kohl as his mentor, who excitedly brought August into a groundbreaking new study. Dr. Kohl spent some time treating patients for syphilis by way of mercury. The severe mental and physical deterioration caused by the syphilis improved, which led the doctor to believe that all mental illness could be treated through the ingestion of mercury compounds.

A cure, and August was going to be on the frontline of fighting the disease that took his mother from him.

For seven years, they fed mercury to their patients. Ages ranged from young to old, with an array of symptoms from irritable and irregular moods, mutism, to vegetative states. Both male and female. The work they were doing would balance out the toxins that made them ill and cure them of their mental health struggles.

Over time, August noted that the patients became volatile. Their moods fluctuated in an instant. They showed both cognitive and physical decline with each test they ran. Their hands were the first to shake, then their whole bodies. August was meticulous in his note-taking and noticed the patients seemed to be getting worse, not better.

August became worried enough to mention his concerns to Dr. Kohl.

"See here," he said, opening his notebook and pointing to the most recent entries. "Ida's tremors have expanded from her hands to her entire body, and she has become more ill-tempered of late."

"You know how women can be, always so emotional," Dr. Kohl said, waving away his concerns. "Up her dose a bit. Besides, the mercury still needs to work its way through her system. We expected it to get worse before it gets better. This is how we know it is working."

Despite his objections, he trusted Dr. Kohl.

His mentor and, as August liked to think, his friend, continued to reassure him that it was for the greater good of mental health everywhere. They were going to prove the theory that mercury worked to cure the disease, and it was going to be their names at the top of the publications. For a while, August convinced himself they were on the right path. After all, Dr. Kohl was an accomplished doctor; they were at the forefront of a huge medical discovery. He would help to cure thousands around the world struggling with mental illness. Not every patient would react the same, and if some suffered, it was for the greater good.

As time went on, August watched as his patients grew more and more sick. He desperately held on to the trust of his mentor. If all they had done was for nothing, then all they had done was hurt people. Dr. Kohl held strong to his belief that they were doing the right thing, and so August held strong. It couldn't have all been for nothing.

Josef, a young boy of the age of twelve, was sent to them for his extreme case of melancholy by his parents, afraid that all hope was lost for the boy. August was married to his work and never had children of his own, but Josef was a sweet kid whose parents' desperation tugged heavily at his heart. August took an instant liking to him and often treated him in a paternal way.

"You are getting quite good at this," August exclaimed during yet another game of dominoes. He enjoyed playing games with the children while he evaluated their progress, but Josef was a quick learner and provided a challenge for August that he rather enjoyed.

Josef smiled. "None of my siblings will play with me at home, and my parents are always working."

"Well, then," said August. "I am happy we have the time here to play."

August promised Josef's parents that he was in good hands.

It wasn't long before Josef began to take in deep, heavy breaths more and more often. August noted this particular symptom as heavy sighs, and shortly after that, Josef began to close himself off from the others. He wouldn't talk or participate in the group therapy sessions, even refusing to play games with August. He soon developed tremors, which progressively became stronger as the months went on. It was Josef's parents who stopped the treatment, which Dr. Kohl protested heavily, and even got angry at the sheer accusation that his treatment was not only not working but making things worse.

That was one of many situations that August would look back on with deep regret for not paying closer attention. Years passed, and he never heard what came of Josef–he could only pray he got better.

It wasn't until sometime in the 1860s when asylums and the treatments being performed began to be more heavily regulated that August learned Dr. Kohl's methods were not sanctioned. Rather, he was a man who believed so heavily in his ideas and theories that he was willing to risk the lives of hundreds of patients until he got the results he wanted. The rise of the Austrian

Medical Association helped further regulate the experiments within the mental health asylums, but by that time, August had done incredible damage, and there was no taking it back.

Norah came to, sprawled out in between her desk and Barb's, staring up at the ceiling, in a manner she was certain was not embarrassing at all.

"She's okay, she's okay!" Barb shouted, relief heavy in her voice. One of the nurses, Mary Anne, rushed over with a small Dixie cup. "Sit up slowly, and try to drink some water," Barb said to Norah.

Still on her back, Norah made her way to her elbows and into a seated position. "I'm fine, really," she said, embarrassed that she caused such a fuss. "How long was I out for?"

"Just a quick second, but my goodness, girl, you gave us a scare. Went down like a bag of bricks." Norah groaned as she stood. "Go home, go get some rest," Barb insisted. "It's a good thing you've got your trip coming up. You need a break."

Norah was happy for the chance to get home. There was no doubt in her mind about what happened that time. The smell, the visuals, the weight of the grief and guilt were all so real. She didn't know how many more of these memories she could live through, or rather re-live through, before it pushed her too far.

Visiting the Bryers *needed* to be the answer.

# CHAPTER 36

## Celeste

NORAH ASSUMED FLYING WAS OUT OF THE QUESTION because Celeste wouldn't have a viable ID, but Celeste reminded her how the things she needed simply appeared for her. Which was a relief, that would have been one hell of a drive. Celeste said she could technically do the same with a plane ticket, but Norah, too concerned with what could go wrong, purchased two tickets together. Clicking the button made it all feel so real.

Celeste's story about the library and how she managed to get the address put her in tears with laughter. It was an odd relief to now know who, or rather what, Celeste was. All the quirky and goofy things about Celeste that Norah found endearing, like when she squealed in excitement at having seen a kid on the trail blowing a bubble with their gum up close for the first time, were now a little more explained.

For instance, Celeste had a difficult time wrapping her head around the airport process. Her small luggage bag was filled to the brim with mini bags of cheese puffs. Luggage was unnecessary for Celeste, but she was concerned that her lack of luggage would appear odd, and also didn't expect the TSA to check her bag.

Norah watched Celeste's cheeks grow pink as she fumbled her way through the very believable explanation that the friend she was visiting had a baby who happened to be obsessed–"Easy on the gums, you know"–and so she was bringing them as a gift. Norah had to stifle a laugh as the security guard, very visibly, could not give a shit as to her reasoning for having an entire carry-on bag full of cheese puffs.

Norah was thankful to have Celeste there for comic relief. Norah thanked Celeste every step of the way until Celeste told her that if she thanked her one more time, she was going to leave her there.

"This is," she said, "quite literally, what I am here for."

It wasn't until they were comfortably seated, after Celeste hit every button above her head, adjusted the seat every way possible, opened and closed the window shade several times, and disturbed everyone by using the bathroom mid-boarding, that Norah was able to explain about Dr. August and his awful experiments.

She had cried for those patients, wishing they were still alive so she could apologize to them. She had the brilliant idea at about 2:00 in the morning to try and track down some distant relatives and apologize to them. There were a ton of those ancestry tools available.

She could do a whole World Tour of accountability-taking—for not only this life, but all of her others.

Norah fiddled with her fingers in anticipation of Celeste's reaction as she relayed August's story. Celeste's eyes bounced from the gentleman across the row fighting with the flight attendant about his seat, to her seat belt fastener, to the tray in front of her. "So," she said, bringing her focus to Norah. "This was another *full* memory? More like Eugène, less like Peggy?"

Norah nodded.

"And again, I didn't touch you or send the memory to you in any way."

Norah continued to nod, eyebrows pinched tight.

Celeste shook her head slowly. "I don't get it. I thought maybe it was my touching you, but now you've seen two memories without me. I don't know what started it, let alone how to stop it."

"I wish you did. This is all just so surreal. I come out of these holding onto all those feelings and emotions. One person is not supposed to feel all this. I might explode."

Celeste patted Norah's arm assuringly. "I just don't understand why..." She opened her mouth to speak, then closed it, then opened it, then closed it. Norah nudged her encouragingly, but with a shake of her head, Celeste said, "No. I shouldn't say."

Norah's eyes bulged. "You absolutely should say. I am going crazy here. If you have any idea about what is happening to me, I need to know."

"I can't. Not only would it be saying too much, but I also don't know for certain—and I don't want to be wrong." Norah groaned and sank into her seat. "I have someone looking into things for me. If I can tell you what he finds out, I will."

Norah looked out the window.

"It does seem as if you are going through your last few lives, albeit a little out of order. I wonder if you'll eventually remember all twenty-four."

Celeste's concerned look did very little to ease Norah's nerves. Her head hit her hands heavily. "Oh, God, I hope not."

They paused their conversation for takeoff. Celeste gripped Norah's hand tightly as the plane made all the typical noises and shook the typical amount. "Why are you nervous? Can your physical form get hurt?" Norah's eyes grew big at the thought.

"No, but being entrapped in a giant tube while up in the air isn't exactly a feeling I'm used to."

Once in the air, Norah opened the window shade, hoping the blue sky and clouds would bring Celeste some comfort. After yet another Life remembered with August, there was simply no denying what was happening to her. The memories were all too real. Celeste was all too real. Taking accountability for Sam had to be the final Lesson.

They sat in silence for a minute before Norah continued their conversation.

"It might be cool to see back all the way to my very first life. I guess I haven't had the chance to really appreciate everything I am seeing. When would that have been?"

Norah scrunched up her face. "I need to figure out what my average life span was to do the math."

"It doesn't work like that," Celeste explained, her breathing returning to a more normal rhythm. "It's not always an instant rebirth. It could happen where your current life ends and you are reborn automatically, but it could also be years, centuries even, before you're reborn. There are so many things at play there. The right timing, the right family to be born into. A 'stars align' type of situation."

Norah nodded her head. "Makes sense," she heard herself say—which, really, couldn't have been further from the truth. How did *any* of this make sense?

"Are you learning anything at all from all this? Anything jumping out at you?" Celeste asked hopefully.

The flight attendant interrupted, handing Norah a water, Celeste a can of lemonade, and each of them a pack of pretzels. "Look how absolutely adorable these are," exclaimed Celeste before popping a little pretzel in her mouth.

Norah, in answer to Celeste's question, spread her arms out wide around her. "Why do you think we're on this plane? I have to take accountability for my actions in all this. I have to apologize to the Bryers for the part I had in Sam's death...and I need them to forgive me."

Celeste's face fell, and Norah's stomach followed. Norah asked, "What? Is that not right?"

"No, I was just...I can't *tell* you if you are wrong or right, Norah. You know that already. You have to learn your Lesson on your own."

Between Celeste coming here, interacting with her, and now Norah's ability to see and feel her past lives... "Aren't we past breaking the rules already?" Norah asked.

Celeste fell silent. Norah worried she had taken it too far.

Norah eventually dozed off in fitful sleep until they landed in San Diego, California. Norah would have given anything to stay on the plane. To turn around and go home.

# CHAPTER 37

# Celeste

CELESTE WAS NERVOUS, VERY NERVOUS. SHE SETTLED in her hotel room with two new concerns. One: Silas. He'd reached out to her while she was on the plane and told her he needed to talk to her as soon as possible. Two: Norah. She couldn't stop thinking about what she'd said on the plane about having already broken the rules.

She lay in her nice hotel room, unable to do anything but panic. She couldn't even enjoy the ginormous soaker bathtub in her en suite.

Suites were the only options left, and Norah said if this was going to be her last life, then she really didn't care about credit card debt anymore. How cool was that? And yet here Celeste was, not enjoying a luxurious night of bubbles, but instead thinking about the mess she'd gotten them into.

Had they already broken too many rules? Not they–*she*. Had she already broken too many rules?

She was so consumed with Norah not learning the Lesson on her own that at first, she didn't think through the implications of her coming to Earth. Each time she turned around, she caused more trouble. Although she knew it, she couldn't seem to stop making things worse. Putting Benny's position on the Council at risk, putting her own position as a Guardian at risk, Silas getting involved. Even Benny wouldn't be able to fix this mess. They were able to hop worlds, but not turn back time.

Celeste replayed the voice note from Silas because why not torture herself over and over again?

Silas's voice snaked its way out of the pendant.

> "I need to meet with you immediately.
> My place this time."

When Celeste first felt her left pant pocket grow warm, where she kept the pendant for Silas, she and Norah had still been on the plane. Celeste quickly excused herself to go to the bathroom.

"Again?" Norah had teased. "It looks the same as the other two times, I promise nothing's changed."

"I like the quick swoosh of the water; it both scares and excites me." It was easy to lie about liking to go to the bathroom when there was so much truth to it. So many things she experienced through a hole in the sky were way more exciting in person, even toilets flying thirty thousand feet in the sky.

The pit in her stomach had grown to the size of a watermelon in anticipation of seeing Silas, and it hadn't gone away since.

In her hotel room, Celeste repeated the same thoughts she had before; maybe he had good news! Perhaps Silas figured out why Norah's memories were resurfacing!

Or, it was bad news—which meant the end of everything.

She quickly sent a note to Benny asking to check in, requesting to go to her living quarters first to give herself the time to meet with Silas, then returned to her seat. She'd think of a reason she wanted to talk with him before getting to him.

One thing she knew for certain, she wasn't going to change anything by worrying. She had some time to kill before she needed to go meet with Silas, and that bathtub really was calling her name.

CELESTE TOLD BENNY TO PULL HER BACK AT A TIME SHE was certain Norah would be settled. As a way to check if she was in for the night, Celeste called her to offer her a nighttime tea from the cafe in the lobby.

Norah said, "I'm good, thanks. Between the travel and the emotion of the day, I am either going to be wired or out as soon as my head hits the pillow."

Celeste couldn't help but worry for her. The next day was going to be full of dread and excitement. She was certain Norah was scared and nervous, but she had more immediate concerns to tend to.

She sent Silas a quick voice note letting him know she'd be there shortly. The sooner she could get there, the sooner she could return.

She popped into his place, thinking he was expecting her. Unfortunately, he didn't receive her voice note. Very unfortunate.

Silas stood completely naked in front of his hallway mirror, belting out Frank Sinatra's *My Way* while he used his blow dryer as both its intended tool and a microphone.

Celeste yelped in surprise and frantically rubbed at her eyes.

She heard Silas turn off the blow dryer and shuffle to grab some clothing, as calm as could be, as if Celeste seeing him naked were a completely typical occurrence. "Stop being so dramatic," she heard him say.

"My eyes—they're burning," she cried. They were. They were actually burning. Silas sighed dramatically. "I sent a voice note that I was on my way," Celeste said, still dabbing at her eyes.

To Celeste's relief, Silas had thrown on a robe. He was tying it tightly around his waist as he said, "I was getting ready, Celeste. You got here before I was done with my evening routine." Silas walked to his sitting room.

Celeste followed him close behind. "I am really never going to get over this. We need to take yet another thing from the humans and get therapists here."

Celeste made herself even more uncomfortable as she sat on one of the plastic high-top chairs that lined the back wall. She knew their options were limited for their living quarters, but of course, Silas went for more style over comfort.

Except for one oversized white chair, tucked neatly in the corner of the room where Silas sat. The chair was shrouded by a big white blanket and white throw pillows, and the image of a throne came to Celeste's mind.

"Will you please stop?" he asked. "You are ruining my maniacal plan to destroy you."

Celeste froze. "What?"

A smile crept across his face as his left eyebrow practically kissed his hairline. Silas's eyes glistened with excitement as he explained. "I had a hunch when you first described that Norah was seeing her past lives, but I couldn't be certain. I was just about there, the last time we spoke, based on some of my questions to Reginald, but still, I needed to be one hundred percent sure. I've done even more digging, deep into the archives, and now...now I am certain. You've been bending more rules than you've let on, dear Celeste."

There was no way. She had been so careful. There was no way he was talking about what she thought he was talking about. Even Benny never put it together.

"Silas, please," she said, feeling her voice shake. "You don't understand."

"Oh, I understand," he laughed. "You knew your Soul before they were assigned to you, and I understand that is against the rules. You started your training in a way that is not allowed. I don't know how you've gotten away with it, and honestly, I don't care, but one word from me and you lose, stripped of it all. No more Guardian role for you. Even Benny can't save you."

How could she have been so stupid? But, seeing past lives was never mentioned as a risk to knowing the Soul a Guardian is assigned to. In fact, Celeste nearly forgot it was a thing in the first place. It never impacted her role as a Guardian in all these years. Or had it, and she just chose to ignore all the signs?

Stupid signs.

Celeste gripped her hands tightly together to stop them from shaking. "Even if it's true, why does it matter? What's the harm exactly? Nothing bad has happened." *Yet.* "Can you please just help me figure out if this is why she is seeing her past lives, and if I can stop it? Norah can then move on, and no one needs to know."

"Celeste, of course, this has something to do with what is happening to Norah. What else can it be? You lied to the Council from the very beginning. That has consequences. Rules exist for a reason. Not to mention Benny's involvement in all of this."

No relief came from learning why Norah was seeing her past lives. Celeste only felt worse. It was her fault.

"Silas," she pleaded, swallowing hard. "Please don't say anything. Not yet. Not to cover for me, but for Benny. He doesn't know my and Norah's Souls knew each other in a previous life. He had nothing to do with covering that up, and I don't want the Council to think he did."

"But he did let you go down to Earth, and I will certainly be telling the Council about that."

Celeste sat forward in her seat. "Silas, I am begging you. Give me time to figure this out. I can prevent Benny from getting into trouble, and I can make sure Norah learns her Lesson. I just need time."

Silas giggled. "And I doubt you even understand just how much you need Norah to learn her Lesson."

"What is that supposed to mean?" she asked.

"As if you don't know," he scoffed, turning his nose up at her. "Clever Celeste, won't be finding her way out of this one."

The room swirled around Celeste as she gripped her chair, trying to keep her balance. "Why are you trying to hurt us? As foolish as it was, I trusted you to help me, and I *thought* you were getting what you wanted out of it. You were getting on Benny's good side to help you become a Guardian. What good does it do you to hurt us?"

Silas placed his hand to his heart. "Gee, thank you so much, Celeste, for your concern regarding mine and Benny's friendship, but where *your* plan had me sucking up to a member of the Council who I know doesn't like me, *my* plan guarantees me that I won't have to do that anymore. If the Council finds out your precious Benny was a part of this, he gets kicked out, and I no longer have to worry about Benny holding me back from becoming a full-fledged Guardian. It's that simple."

"You're willing to ruin us because you assume Benny won't vote for you to become a Guardian? I know I used your fears as a way to get you to help me, and I shouldn't have. I am sorry. But Benny would never do that just because he and Reginald don't see eye to eye."

"I cannot take that chance."

Pleading wasn't working, so she needed to try and beat him at his own game. "You were the one sneaking around, asking questions to dig information up on me. If you go to the Council, I'll tell them that you—"

Silas cut her off. "That I what, Celeste? Asked Benny a few times where you were. You caved so easily. It was like taking candy from a baby, or beating you at bingo night." He smirked. "I searched for information just as you asked me to do, in places I am allowed to look, mind you. I spoke with Benjamin just as you asked me to do." He settled deeper into his throne, as casual as if he were simply chatting with an old friend.

Fiddlesticks.

"My going to Reginald is a good thing to do. You've handed me both of your demises on a silver platter. Well, it's for me, so I'll say a gold platter. Thank you."

She had to fix this.

"What can I do? How can I fix this for Norah?"

"Find a way to pin this on Benny, get him off the Council. That simple. I won't ever mention a word about you or any of this."

# CHAPTER 38

# Celeste

Death. It was not how they described it, because there was no way to truly describe it. In fact, it was possible that death was experienced differently from person to person. Celeste could see how it might be terrifying for some, a relief for others. Knowing exactly what was happening, while others were uncertain. Some who enjoyed running through their lives, even the bad parts, as if sitting down to watch their favorite movie. Others felt as if they were walking through an unhinged hall of mirrors in an unimaginably terrifying carnival experience.

At the time of Celeste's death, she was a man named Duncan living in rural Scotland. He had a quiet life wherein he grew up, lived, and died on the same land. Kept to his family, married to the love of his life with whom he had two fiery and fierce daughters. It was a simple life, but a very good one.

When he passed, it was nothing short of magical. He walked through all his lives with joy and pride in his heart. Dying, for him, took the length of a lifetime and it took no time at all. In his past lives, he got to be a faithful husband, a doting mother, had a very best friend, and he saved a life in more than one. Hard to say any of his lives were grand, but he was rich in love. The best kind of riches. It had been a long and beautiful journey, and he looked forward to what awaited him.

In a flash of a moment, Duncan found himself in the brightest white space he'd ever seen. The endlessness of it all was unsettling. Once his nerves settled, and he found himself in a moment of solitude, the whirlwind of his memories no longer swirling, he was struck with a strong sense that he was waiting for something. A pull at his heart as he looked around the vast whiteness, tapping at his person as if he expected to find things in his pockets.

*Did I leave something behind? But what could it be?*

Something popped into his line of vision, distracting him from his thoughts, and standing before him, who he would soon learn to be, was Kinsley.

"Hello." She smiled warmly.

"He–hello," he stammered, eyes as big as saucers. "Are—are you God?"

Kinsley laughed. "I am here to greet you and bring you into your afterlife, Duncan. Or Achara, Baako, Celeste, or Theodore. Whomever you prefer to settle here as."

Duncan thought for a moment, the list of names the woman had noted mixed with several others, as he contemplated all the forms he had before. He looked down at himself to find a familiar form. She was his favorite life, and so it wasn't surprising that this was the form he'd chosen.

Duncan, now Celeste, looked around at the nothingness that surrounded them. When her eyes landed on Kinsley, Kinsley looked back with a knowing smile.

"Are you taking me somewhere?" Celeste asked.

"I'd like to show you a place, yes. You see, I don't greet all Souls who come here. Most go straight to their own afterlife, a place of their very own choosing to settle here, however they envision their afterlife to be. You'll have the same option, too— but first I'd like to make you an offer."

And with a single wave of her arm, the white space faded away, and they found themselves in the most beautiful garden Celeste had ever seen.

"This is the home of the Guardians," Kinsley said. She opened her arms and spun around slowly before coming to a full stop. "Celeste, I would like to offer you a place amongst our most treasured. We don't offer this to everyone who comes here, so don't take the offer lightly." Her face grew stern. "But we do offer the role of Guardian to those who we know would value and uphold what we do here. You've led honorable lives. You've treated those closest to you in all of your lives with love and care, and you have proven yourself to be a natural caretaker in many of the lives you've led. We feel you'd make an excellent Guardian."

Celeste marveled at the thought of her, of all people, getting the opportunity to become a Guardian Angel. Never, in all her lives, did she imagine getting to do such a tremendous and honorable job. It was an emphatic "Yes!"

Kinsley gave Celeste a tour of the grounds. Back then, the grounds looked slightly different. The Great Hall looked like another building entirely, and the Guardian Tower was much smaller (demand had certainly grown over the hundreds of years). Kingsley took great care to show her everything and answered all of Celeste's questions.

Kinsley ran through all the rules Celeste now knew so well. A Trainee gets one Soul to look after while they learn to become a Guardian, guiding the Soul through their Life Lessons. A Mentor is assigned to each Trainee to help them learn. The Council will test their capabilities and decide if and when a Trainee is ready to become a full Guardian. It is important to keep distractions low: White garments only, white decor in their living quarters, and while friendships are encouraged, a Trainee may not guide a Soul they have known in a lifetime.

The rules were tough but reasonable. Besides, when a person lives so many lives in a world of progressive order, true free range and free will can be a bit unsettling. Celeste was happy to have the structure if it meant she was going to get to be a real Guardian Angel, to help souls learn all their Lessons and crossover to their afterlives.

The last Rule, however, did give Celeste pause. Like most new Trainees, she didn't understand why Guardians were not allowed to guide a Soul they knew in one of their lifetimes.

"Because," Kinsley explained, "while we are here to guide, it is imperative for Souls to learn their Life Lessons on their own. If they are guided too directly, then the Lessons themselves are never truly learned. It's been proven over and over that if a Guardian–or a Trainee–knew a Soul in a previous life, it creates a bit of a bias. It's difficult for the Guardian to separate the work they are here to do from the Soul they knew in life. It ultimately ends up hurting the Soul, not helping them."

Celeste's first order of business was to meet the Council, the mentors available to the Trainees, and to be assigned a Mentor. The other seven members of The Council were undeniably intimidating, although not quite as intimidating as Kinsley. Reginald, Benjamin, and two other members, Beatrice and Demetrius, were the four (out of the eight total) members of the Council who also served as Mentors.

Celeste instantly wanted Reginald as her Mentor. A man who knew the rules, followed the rules, owned the rules, was sure to be someone who was going to train her to be the very best Guardian this afterlife had ever seen.

When Celeste was called into Benjamin's Trainee group, along with four others (two of whom would not complete the program, deciding it was too much responsibility and they wanted to live the afterlife of their choosing), she was instantly disappointed. This Mentor wasn't going to take anything seriously, always laughing and being playful with his Trainees. How was she supposed to learn to be the best from this one?

It was that distracted frustration that Celeste would later blame the mix-up on. Too busy grumbling in her self-pity to pay close attention when she was handed her first Soul assignment.

She would later learn that an announcement was made: If any Guardian received a Soul they knew in a previous life, they must report it to their Mentor for a change in assignment. They tried their best, but millions of souls in billions of lives came through, and sometimes things slipped through the cracks.

But she hadn't heard the announcement, and she hadn't paid much attention to the Soul she was assigned to. She was far too busy gazing longingly at the group who were lucky enough to get Reginald, and glaring back over at her group and Benjamin.

Training started the following day. Benny gathered her and the other new Trainees in his group, five of them total. They stood on the first floor of the Guardian Tower. Celeste was still getting used to the no-walls, open spiral staircases, and was grateful for the first floor. Benny showed them how to pull up their view into their Soul's life down on Earth.

He started with his fists together, then expanded his hands and fingers out wide as he spread the space before him. A hole opened up, revealing the perfect picture of an older man, slim with dark brown skin, bent over an intricate ivory carving. The entire group of Trainees gasped as Benny beamed with pride. He spread his hands out further, and the view he could see enlarged; he brought them closer, and his view got smaller. He could move the hole to see around the old man, but was not able to track beyond him. He could also zoom in or out of the image with just a pinch or a spread of his fingers. All without the man being aware of an audience.

"Who wants to try?" asked Benny, and all hands went up.

Benny chose two of the Trainees before finally having Celeste try. She was so nervous she thought she could be sick, right then and there, in front of everyone. What if it didn't work for her? Would that mean she wasn't meant to be a Guardian? Could all this be taken away from her?

She was able to produce her view into Earth on her second try; it took the others at least three. "Wow," she gasped, as a young man named Thomas ran the streets of London. His laughter, so loud and pure, Celeste's eyes welled with happiness.

She toyed with how to command the space in which she could see, concentrating so hard her tongue stuck out of the corner of her mouth. The other Trainees cheered her on, and Benny clapped beside her. She paused for a moment and took Thomas in.

*Could it be?*

She looked up to her peers and ran her gaze to where Benny stood.

*No. It can't be.*

"Okay," Benny shouted, "who's next?"

She couldn't bring herself to tell anyone. She knew she should, but couldn't. She thought, what could be the harm of waiting just a little, just to be able to check in with the Soul? Once she knew the Soul was okay, of course she'd come clean, explain to them she hadn't realized at first, which was true.

But time went on, and the longer it went on, the more difficult it became to tell someone. Celeste began to actually *like* Benny—she was learning how to properly guide. What if he became upset with her, and she was assigned a new Mentor? What if she were banned from checking in on her Soul?

Then...well, nothing.

No one noticed. No harm ever came of it. And Celeste got to watch over this Soul for five full lives. She couldn't believe she could have ever been so lucky to be a part of it, even if only from a distance. In each life, Celeste was certain they would learn their Lessons and pass over, and then she'd get to see them face-to-face once again. But each Life ended more heartbreakingly than the last. How could she possibly have ever stepped away?

She needed to make sure this Soul learned their Lesson, and going to Earth was the only way.

# CHAPTER 39

NORAH TRIED, BUT FAILED MISERABLY, TO FALL ASLEEP. She took a shower and made a cup of chamomile tea, but she couldn't settle her nerves enough to relax.

She sent Chris a text telling him she made it to California, that she was there to see Sam's parents, and how nervous she was to see them in the morning. She didn't expect a response back. Truthfully, she didn't think too hard before sending the message; she just knew she wanted him to be a part of it somehow.

She certainly never expected a phone call, so when her phone rang twenty minutes later and Chris's name appeared on her screen, she almost panicked and hit the ignore button. Almost.

"Hey," she whispered, tucked deep in her sheets. Something about a hotel room made her feel like she needed to be quiet.

"Hey, how are you?"

"I'm...umm. I'm okay." She felt countless emotions, and not one of them was *okay*. There was no need to hide it. "I'm scared shitless, actually."

"Norah, from what I've heard you say, they treated you like family. I'm sure they're going to be so excited to see you."

She scooted down even more into the blankets and groaned louder than she intended. She could hear the smile in his voice. "I'm serious. This is a great thing you're doing. They are going to love seeing you, and I think this is going to be really good for you, too."

Norah heard a male voice in the background. "Is that Joey?"

"Yeah, we're at Frank's place watching the game. I just saw your text and wanted to call."

"Well, thank you. I really appreciate it."

"Of course."

And because there was nothing else to say, she said, "Well, tell them I said hi." Without thinking, she added, "I miss you."

There was a long pause that made Norah ache in a way she hadn't yet that day, as if every other emotion just wasn't enough and she needed one more punch to the gut.

"I'm proud of you. For flying to California, for telling me about it. I'm really proud of you. We'll talk later, okay?"

"Yeah, okay." And with that, they said their goodbyes. Norah was left alone with her thoughts once again.

She spent the rest of her night talking to Sam.

She told him how much she loved and missed him. She told him, as she had so many times before, how sorry she was. She asked him for help with his parents. To give her strength to survive the conversation the next day, she begged him to make sure they were understanding and forgiving.

She thought back to the time when she convinced Sam to borrow the car without asking. Sam was a new driver and only had his license for a few months. He hadn't yet earned his parents' trust to have car privileges. They wanted to go to the mall and then to the movies, but the Bryers were out and Sam couldn't get a hold of them to ask.

*"What's the big deal? You have your license, the car is technically yours, or it will be soon. Let's just go."*

*"If something happens, they'll kill me. I can't just take the car."*

But they did take the car. Because, as Norah knew, she could get Sam to do almost anything. A fact that would haunt Norah. Sam always listened to her.

And something did happen because, as much as Norah wanted to believe she was always right, it was usually Sam who was right.

*Sam backed into another car in the movie theater parking lot. Thankfully, the other car was fine. The driver was a very understanding woman who said she had a new driver at home, too, and hoped their first accident involved an understanding party. Sam's car, however, had a nice dent on the bumper. Hiding the fact that they took the car from his parents was impossible.*

*They were pissed, to say the least, and scolded Norah just as much as Sam. Being treated like family comes with all forms of love and support, including the punishments.*

*When Sam was sent to his room, Maureen turned to Norah and said, "I'll leave the discipline to your mother, Norah—but I am very disappointed in you." Those words stung Norah more than anything her own mother could say. Maureen took a deep breath and softened her tone. "Norah, I know Sam is not your responsibility; he's old enough to make his own decisions, but he has always been impressionable, and you have always been his rock. I am asking you to make good decisions. Help keep him on the right path. He listens to you."*

*Sam was grounded for a month, and though Norah's mother never even acknowledged the incident, she still felt punished, too. Norah spent that whole month worried that the Bryers hated her and that she ruined their trust.*

*When the month was up, Norah went right back to the Bryers. It felt like coming home. The Bryers welcomed her with open arms, not a hint of anger on their faces or disappointment in the set of their shoulders.*

Seventeen years later, she hoped their arms would be just as open for this homecoming, but she wasn't naive. She caused a lot more damage than just a dent in a car's bumper.

Norah's stomach turned all morning as she prepared to head out. She regretted not calling first, envisioning a look of utter disdain when she'd surprise them at their front door. But if she'd called, would they have just let the phone go to voicemail? She was more afraid of them avoiding her than a door slamming in her face. She convinced herself that showing up unannounced was the only way, when in truth, she was stretching out every possible second before seeing them face-to-face.

She talked with Celeste that morning about going with her. The past few days had gone quickly: from deciding to go to California, to getting on the plane, and now preparing to leave the hotel, she'd never had a second to ask if Celeste would go with her to the Bryers' home.

Norah was immensely grateful to have Celeste travel across the country with her. She wouldn't have been able to take the first step off the plane if it weren't for her support. Ultimately, though, she felt it was best to go see the Bryers alone.

"I promise, I agree it is better for you to go on your own. This is between you, them, and Sam. They don't know me, and it would be weird to have me hovering. Well, you know, knowingly hovering."

Panic surged through Norah's core right before she left, and she almost changed her mind. She nearly begged Celeste to join her.

She set her shoulders. If she was going to take accountability and ask them for their forgiveness, she needed to do it on her own. After all, wasn't that a part of learning the Lesson?

THE DRIVER PULLED UP TO THE ADDRESS, AND NORAH sat quietly in the back seat. It wasn't until the third time the driver cleared his throat that Norah found the courage to get out of the car. But as she reached to open the car door, John came walking out of the garage, carrying a five-gallon bucket, and Maureen came walking around the back, gardening gloves on both hands, pants dirty, sun hat resting on her head.

Norah's heart stopped. She expected each slow step towards the house to be a quiet moment to herself; she expected the chance to collect herself at the door before knocking. She did not expect to see them so quickly.

She watched, frozen, as Maureen kissed John and grabbed the bucket. Norah smiled. It warmed her to know that if nothing else, their affection for one another hadn't dulled. They walked together to the flower beds in front of the house, a display of rock and succulents, and placed the bucket upside down as a place for Maureen to sit while she dug.

The driver cleared his throat once more. Norah jumped, spurred out of her thoughts. She smiled politely as he pursed his lips at her. She scrambled out of the car and shut the door behind her. The noise caused both the Bryers to look her way, and Norah watched with a racing heart as recognition crossed both of their faces.

MAUREEN HANDED NORAH A CUP OF COFFEE, THEN SAT across from her, snuggled beside John on the couch. Norah couldn't help but wish it were a mimosa or a Bloody Mary.

They had embraced her, both of them together, when she approached them in their yard. They had, literally, welcomed her presence with open arms. Still, Norah couldn't stop shaking.

Maureen smiled from ear to ear and said, "We cannot begin to tell you how happy we are to see you, love."

Norah's throat tightened, and tears welled in her eyes. She tried hard not to release them as she looked anxiously around the room. It was a small home, the perfect size for an older couple with no kids or grandkids to accommodate. It was an open floor concept, and the living room was just big enough for an L-shaped sofa and a small reading chair. It looked right into an all-white kitchen featuring a breakfast nook tucked deep into the corner, complete with a small round table fit for two.

Some familiar items popped out at Norah, like the old white-and-blue plates that hung on the walls of their old kitchen, a plaid wool blanket draped neatly on the back of the chair. The fabric was worn thin from all the years of use. Norah remembered quite a few occasions where she tucked herself into the old Bryers' couch with that blanket wrapped tightly around her.

Norah noticed the pictures last. Sam from all ages looked at her from the side table, the back wall, the refrigerator. One stood out, in particular. Sam and Norah on graduation day. The framed photo both proved the Bryers' acceptance of Norah and mocked her failures.

"I'm sorry I haven't been around," she said, unable to look either of them in the eye.

"We're just happy you're here now," John said. "We've missed you, Norah."

The tears fell slowly; there was no stopping their escape.

John continued to talk as Maureen held tightly to his right hand. "We tried to reach out a few times, but understood why you didn't want to talk right away. We kept telling each other to give you space, that you'd come around eventually." He smiled, and Norah noticed him release Maureen's grip and wipe his hand along his knee. " We're sorry for not trying harder." John looked at Maureen, and she nodded assuringly.

Norah took a deep breath. "I am so sorry I let Sam down. I am so sorry for my part in all of this."

Maureen scooted forward so she was halfway off the sofa and placed her hand on Norah's knee. She said, "Norah, honey, what on earth do you mean?"

Norah wiped her nose on her sleeve, and John hopped up to get her the box of tissues off the side table that held Sam's college graduation photo. Tears lodged in her throat, Norah said, "I was so excited to start my residency...I was so focused on my own next steps."

"Norah, no," Maureen said, but Norah cut her off with a fervent shake of her head.

"Sam and I had been distant during my last year of medical school. Sam was struggling at work, frustrated with where his career was going. He just broke up with Danny, the first guy he'd dated openly. It bothered him that, at thirty years old, he still hadn't had a lasting relationship—*that's* what crushed him about the breakup. He didn't really even like Danny all that much. And I knew Sam was struggling in other ways, too, but I was so focused on my own life, excited for *my* own next big thing. I saw him shutting down, and I ignored it."

"Norah, you couldn't have known. Sam was such a private kid."

"Not with me," she said. "Not with me. I knew how hard things were for Sam growing up. I knew he had the habit of retreating into himself. But at least he always had me. He got through it because we were together. Then we weren't. I wasn't there when he needed me most."

"I'm sure that's not true."

"He called me the night he..." Norah squeezed her eyes shut. "He called me. Did you know that?"

The pain on Maureen's face was like a punch to Norah's gut. Her voice shook uncontrollably, but she continued. "He called me, but I was preparing for the interviews I needed to do for the residency match, and I told myself I'd call him later. I never did. I never called back."

"Norah," Maureen said, shifting her body toward her. She wrapped her arm around Norah's shoulders. "We understand how you feel. But none of us could have known for certain that Sam was going to take his own life."

Norah continued to shake her head, eyes downcast. Her ears grew warm and her heart began to race. "No. I need to take accountability for my role in Sam's death. I need you to understand how sorry I am. Sam trusted me. He always listened to me. You always told me that. Sam would have listened to me had I talked to him that night."

They let her cry then. No one said a word as Norah released three years of sadness into the arms of Maureen.

# CHAPTER 40

## Celeste

Fter she met with Silas, Celeste touched base with Benny as intended, making up the need for some silly advice. She barely remembered her walk to his office, so consumed with Silas's blackmail. If she didn't need Benny to get back down to Earth, she would have canceled entirely. Instead, shortly after arriving, she feigned not feeling well and asked to return to Earth earlier than anticipated. Benny was concerned, and she knew at some point she'd have to give a better explanation for her strange behavior, but she couldn't bring herself to focus. She needed to get away from Benny to think—and think she did, all night and into the morning, but to no avail.

When she spoke with Norah the next morning, it was a good thing that she asked Celeste not to join her at the Bryers.

After her conversation with Silas, Celeste wouldn't have had the energy to support Norah the way she needed. Besides, it was important for Norah to go see the Bryers without this strange new friend tagging along.

There was a part of her that wished she could have gone. She'd gotten used to her inability to watch over Norah's every move, but as she said goodbye to Norah that morning and told her how proud of her she was, she was struck with the odd feeling that she was missing out on something she should have been a part of.

Perhaps the weight in her chest that suffocated her more with each passing second was less about fear of missing out and more about the looming possibility that it was all coming to an end. Not only her time here on Earth with Norah, but the very real possibility that Celeste's time as a Guardian could be over.

Unless, of course, she betrayed the one being who had always been her biggest supporter.

WHEN THEY MET IN CELESTE'S HOTEL ROOM THAT EVEning, Celeste could feel Norah's eagerness to tell her all about her day. She described every detail to her, from the moment she pulled up to the Bryers' house to the moment she left. She explained how happy they were to see her, and how relieved she felt to apologize for her role in Sam's death. What a relief it had been to say it all out loud and to the two people who mattered most.

Celeste listened closely to her words as she watched a shadow creep across Norah's face with every forced lilt in her tone.

"They invited me to stay the night," Norah said. "But I had already told them all about you, and I explained I didn't want to leave you here alone."

Celeste reached for Norah's hand and squeezed. "You could have," she said.

A part of her was elated; Norah hadn't run off and forgotten all about her the second the Bryers welcomed her in, but another part of her wished she *had* stayed with them. She wasn't sure how she could hide her concerns over what Silas discovered from Norah. Although from the look on Norah's face, she couldn't hide that she was concerned about something, as well.

"I promised them I'd go back tomorrow. We've got one more day in California, and I'd like to make it count, if that's okay? Of course, I'd love for you to meet them—well, officially meet them," she said with a wide smile.

"I'm really happy for you, Norah. Not only that, I'm proud of you," Celeste said. "I know how much you've been struggling. I know it wasn't easy for you to do what you did today." Celeste felt Norah squeeze her hand back in thank you after sighing heavily.

Celeste asked, "Are you okay?"

"Yeah, I am," she said, before going quiet. Celeste embraced the silence.

For only a moment.

"It did feel *good* to talk with them. To take accountability and have them accept me back into their lives." Celeste nodded encouragingly. "I'm excited to spend the day with them tomorrow, and they seem genuinely excited, too." She tucked her dark hair behind her ear and focused her gaze on her knees.

"It's just, on the way back here, away from them and the adrenaline of it all, it doesn't feel complete." She sighed, released Celeste's hand, and shifted her weight a bit. "Maybe I will always feel the loss of Sam. He was the one person who truly needed me, and I let him down. I loved Sam so much. Maybe that guilt, that grief, will never go away."

Norah shook her head, deep in thought. "If today wasn't about taking accountability, then I don't know what else I am supposed to do to learn this Lesson. If what I need is forgiveness from Sam, well, I'll never get it. He's gone," she said and threw her hands up. "All of them are gone. Luisa's parents, Serge, Amelia, all those poor patients.

"I was responsible for torturing people, Celeste. How am I supposed to fix *that* unresolved accountability? Is that why I am seeing these memories? How do I make up for all of the wrongs I've done in every life? I just have this one left. I've already failed Sam. I'm hopeless. And isn't it selfish to want to fix all this in order to learn my final Lesson, considering all the lives I've ruined along the way?" Norah wiped fresh tears from her cheeks with her shirtsleeves.

Celeste sat quietly, picking at her nails. She didn't want to say too much, for fear of making things worse.

"Is this it?" Norah cried. "Did I ruin it already? Am I too late?"

Celeste rubbed her hands along her face in frustration and, for the first time in a very long time, felt tired. She said, "Norah, you didn't ruin anything. There is no light bulb moment for the Lessons. You are *human*. You'll have a mix of emotional ups and downs. One day you'll feel amazing, like you're nailing this crazy thing called life, and another day you'll feel lost and confused. All you can do is do your best, and that, I have no doubt, you will do."

Norah sniffled and continued to wipe at her cheeks with her sleeve. "You know the worst part about finding you, and finding out that this," she pointed up to the ceiling, "is real?" Celeste gave a look of encouragement to continue. Norah said, "It's knowing that I never will see Sam again."

Celeste took a moment to try and understand what Norah meant, but couldn't quite get it. "What do you mean? How does meeting me lead you to know you'll never see Sam? Should be the opposite, right?"

Norah's voice shook as she said, "Sam committed suicide. Doesn't that mean he goes to Hell? I don't know, fuck, I probably shouldn't assume I'd go to Heaven even if accountability is the last Lesson."

"Oh, no. *Norah*." It pained Celeste to know she carried the weight of this thought with her. "First, there is no Hell. This is the cycle," she said, gesturing at Norah. "What you are going through now with all the Lessons, learning, and growing in each life." There was a brief moment Celeste thought of telling Norah the truth, that taking accountability for Sam's death was not the lesson she needed to learn, but she thought better of it.

She was done making things worse. No, really, for real this time.

"Secondly, do you think that there would be a God who created you only to then punish someone eternally for being so immensely lost in this world that they would take their own life? That's when humans need us Guardians the most, and, in my opinion, that's when we fail the most."

Humans. For as much as they tried, and as much as they've done good, they sure did mess up on some of the really big stuff.

Norah's shoulders shook as she began to sob. The emotion of the day, the certainty that this was not the first time Norah found herself drowning in uncontrollable tears, was not lost on Celeste. She wrapped her arms around her tightly and gave her a big squeeze.

And because Celeste was Celeste, and simply couldn't help herself, she added, "You aren't accountable for fixing things that happened in the past. The goal is to learn in the current life." She squeezed her once more for good measure.

After a few moments of silence, Norah excused herself to go to the bathroom and splashed her face with cold water.

"I think I'm going to head back to my room. I'm exhausted, and I'm either going to sleep like a rock tonight or not at all. Can't wait to see which one," Norah teased as she walked out of the bathroom.

Celeste watched her walk to the door, and relief washed over her at the thought of sweet reprieve from having to lie to Norah about her day.

"I'm so sorry," Norah said, right as she was about to grab the door handle. "I didn't even ask you how your day was." Norah turned and made her way back towards the bed where Celeste was still sitting.

Fiddlesticks.

Celeste waved her off. "Fine, fine, it was fine," she said, her voice cracking on the third fine.

Norah crinkled her nose. "I'm sorry. That boring, huh?" she asked.

"Yes," Celeste exclaimed. "I mean, not terrible," she said, and ran her fingers through the tips of her hair. "No worries for me, really. Just not much to do today. But that's totally okay, I knew it would be like this, and I'm happy to have hung around here."

Norah nodded slowly. "Okay, well, I'm sorry, but I do really appreciate you letting us have our space. Really, it meant a lot."

"No problem."

"We will have a lot of fun tomorrow," Norah said, perking up a bit. "I think I subconsciously expected a wash-of-light type of feeling to come over me after taking accountability. I've felt so bad for so long, I think I just need time to process the good."

Celeste smiled. "I'm really proud of you," she said for the third time. And she meant it. If only she could say the same of her own actions.

Norah said her goodbyes and was barely out of the door before Celeste grabbed the nearest pillow, buried her face into it, and screamed.

There was no way she was going to be able to hide her worry about Silas and Benny in front of Norah tomorrow, let alone the Bryers.

THE NEXT MORNING, CELESTE WATCHED NORAH SWIRL syrup on her waffle as she worked to discern the best possible moment to tell her.

There wasn't one.

"You're going to love Maureen. She's so welcoming." Norah seemed to be in a more cheery mood than last night, the excitement of seeing them again showing brightly. "And John is hilarious. Oh," she stopped herself. "You probably already know all this, huh?"

Celeste smiled and sipped her tea. It took everything in her not to run.

They sat at the hotel cafe, eating the continental breakfast and preparing to leave for the Bryers before then returning home that evening. Their flight back to Greenville was that evening, so they had most of the day to spend with them.

That had been the plan anyway.

"Norah," Celeste said softly. Norah looked up from her plate as she took a big bite of her waffle. "I'm not going to come with you to see John and Maureen today."

Norah frowned as she swallowed her last bite practically whole. "Why? You said you were bored yesterday, don't just sit in the hotel. I promise I want you to be there."

"That's not it, but also, thank you, you're the best." She smiled, though she knew it looked as stilted as she felt. "Um, I'm actually going to return home. To *my* home."

Norah paused, fork raised in waiting. "You're leaving? Like... leaving-leaving? Why?" she asked.

Celeste dropped her eyes to her hands wrapped tightly around her cup. "I think I really messed up by coming here. Not just for you, but for other reasons that I can't explain. I need to make it right."

"You can't explain? Celeste, you can't leave. I'm finally making progress on taking accountability and cleaning up my life. I need you, and not just as my Guardian Angel, but as my friend."

Celeste's heart nearly exploded. How was she supposed to leave after that? But no, leaving was the right thing to do. She had to find a way to make things better.

She reached across the table for Norah's hand. "I'm sorry," was all she could say.

"You're sorry? I need help. What happens if taking accountability for Sam isn't the Lesson? You won't tell me what the Lesson is, so I don't know if I'm even doing what needs to be done. Guide me! Tell me what to do!" Norah leaned forward, and Celeste fought the urge to reach over and stop her hair from getting into the syrup. It didn't. Close call.

"I am trying to guide you, but coming down here was wrong. I need to guide you the right way–from afar. You're going to be fine without me here, Norah. You have a long life ahead of you."

Norah narrowed her eyes at Celeste. "Do you know that for sure?"

"No." She smiled. "But I am sure you will live your life and learn your Lesson the way you should have. I should have never interfered."

Celeste felt her heart break as she watched Norah process. The thought of failing her, the thought of going back home and leaving her behind, not knowing for certain she was going to make it, hadn't crossed Celeste's mind before they sat down to breakfast. But she knew she was making the right choice..

"So this is it? You just leave, and I never see you again? I live the rest of this life and hope I've come to the right place in the end?"

"I am so sorry that you even know of Life Lessons, past lives, and Guardian Angels. This is my fault, and I promise to do all I can to make it up to you. I just have to do it from there and not down here."

Norah stood and grabbed her plate. "Sure, I get it," she bit back. "My Guardian Angel randomly shows up one day, tells me I am about to run out of lives if I don't learn a vital Lesson, makes me see my past lives where I've equally ruined things, tells me she can't help me with what that life Lesson is, then says 'oops, I shouldn't have come.'"

"I'm–"

Norah held up her hand to stop Celeste. "You're sorry," she said.

Without another word, Norah walked away. She didn't look back.

# CHAPTER 41

## Norah

THE FLIGHT BACK HOME FELT MUCH LONGER WITHout Celeste. Norah tried to focus on the positive. The trip was, after all, a success. She went back to the Bryers' that day and had a wonderful time. They had lunch together, and Maureen took Norah for a beautiful walk along the beach. It was chillier than she thought it would be, and she had to borrow a cardigan from Maureen.

They were a few feet along the beach when Maureen asked, "So, tell me everything that I've missed. Gosh, you're probably done with your residency, right? Or do you have a couple more years? Are you still leaning towards emergency medicine? Are you enjoying Greenville? Are you seeing anyone?"

Maureen's excitement grew with each question, and Norah desperately wished that she could tell her good things. That she was now halfway through her residency, she loved working in the emergency room as much as she thought she would. That she had a great group of friends in Greenville, and they all hung out on her off days. That she was happy and in a committed relationship with a man who loved and respected her.

Norah knew that for Maureen, it was more than just getting to hear Norah's life; it was getting to hear the life Sam may have gotten to live, too.

Norah's chin quivered as she failed miserably at faking a smile.

"Truthfully, Sam would be ashamed of what I've done with my life."

"Oh, honey, don't say that. Sam was never one to judge, and certainly never judged you. I know he is looking down on you, and he is very proud of you."

Norah shook her head as she explained the past three years of how she had screwed up her life. She described every detail, every feeling, and every misstep. The quitting, the shutting down, the drinking, and all the ways she pushed anyone who ever cared about her out. "It wasn't just you two I ruined things with," she explained. "Although, given how much you took me in when I was little, you are the worst of it."

She told her all about Chris. How caring, gentle, and patient he was with her. And how she pushed him away. She thought of Barb and how she continuously turned down her offers of friendship. She thought of Celeste. Was Celeste her fault, too? Did she ask too much of her, expecting her to fix it all instead of taking accountability for her own work she needed to do to get her life back on track?

"I'm starting to see how much I push people away. I shouldn't have cut you out of my life."

"You did not ruin anything with us. John and I both love you and always will. We're together now, and that's what matters. We all do things in our lives that take us off our paths. We mess up, make mistakes, hurt people, even when we have the best intentions. No one is perfect." She squeezed Norah's hand as they continued to walk. "And dear, if we're the worst of it, then it sounds like nothing you've done can't be fixed."

They walked a few steps more in silence, and Norah thought of Sam and her missed opportunity to set things right with him. The heaviness hung on her shoulders like a wet sweater.

"You know, Norah," Maureen said, breaking the silence. "Sam would want you to find happiness. Sam would never want

something he did–and please understand it was *his* decision—
to hold you back for the rest of your life. I know, and he knew,
you deserve happiness. You deserve success in your career. You
deserve love."

*Not yet,* Norah thought. But taking accountability for all
she'd done to others was her first step towards deserving it all.
Maybe one day, Maureen will be right.

When she and Maureen returned to the house, the Pirates
versus the Padres game had just started.

"Hey!" John exclaimed. "Come watch the game with me,
just like old times." He beamed.

Fun fact: Norah never liked baseball, and Sam hated to
watch it. Yet, they always watched with John. It was important
to Sam to have something with his dad, even if it wasn't for him,
and Norah loved to be included.

"That would be great," she said.

And she meant it.

Norah stayed long enough to have dinner with them, but
left shortly after. They offered for her to stay the night once
again, but–as wonderful as the day was–she was longing for
some time to herself to process the last forty-eight hours. She
explained that Celeste was expecting her back at the hotel.

Was it a lie if deep down she was hoping it was true?

And there she was, sitting on the plane, thinking about the
last two days. She'd apologized for her part in Sam's death, and
the Bryers were back in her life, to the extent they could be living across the country, anyway. Mission accomplished.

She did get forgiveness from the Bryers, and while she
couldn't get forgiveness for the mistakes she'd made in her
past lives, she understood she needed to fix the other things in
her current life she'd messed up since Sam's passing. Chris, for
starters.

She called Chris the night before to tell him all about her
reunion with the Bryers. She tried to relay the excitement but
couldn't hide the off feeling she still had, and admittedly, she'd

been the same with Celeste. She feared the hesitation came across as being distant, as if she was holding back from him yet again, when really she could not find the words to explain the sense of disconnect she was feeling. Celeste explained that it wasn't going to be a light switch, but the sense of guilt she felt over Sam's death still lingered heavily.

Norah swiveled her head to the right, excited to tell Celeste how she was going to make it up to Chris. Her stomach dropped as she stared at the pile of unused yarn and knitting needles piled in the empty seat next to her—where Celeste was supposed to be sitting. She sighed. She brought the yarn and needles to distract her, but clearly, her mind had other plans.

She spent the remainder of the flight in a mess of emotion. She wanted to be hopeful she could win Chris back, elated that the Bryers accepted her apology, angry at Celeste for abandoning her, and scared of what would happen if accountability wasn't her final Lesson. And yet each time she forced herself to think on one of those thoughts, she ultimately came back to the very simple fact: the seat beside her was empty, and she'd never see Celeste again.

# CHAPTER 42

# *Celeste*

Without much else to do, Celeste returned to the hotel room after Norah left that morning. She racked her brain the entire evening before and still didn't know what to do about Silas's blackmail scheme.

She couldn't betray Benny.

On the other hand, if she didn't, then she risked losing Norah forever. She threw her hands up. There was, quite simply, no way the Council could find out about what she'd done. Going against their orders, directly interfering with her Soul, never telling anyone she knew her Soul in the first place, showing her Soul her own past lives. Could the list get any longer? Celeste was certain the Council would banish her from the Guardian afterlife, which meant she'd never be another Soul's Guardian. Even worse, she would never see Norah again.

Either way, Benny's involvement in Celeste's shenanigans was going to get him punished. Should they both suffer for all eternity?

She knew what she needed to do, and it was best to simply–as they say–tear off the bandaid.

She first sent a voice note to Benny asking to schedule yet another check-in, apologizing for leaving so abruptly the last time. Not a moment later, she sent a voice note to Silas.

Celeste rapped gently on the door in front of her as if it were made of the thinnest glass and the slightest touch would shatter it. Then she held her breath.

*Don't be home yet. Don't be home yet. Don't be home yet.*

Coming clean to Benny was the right thing to do, she knew it. She'd always known it. It didn't make the actual act of confessing to him any easier. Ironically, it was Celeste taking a lesson from Norah this time; she needed to take accountability.

Her stomach turned as footsteps approached from the other side of the door. Benny swung the door open and stood before her. Celeste swore he had the brightest smile she had ever seen strung across his face. Was it just her, or was his glow brighter than usual, too?

"Celeste!" He exclaimed, stepping aside to let her in. "You could have just popped in, no need to knock on the door. I knew you were coming."

"Oh, no, I'll never do that to anyone ever again." She shuddered at the thought of Silas in his apartment.

As Celeste passed him, Benny's eyes tracked across her face, and she noticed his brightness dull. "Everything okay? You don't look great."

He closed the door behind her, and they made their way to Benny's living room. Celeste was acquainted with his home, but it had been a while since she'd been inside. They typically preferred meeting at his office in the Great Hall or the garden. As a member of the Council, he was able to add a little more personal touch than the others, but he still chose taupe and jade. He always said he liked to be surrounded by the "Earthy" tones in his home, something Celeste never could understand.

She sat quietly at his writing desk, not allowing herself the comfort of his sofa.

"I'm glad you reached out today. I was disappointed you had to leave yesterday. I've got Silas to keep me updated, but he's not nearly as fun to visit with as you," he teased, but his smile fell flat at Celeste's silence. Benny cleared his throat and sat across from her, his conscience clear enough to choose comfort. "Seems like the plan to keep him entertained has worked," Benny added as he smiled cautiously.

Celeste groaned and dropped her head into her hands.

"Celeste, what's going on?"

She took a deep, shaky breath. "We need to talk."

And so she told him. Everything.

The worst part about Benny's reaction to Celeste's confession, what made her feel even more terrible than before, was that he was more crestfallen than angry. He didn't yell, he didn't turn red, and steam didn't shoot from his ears. When she finished talking, he simply sighed, pressed his hands into his knees, and sat silently for what felt like an eternity.

"Can you please say something?" Celeste begged.

He picked his head up and looked at her directly. The hurt in his eyes cut far worse than any words he could have said.

"All this time and you didn't come to me," he said. "You could have explained the mix-up; you could have asked me for help. I would have assigned the Soul to someone who would have taken good care of them."

Celeste tried to blink back tears. Being in his space, so warm and inviting, humanized him, for lack of a better word. It made her guilt sit thicker in the air.

"You are right," she said. She wanted to dive into more of an explanation, but Benny continued to speak.

"And to think," he sighed, "you felt more comfortable telling Silas than me." Celeste hung her head in shame as he continued. "If you had come to me from the beginning, it wouldn't have been on you to deal with. There was a glitch in the assignments. This stuff happens—not often—but sometimes the process fails and things get mixed up."

Celeste thought back to their boardroom conversation and how they emulated the humans in that regard. From what she has seen through the years, there's not much difference in the way they run all their *processes,* either, including the mess of them.

"It's why we stress that you need to be diligent when it comes to the Souls you receive. *You* should have spoken up when you were assigned a Soul you knew. You agreed to this rule in your onboarding."

"I know," she said. "But I really was distracted." She didn't tell him *why* she was distracted; she'd hurt him enough for one day. "And then by the time I realized who my Soul was, I...I couldn't believe it. Out of all the Souls out there, theirs was the one I got. At first, I was just going to check in, make sure they were doing okay, but then it all got out of hand." She hung her head low.

"And this," he said, thrusting his hands out before her, voice raised for the first time, "is why we make sure you don't get Souls you knew in your lifetime. Now, there is a very real chance we've ruined everything for your Soul if the Council deems this too much interference, and that's on us."

"If I could take it all back, I would."

Benny took a deep breath. "That was unfair. I shouldn't say we've ruined everything. I am certain we can fix this. I just have to figure out how."

"You said members of the Council have gone down before. Do I just happen to be the first Trainee to interact with a Soul I knew in one of my lifetimes?"

Benny shrugged. "I'm honestly not sure. A Soul seeing all past lives after interacting with a Guardian is new to me, too. Why do you ask?"

"I'm trying to understand if it is because I knew her in a past life. Does that alone cause such a strong connection?"

Benny looked at her thoughtfully. "I'm not sure. Maybe I can look into that before losing my seat on the Council."

Celeste grimaced. "I can try to convince Silas not to talk, or at very least leave you out of it completely. I'll find a way." She hoped they could convince Silas to say Benny had no part in any of it. After all, he only knew of a small part in the grand scheme of things.

Benny shook his head. "There's no way the Council would ever believe I had no part in you going down to Earth. It would be impossible for you to go down by yourself undetected."

He told her he would try and think of something, but the doubt between them was palpable. Right before she stood to leave, he said, "I do get it, you know. You barely had a chance to adjust to your world here, to your new role as a Trainee, and to your enlightened state, before being thrown into a very unique situation that anyone would have had a hard time walking away from. But that is why I am here. To help you."

Celeste nodded. "I should have come to you. In the beginning, there were several times I almost *did* tell you. Day after day, things were okay, and I'd think *tomorrow, I'll tell him tomorrow*. Then, nothing bad happened. It all seemed fine. And the longer I watched over them, the harder it was to give them up."

"Which, again, is why you aren't supposed to be assigned a Soul you knew." Benny rolled his eyes and brushed his hands through his hair. "Truthfully, I did think you were a bit over-the-top with this Soul. Too persistent. I thought you just needed to get your first Soul across. I really thought you just loved being a Trainee that much."

"I do," she protested. "Really, I do."

But was there more to it than that?

SHE LEFT BENNY'S, WEIGHT HEAVIER THAN WHEN SHE arrived, but she didn't doubt that she did the right thing. The pain of hurting him with the truth was nothing compared to if she betrayed him. Still, knowing she hurt him at all filled her with shame.

At least she could use the emotion as fuel. She'd approach Silas and tell him to take his awful blackmail plan and shove it where the sun didn't shine.

She went to Silas's living quarters right after leaving Benny. She was sure it would upset Benny if he knew. She should leave Silas alone to give them time to sort things out, but she needed to talk with him.

She chose to knock on his door this time. She did not want a repeat of the last time she'd been here. He swung open the door to Celeste with her right hand firmly over her eyes. She heard him scoff as he told her to stop being so ridiculous.

The sound of his voice made her blood boil, and the heat only increased when she released her hand to look at his mousey face. "What do you want?" he asked. "We aren't supposed to meet today."

She tucked her hands into her armpits to keep them from shaking. Whether from anger, shame, or simply the adrenaline of the day, she didn't know, but she sure as heck wasn't going to allow Silas to see any weakness.

"This will be quick," she said, grateful that her voice wasn't also shaking. "I came to tell you that I have just spoken with Benny."

Silas looked at her with an air of boredom. "And?" he asked.

"And, I told him everything."

It took Silas a split second to register her words before his eyes bulged and his jaw practically hit the floor. "What do you mean you told him *everything*?"

The shocked look on Silas's face gave her the confidence she needed. Arms released and voice raised, she let him have it.

"I mean *everything*. That you were snooping around trying to catch me doing something I shouldn't have been doing, that I panicked and brought you in on it. That I've been working with you to hide my interactions with Norah. That you tried to blackmail me into betraying him, and that I knew Norah from my last life before becoming a Trainee. Everything."

"Are you going to tell the Council about all this? Is Benny?"

Celeste shrugged her shoulders, a genuine gesture. She hadn't gotten that far. It would be the right thing to do, but she also wanted to do her best to fix things for Benny, without any of it ever getting back to the Council.

Silas stammered. "You cannot tell the Council I was involved."

His panic grew with every word.

"How do I know you won't tell the Council?" Celeste countered. "If you keep your mouth shut, I'll keep mine shut." Silas scowled and held her gaze long enough to make her fidget. "Fine," she continued, "I take full blame for all this; this whole situation is my fault. If you promise not to tell the Council about Benny's involvement, I won't tell them about yours."

"So I get nothing out of this whole deal?" Silas protested. "I've done what you asked of me, for nothing?" He shifted his weight from one side of the doorframe to the next. No sign of inviting Celeste inside for their conversation.

Leave it to Silas to always work an angle.

"Might I remind you that if you hadn't gone snooping, I never would have asked for your help, and if you hadn't blackmailed me, we'd be fine. You wanted to only look out for yourself."

Silas laughed, but he couldn't hide the shake in his voice when he said, "Well, all I have to do is tell the Council before you do, then. Great job, Celeste, you just ended your own Guardianship before it began."

Celeste cast her gaze down and softened her voice. "I ruined things for myself before I even started, Silas. I'm ready to own up to that now, but don't ruin things for Benny, please." She was done playing this game. It was a game she started, yes, but now it was time she ended it.

"Wait, did you say you told Benny you knew Norah in your *last* life?" The softness in the way he spoke drew Celeste's gaze back up at Silas, eyebrows pinched tight. "You don't know, do you?" His wicked smile spread across his cheeks.

"Know what?"

"This is even bigger than you realize, Celeste." He stepped back and reached for the door. "Enjoy your new afterlife, wherever you end up." He slammed the door in Celeste's face.

Celeste huffed and stomped her foot in aggravation. She contemplated going in after him, but thought better of it. He didn't know anything. He was just trying to get under her skin. She took away his power, and now he was acting like a giant child about it.

There was nothing else to know.

# CHAPTER 43

## Norah

NORAH WIPED THE TEARS THAT POURED DOWN HER face. "I don't want to explain my behavior and sound like I'm excusing it. I am genuinely sorry for the wall I put up, and the distance that I forced between us."

Norah sat on Chris's kitchen counter, knees pulled to her chest, while he stood across from her, leaning on his fridge, body stiff.

Her eyes scanned him while he focused on the floor in front of him. His lean runner's body appeared fuller with muscle, and she wondered what all had changed about him that she didn't know about. She longed to slide from the counter and wrap her arms around his waist.

"I really appreciate you telling me stuff lately," said Chris. "Going to see Sam's parents, our phone call after. I know that wasn't easy for you, so I really do appreciate it. It's just...I tried for a long time to talk to you, and you wouldn't let me in. I wanted to be there for you, and you never allowed me to be. Now, all of a sudden, you want to...what? What is it that you want here?"

Norah raised her shoulders to her ears and left them there for a moment. "I don't know, Chris," she said, finally releasing them. "I know it's taken me a while to climb out of this, but I'm trying to get there."

It had taken him nearly a day to respond to her text asking to meet up, and then nearly another half day to say whether or not he would. She couldn't blame him. It was one thing to respond to a text, another thing to talk on the phone, and a whole other thing to meet up in person. He didn't owe her anything, and she wasn't entirely certain what she expected out of meeting with him, but she knew he deserved an apology face-to-face.

Chris ran his hands through his long, dark hair as he tried to find the next words to say, like he so often did when dealing with her. "I'm honestly just not sure what to do with all this right now."

"I don't expect you to do anything. You deserved an apology for the way I treated you, and that's all I wanted to say." She noticed their picture still tucked behind the Cancun magnet on the fridge, and found some encouragement in that. "But, if you'll let me, I'd like to tell you more."

He watched her for a moment, their eyes locked on one another, and she hoped her heart wasn't racing too loudly.

"Okay." He nodded. "Let's start with you telling me about Sam."

And so she did. She talked for a long time about the first time she and Sam met, how he was the first boy in the neighborhood to play with her. She talked of the Bryers taking them camping when they were younger, their movie nights (she got a sideways glance for that one), and how they would go to parties only to sit in a corner talking to each other and then leave early. She talked about how they stayed close through college, despite their different paths.

"Sam always had the tendency to sit in his moods too long. He'd get into these funks and wouldn't know how to get out of them. I could get him out, get him feeling better. I was the person who made him feel understood. Until I wasn't. Somewhere in between graduating from college, his starting work in an office, and me moving on to medical school–the phone calls slowed."

Chris tore a paper towel from its holder and handed it to Norah before settling once again against the fridge.

She wiped at her tears. "If I had been able to anticipate his moods like I could when we were younger, I would have known the importance of that phone call. I would have dropped everything I was doing to talk to him." She thought of Mrs. Bryers and how great she felt when she left their last conversation. But now, thinking back on Sam..."I feel like I don't deserve to get close to another person. Like I don't deserve happiness and love."

"Norah. I hope you know–" He tried to interject, but now that she'd started talking, she couldn't seem to stop the words from pouring out of her.

"But just because I don't deserve those things, doesn't mean you don't. I've treated you unfairly, Chris. By trying not to hurt myself again, I hurt you. I am so sorry."

Norah watched her words wash over Chris. She watched him struggle to respond to her.

"I knew you lost your best friend. I tried to be understanding, but if you had talked about him, if you had told me about the day he died, I would have understood why you shut down. Fuck, I would have tried more to find a better outlet instead of just getting angry with you." He took a sharp intake of breath. "Now that's me giving excuses," he joked. "You deserved to have someone be there for you, not lash out like I did. I'm sorry, too."

"You really don't have anything to apologize for; you gave me a lot of chances. You were as patient as you could be. You know, a friend recently told me that no one is perfect, and it's how you handle something moving forward that counts." Norah smiled at the thought of Celeste. She missed her friend terribly.

"I guess we both have some things to learn."

Norah sat up straighter, her back stiff from sitting on the granite, and the urge to tell Chris about Celeste heavy on her lips. She opened her mouth to speak, then thought better of it.

Would he believe her? There were moments when she hardly believed it herself, and she had weeks to come to terms with it. But if they were going to fix this relationship, like Norah hoped to do, she needed to be honest with him. This was far too big to keep from him. She opened her mouth once more, but hesitated again. *How on Earth do I begin?*

Chris watched her quizzically. The softness had returned to his eyes. A softness he'd held for her in times she didn't deserve it, and Norah knew she didn't want to lose that ever again, even if she risked coming off as crazy.

"I told you a little about the friend I met. Her name is Celeste. She's funny and odd, in the best way, and I've really enjoyed hanging out with her lately." Norah felt herself light up as she described Celeste. "I think I told you she's the one who talked me into going to see Maureen and John. She's really helped me open up a bit. I always felt comfortable with her and, for whatever reason, found myself sharing a lot with her almost as soon as I met her. It's strange, really. I feel like I've known her for so much longer than the last few months."

"That's great. Sounds like I owe this woman a thank you," Chris joked.

"Well, that's the thing," Celeste hedged. "She's gone home and won't be around anymore."

"And y'all can't visit each other?"

Norah struggled to find the words to explain. "So after I started hanging out with her, I started to get these visions... no, they were memories, really. They were my own past lives." Norah fumbled her way through explaining her lives and the life Lesson she needed to learn. To Chris's credit, he never laughed, just listened. "So, yeah. Celeste is actually my Guardian Angel."

It was the first time she said the words out loud, and she wished instantly she could take them back. There was no way he was going to believe her.

"So..." He dragged the word out, clearly processing. "You met your real-life Guardian Angel, and you're trying to figure out the Life Lesson you need to learn in order to move on, and if you don't, then you're done? You just finish this life and never come back?"

"Right."

Chris nodded. "Okay." He kept nodding. "Can I meet Celeste?"

Norah grimaced. "That's the thing. She's gone. She went back to–Heaven, I guess?" Chris gave her a look that made it clear he didn't believe her. "I know how crazy this sounds, but you have to believe me."

"Let me just be clear–the only proof of your new friend, your Guardian Angel, is now gone. She went back to up there." He pointed up. "And I can't meet her." Chris let out a laugh. "I'm sorry, I'm not trying to be a dick. This is just–"

"A lot, I know." Norah hopped down from the counter and walked over to Chris. She racked her brain for a way to prove it to him. "Barb met her, actually. She worked at the pet store by my place."

Chris simply nodded his head, dubious.

"Look, she knew things about me that there was no way she could have, but beyond all that, these lives, Chris, I wish I could explain the feelings. How real it all was. And she knew details about those without me needing to explain it all."

"Okay, okay. Say it's all real and you really only have one more life left. Do you think that remembering your past lives puts you at a disadvantage? Like having someone tell you your fate and then you try to avoid it, but it ultimately leads you to that fate."

"Macbeth?"

"Exactly."

Norah sighed heavily. "I have thought about that. I mean, going to the Bryers was probably the wrong thing to do. I have no clue if accountability was the right Lesson. The more I stress about this, the more I am probably going to go down the wrong path."

Chris inched forward. "I'm not saying I believe all this yet, and I have a lot of questions, but one thing I know for damn sure, Norah, is there's no way going to see the Bryers was the wrong thing to do. I am really proud of you for going to see them."

Norah stopped herself from reaching out to grab his hand. "Do you think you could believe me?"

Chris hesitated. "I don't know, Norah. This all sounds unreal. I can't tell if you just met this crazy person named Celeste, or if the stress of everything has finally gotten to you, or what this is."

"I get how insane this sounds, trust me. I rehearsed this conversation a million times in my head. It never sounded sane to me either, and I know it's the truth."

"I am proud of you for making a friend, though." He smiled. "Even if one or both of you are batshit crazy."

"I hate that she's gone. I miss her." Norah could feel the rawness from all the crying she'd done over the last few days, but she had to admit it was cathartic. She'd been holding in everything for too long.

"If I am being honest, Barb being your only credible witness to your Guardian Angel does not lend much credit to all this," he teased.

Norah playfully shoved at his arm, causing him to sway and settle closer to her. She felt her heart skip a beat.

"Fair," she said, and smiled. "But she's real. I promise. I wish I could prove it to you."

After a moment of silence, Chris said, "Well, real or not, I think it's great that you're working on yourself."

"Thanks, but you deserve better than me," Norah said with a shaky breath.

"Norah, I don't deserve better than you because you are amazing. You need to understand that you deserve better than this."

Norah thought back through all of the lives she remembered. How could she deserve anything good if she's done nothing but hurt people? She left one disaster after another in her path.

Chris reached out and gripped her hand tightly. Norah wasn't sure if this was his way of saying he forgave her, but for now, it was enough.

A WEEK LATER, NORAH SAT QUIETLY ACROSS FROM BARB as she blew her nose and dabbed at her eyes. She asked Barb to lunch, hoping to continue connecting with people. Barb, someone who always tried to be there for her, was a great place to start.

Their lunches sat on the table in front of them, nearly untouched since Norah began talking. They sat on the restaurant's patio, and a cool breeze hit them nicely, balancing the summer sun.

"You've been dealing with all of this since I've known you? All alone? No wonder you were overwhelmed to the point of making yourself sick."

She'd just finished filling her in about Sam and their life together. Norah had sat down for lunch with the plan to gradually open up to Barb, but once she started talking, she couldn't stop.

She didn't tell Barb the full truth about Celeste. Only stressed their friendship and how much she had helped her these last few months. She was still doing everything she could to convince Chris, although she believed she was getting somewhere.

Norah nodded and shrugged. "I was on my own by choice. Like you've said before, I had my ways of keeping people at a distance, including Chris."

Barb smiled gently at the mention of Chris's name; Norah knew she was happy at the news that she and Chris were talking again.

And it was great to talk to Chris again, to have someone she was able to confide in about Celeste and all the craziness of the last few months. She enjoyed opening up to him finally. But it was different talking to him versus a girlfriend. She missed Celeste fiercely.

Not a moment went by that she didn't hope Celeste would pop in. She still wanted to be angry at her for abandoning her. She was no expert on Guardians, but something didn't seem right about her Guardian Angel abandoning her. At the heart of it all, though, she knew she just missed her friend.

"Well." Barb sniffled and placed her tissue in her pocket. "The important thing is that you are learning to let people in."

"Thank you." Norah smiled and reached for her fork, picking at her salad.

"Have you talked to Sam's parents much since getting back into town? Do you think you'll keep in touch?"

"I have talked with Maureen over the phone. It's been nice to be able to do that. They live across the country, so it won't be easy, but we talked about taking turns visiting once or twice a year, which I'm excited for."

Barb studied Norah closely for a moment. "You still seem a little sad. It's all a lot to take in, I'm sure."

Norah thought about Barb's words while they both took bites of their food.

"How is your friend Celeste, by the way? I didn't see her at the pet store last time I was there," Barb said, with a tone of affection.

Norah looked out along the patio, feigning distraction as servers worked their way along the tables. "Um, she had to go home for a bit. Visit family. I'm sure she'll be back soon."

Norah hadn't seen any past lives since Celeste left, since talking to the Bryers, really. Perhaps it was possible that talking with them and taking accountability *was* the Lesson. Celeste explained she lived five other lives dedicated to learning this Lesson, which meant she had one other one to see. She was a little disappointed not getting to see the last life, not knowing this person's story. She had been so caught up in why it was happening, her frustration with herself at not learning what she needed to, she hadn't had a moment to process just how very cool it all was.

To see herself in these individual people, to feel what they felt, to have such a connection to them and herself. The confirmation of something greater than her, to know that there really were people up there looking out for the people down here.

It was overwhelming and it was beautiful.

"Good," Barb said. "She seems like a good influence on you."

"Yeah," Norah agreed. "She really helped me get back on my path. I am very lucky to have met her."

# CHAPTER 44

## Celeste

IT HAD BEEN A FEW DAYS SINCE SHE SPOKE WITH BENNY. She hadn't had a chance yet to tell him about her most recent conversation with Silas. She knew Benny was trying to figure out a way to fix her mess. She wouldn't blame him if it were more because of the impact it would have on him than because of his wanting to help her out of it. She deserved whatever fate had in store for her, but Benny didn't. He'd trusted her to do the right thing, and she blew it.

Celeste was back home—her real home. No longer in her brightly lit apartment so close to Norah. That place was never truly hers, yet she missed it terribly. She groaned at the drab setting around her. No colorful pink walls, no plush teal couch. It no longer felt like her home, but it probably wouldn't be hers for much longer, anyway.

The only way Benny could fix things was if he could have convinced Silas not to say a word about what he knew. There was a small chance—Celeste could still see the fear in Silas's eyes when she told him Benny knew everything, and he realized that he no longer held power over her. But what Silas had on them was far more damaging than what they had on him. Helping Celeste dig into why Norah was seeing her past lives, helping Benny keep an eye on Celeste, hiding what she and Benny were doing from the Council. This was nothing compared to blatantly disregarding their orders and potentially ruining a Soul's chance at making it to their afterlife.

There was not much for her to do but sit tight and wait.

Celeste wandered aimlessly from room to room before finally making herself a cup of tea and settling on the porch outside. With their individual living quarters tightly knit together in one area, Celeste's only view was that of the backend of another building just across a courtyard. She grumbled to herself. She appreciated the light breeze, perfect temperature for sitting outside, but the view left little to be desired.

In the midst of all of this, she still worried relentlessly about Norah. Celeste hadn't looked in on her as her Guardian for fear of what she might see if she did. What if Norah was struggling more now that Celeste was gone? She knew before Norah even went to see the Bryers that she wasn't going to leave feeling complete. Her accountability, and their forgiveness, was not the seventh lesson Norah needed. It pained Celeste not to be able to tell her exactly what it was. Not to be down there with her.

Benny popped in beside her, startling her; tea sloshed over the brim of her mug. "Dang it," she exclaimed. "Just when I was adjusting to the gravity down there, here I am readjusting to things back up here." She looked over to find a pile of napkins sitting on the table beside her and busied herself cleaning up the tea from her seat before finally looking at him. The look on her face made her stomach drop. She did not like what she saw.

"Not good news."

CELESTE PRESSED HER SWEATY PALMS INTO THE ENORmous oak door. So much of this scene reminded her of when she was there only a few months ago. She was nervous, but for a very different reason from the first time she was there. Benny stood beside her, his face a reflection of the way she felt inside.

Benny had gone to the Council and told them everything. "I am one of them, Celeste. I am supposed to be held to an even higher standard than you are. I needed to do what was right. Come clean and fix this."

It took a moment for the shock to wear off, but once it did, Celeste couldn't help but admit it was exactly what Benny should have done. He was right, not only was he a Guardian and a Mentor, he was also a member of the Council. He could have never known that allowing Celeste to go to Earth would lead to Norah seeing her past lives, but it was only fitting that he do everything he could to own up to allowing her to go, and correct the situation as best he could.

After he told her they were being summoned by the Council, he left as quickly as he came. He gave her space to collect herself, and Celeste suspected he needed to collect himself, as well. They met back up outside of the Council building a short time later, and Benny met her eyes only once as he approached.

They walked in together and made their way to the long table, the 1960s decor and bright light feeling even more ominous somehow.

Celeste wiped her palms along the front of her white dress and waited for her eyes to adjust to the bright light emanating from the Council members. If it weren't for Benny standing beside her, she would have felt a touch of déjà vu.

Her eyes scanned the length of the table and the eight members sitting at it. She locked eyes unexpectedly with Muriel, a Council Member typically known for her calm demeanor, and her chest tightened. Disappointment lined her face, her eyes cold.

The silence was agonizing.

"I am so sorry," Celeste blurted.

Reginald shot up in his seat. "An apology does not begin to correct the damage you've done."

Benny's hands went up before him. "Now, Reggie–*Reginald*–no real harm has been done."

Reginald turned to address Benny, daggers shooting from his eyes. "No real harm? Her Soul is on their very last Life, hasn't completed her Lessons, and is seeing all of her past lives. She may have ruined all chances they have of ever making it to their afterlife. Celeste did the exact opposite of what we are supposed to do as Guardians."

Muriel's airy voice filled the room. "While I do not condone her–or Benny's–actions, Benny is right. We don't know the extent of the damage just yet."

"Regardless," Reginald protested, "what she has done is beyond repair."

Celeste picked furiously at her fingernails, unable to defend herself.

Whatever punishment they dealt out to her, she knew she deserved it.

"And him," Reginald shouted, pointing his bony finger in Benny's direction. "He is a member of this Council. His actions are unforgivable."

She could not let Benny be punished.

"No, please," Celeste begged. "Please, this is not Benny's fault. I did this. He had no idea this Soul was a part of one of my previous lives, not when I was first assigned, and not when I requested to go see them. I didn't understand the depth of it all when I was assigned my Soul, and I certainly didn't know the impact my going to see Norah would have. I'll take whatever punishment you give me, but Benny shouldn't suffer over my misjudgment."

Benny, perfectly composed with his hands clasped behind his back, head held high. "I am her Mentor, and therefore, I am responsible for her actions. I allowed her to go down to Earth when the Council was clear in their decision not to allow it. I take responsibility for my actions as well."

Celeste began to protest, but thought better of it. Arguing with Benny in front of the Council would do little to help her case.

Kinsley, quietly observant, cleared her throat. She motioned for Reginald to sit, and he obeyed without hesitation. "Celeste, I can understand how the very rare circumstance of you receiving a Soul you'd known in life—as your very first assignment, no less—would present difficulties. Especially given a layer here that you yourself don't quite understand yet."

Celeste shot Benny a concerned look.

"But rules are in place for a reason."

He shot her a knowing look right back.

"You were chosen to be a Guardian for a reason. We knew when we chose you that you would be able to shoulder the responsibilities that come with being one because we have seen your Soul exude those higher standards time and time again. In other words, Celeste, we have an honor system as our failsafe. We expect Trainees to tell us if they were assigned a Soul they once knew because we expect to be able to trust you."

As if Celeste could possibly feel even worse.

Reginald chuckled smugly and leaned back in his chair. Kinsley looked at him sideways. She refocused her attention on Celeste. "There are things at play here that I don't think you understand. This *situation* goes deeper than you realize, Celeste."

Celeste thought back to Silas's comments. *This is even bigger than you realize, Celeste. Enjoy your new afterlife, wherever you end up.*

It felt as if there was a tiny person doing somersaults in her stomach.

"I am certain that as a member of this Council, your Mentor has figured this out, in which case, he understands that while his actions may not have had any intended malice, they very well could have caused more than we all have yet to realize. It was a miss on the Council's part, of course. It happens given the volume of Souls minute-by-minute. That's not an excuse, however. If he had known the truth from the beginning, he may have been able to piece it all together and help to avoid it." Kinsley looked past Celeste, and her strong demeanor broke for only a moment. "Although it seems as if your and Norah's fates were sealed regardless. Nevertheless," she snapped back to attention. "We could have intervened, and now the true impact is unclear."

Celeste stole another look at Benny, but he kept his gaze focused on Kinsley, jaw clenched tight. She wished she could call a timeout, talk to him outside of the room. Clearly, there was something going on that they didn't want her to know.

Ezekiel, a Council member Celeste hadn't heard speak before, spoke up from the other end of the table, his voice stern. "There is a very real chance your Soul doesn't make it across due to your interference. If we are lucky, we may have caught this in time, but we don't know that yet. We will not be able to fully understand and decide if they have learned their final Lesson until the final phase of them moving on."

Reginald scoffed. "We rely on order, and expect such from those who deserve to be here. Neither of them is worthy of their title."

Muriel chimed in, "It is easy to break the rules, thinking you'd be the one to overcome the consequence, until you are the one actually dealing with the consequence."

The room was silent as Muriel's words settled over everyone. Celeste felt the gravity of it all; there was no way what she had done wouldn't cause a drastic impact, one she was going to have to own up to and deal with.

Her muscles began to feel sore from all the tension she held since entering the room. If she had any doubt before entering the Council room, she was certain now: any chance of seeing Norah again was zero.

She was desperate to know if Norah was on the right track or if she was slipping again without her there. After everything she'd been through, Celeste was now just another person she'd lost.

Celeste inhaled deeply. It didn't matter if she ever got to see Norah again, as long as she made it to her afterlife.

Kinsley cleared her throat. Her eyes were on Benny as she said, "I am extremely disappointed in you, Benjamin. Everything I have said to Celeste I could direct at you tenfold." Benny nodded once in understanding, but kept his head held high. "You blatantly disregarded the Council's orders and allowed her to go to Earth. The Council only works if we work as a team. Your loyalties to your Trainees are second to your loyalty to us."

Celeste looked imploringly at Benny, hoping he would defend his actions, but he didn't.

"So," said Muriel, "do we have a ruling?" Celeste could practically feel Benny tense beside her. "Or, do we wait to see if her Soul makes it through to decide what actions to take?"

"Regardless of the impact, they both broke the rules," said Kinsely. Beside her, Reginald smiled. "Admittedly, I haven't come across this before, and as such, I'd like to take some time to process. We will reconvene later. Wait for my summons, and then we will declare what to do with the two of you."

Nausea gripped Celeste's stomach. By the look of Benny's skin tone, he felt the same.

THE TWO STOOD OUTSIDE THE ROOM FOR A MOMENT, unsure of what to do next. Kinsley had explained that all of Benny's Council and Mentor duties were to be placed on hold. They would divide up his responsibilities amongst them and, naturally, Celeste would not be allowed to continue her Guardian Training duties until further notice.

"Well," Celeste said, wanting to lighten the mood, "at least I kept it under your three-month rule."

The joke did not get the desired laugh.

"What now?" she asked.

Benny had yet to make eye contact with Celeste. "I believe my days of giving advice to you are over, Celeste."

No, she refused to believe that was true. She couldn't lose Benny, too. "Benny, you know I didn't mean for all of this to go so far."

"It doesn't matter, Celeste. It's done now."

Benny moved to step away, but before he could go, she asked, "What was Kinsley talking about?" She knew she shouldn't push, but she needed to know. "What was missed by the Council that goes deeper than I realize?"

Benny's head turned slowly to look at Celeste, pain in his eyes, before turning and walking away. He'd finally made eye contact with her.

# CHAPTER 45

# *Celeste*

A BSOLUTELY NOT, NO."

"Silas, you owe me."

"I most certainly do not owe you. You pulled me into this mess, and now I am the one who could potentially get into trouble here." Silas fanned his face with his right hand to stop from tearing up. Celeste had to lock her eyes in place to keep them from rolling.

She sat with Silas inside the Guardian Tower, back in the communal area across from where he worked. It was calm and quiet for the time being.

"Oh, please, you'll get a slap on the wrist. Your ridiculous delusion of power may have cost Benny and me our entire after-lives of Guardianship."

"You've managed to do that all on your own," Silas scoffed. He crossed his arms about his chest, stuck his nose high in the air, and spun his chair so that his back faced Celeste.

She needed to watch her tone. That was not the way to handle a giant-man-baby-angel. If she was going to win him back over, he needed to be treated delicately. She cleared her throat, and Silas looked over his right shoulder.

It pained her, but she said, "I am sorry, Silas. I shouldn't have said that. You are right. None of this would have happened if it weren't for me, and you wouldn't be in *potential* trouble if I hadn't pulled you in. I promise that if you tell me what the Council knows, I will write a letter myself encouraging them not to punish you for your part in any of this."

He let out a sharp crack of a laugh. "As if a letter from you carries any weight."

Celeste rolled her eyes and threw up her hands in defeat. "It has to be better than no letter, right?"

They sat in silence while Celeste looked hopeful at his back. He tip-toed his chair back around to face her.

"Fine," he begrudged. "Write the letter."

Celeste released a sigh of relief and waited for Silas to speak. When he didn't immediately, Celeste said, "Silas, I am only writing the letter if you tell me what they know."

"Fine, fine." He sat up in his chair and told her.

Celeste paced before him as he talked. His words were as heavy as stones, and they settled into the deep cavern of her stomach until the weight of it all made her ill.

"I don't understand," Celeste said slowly. "This isn't covered in training."

"Yet," he corrected. "They haven't taught us this yet. I read it while doing my research in the Archives. It's not something they'll tell us about until we are actual Guardians. If you had turned your Soul into Benjamin as soon as you realized you knew them, he would have dealt with it, and they would have assigned the Soul to another Guardian. But you didn't, and here we are."

Celeste was beginning to wear a path beneath her feet as Silas's grin grew bigger and bigger.

"But," she protested, "this is so much more than me knowing a Soul I was assigned. How didn't they catch this? Aren't they all-knowing? I get it, Souls slip through, blah blah, but this is a huge deal. Especially considering the outcome."

They shared a knowing look, and for once, the two enemies found a common hatred.

"Process," they said, simultaneously.

Celeste sat across from Silas. The communal space remained quiet around them.

"Oh, before I forget," he said. "I'm going to need your half of the communication pendant."

Celeste sucked in a comically large amount of air through her teeth. "About that. I don't have it anymore. And...I kind of need yours."

He stared blankly at her for a moment before he said, "No."

"I'll make sure the letter is *extra* good."

A SHORT WHILE LATER, CELESTE FOUND HERSELF KNOCK-ing on Benny's door. She was certain Benny's door alone was going to begin showing up in her nightmares.

He answered with an air of caution on his face that Celeste couldn't help but appreciate.

To his credit, he stepped aside to allow her through the door with no hesitation. Celeste detected a hint of defeat in his slouched shoulders. She felt terrible that she was the cause of his current state, and there she was, about to make things even worse.

Celeste picked at the edges of her fingernails. "I saw Silas today," was all she said.

Benny sighed and pinched the bridge of his nose. "Celeste, you need to stop all this; it's over." The two had barely made it inside the door.

"I needed to understand what Kinsley meant when she said it went deeper than what I knew, and I knew Silas had it all figured out."

Benny looked at Celeste, not with the expected cold steel of anger, but with sympathy.

"So you do know," she said.

"I only figured it out after you told me you knew Norah in a past life, and that she was seeing her own Lives. You knew her in more than one of your lives, didn't you?"

Celeste hung her head and said, "Yes." Her shame brought tears to her eyes.

Benny nodded. "One life wouldn't have caused this mess. It's still a big deal when it comes to being a Soul's Guardian—the same principle of bias applies. But this is much different. Two Souls who follow each other through many lifetimes—"

"Soulmates," Celeste said, completing Benny's thought. "I wasn't lying about how it took me a moment to realize I knew the Soul." She needed him to understand that part. "I had no idea what we were to each other, I swear. But once I figured out I knew them, I couldn't tell you. I couldn't lose the ability to watch over them, to be there for them."

"No," Benny said, shaking his head. "You wouldn't have been able to keep yourself away. Maybe if it was a Soul you happened to know in one life, but not this. I'm assuming Silas told you how incredibly rare real soulmates are?" Celeste nodded, and so Benny continued, "Humans toss that word around as if they have any clue what they are talking about. I've only ever seen a few true cases of soulmates, but certainly never one who became a Guardian of theirs. If we had caught that you knew the Soul, if you had told the Council right away, we would have transferred the Soul to another Guardian, and you would be none the wiser. When you passed, you experienced the memories from all of your lives, but you probably also felt a longing. One that would not be satiated until that Soul arrived in their afterlife. You wouldn't understand the depth of your relationship with that Soul, or who they were. You wouldn't have been able to discern the Soul that you knew was your soulmate, and therefore never would have interfered in their life on Earth." Benny closed his eyes and rubbed his hands along his face. "Did Silas tell you what this means?"

Celeste had yet to fully process what it meant to be Norah's true soulmate since Silas explained it to her; his large grin and eager delivery did little for the gravity of the situation. But Benny's morose tone and the somewhat green hue to his skin made Celeste feel it all.

"Wherever the Soul ends up, I end up."

"Which means, if Norah makes it through this Life and learns this Lesson, then she goes to her afterlife, and you two get to choose how to spend it together. But, if she doesn't make it, then chances are, you won't either."

"Chances are?" Silas was practically gleeful when he told her that if Norah didn't make it to an afterlife, then Celeste would be gone too, but Benny's words seemed as if there was a chance she could still exist without Norah. Relief washed over her in an instant, but the thought of never seeing Norah again caught up to her. *Could* Celeste continue without her?

"Well, like I said, I've never seen this. You can try and stay here without her, but inevitably, without her Soul around, in any capacity, you will more than likely be unable to cope. The lost connection with Norah's Soul will likely be too painful for you. It's described as...essentially...fading away."

"So, if my interfering really ruined things for Norah, if I messed up her chances of ever truly learning the Lesson and passing over into her afterlife, then I will lose everything, too."

Almost as if he was reading her thoughts, Benny said, "You can't fix this one, Celeste. What's done is done. I don't think the Council is going to go easy on us. All you can do now is hope that you've done the best you could, and that Norah learns her final Lesson." Benny shook his head as if to clear it. "Here I was thinking you were just dedicated, good at your job."

It was a poor attempt at a joke to lighten a very dark mood, but Celeste appreciated him nonetheless. "I am good at my job," Celeste said. "Or I was. Until I messed it all up."

# CHAPTER 46

# *Norah*

Norah frantically searched for her black sandals with the two straps going across the tops of her toes. She could have worn the ones with the single strap that went between her toes, but those ones always pinched. Chris not-so-patiently waited in Norah's living room as she blew through her room, tearing things out from under her bed and the floor of her closet.

"Norah, I am starving," Chris shouted, managing to drag the word out to three syllables.

"Maybe if you kept your hands to yourself all afternoon, we wouldn't have burned so many calories," she teased.

Chris shouted back, "Never!"

Norah stood inside her closet, resigned to wear her less comfortable pair of black sandals, when her eyes fell on the bag she took with her to the Bryers. "Yes!" she shouted. She had taken those sandals with her on the trip.

"What?" Chris called.

"Nothing," she said, as she grabbed the bag and stuck her hand in deep, retrieving both sandals from the bottom and pulling them out in one go. She stepped out of her closet and dropped the shoes at her feet, ready to slip right into them, when a slip of paper and something gold slid out from between the shoes. Norah bent to pick them up.

The gold object was about the size of a quarter, flat and round. On the paper, in Celeste's handwriting, the note read:

"Keep this close to you. If you feel it heat up,
press it between your thumb and pointer finger. – C"

# CHAPTER 47

"OKAY, WALK ME THROUGH THIS AGAIN?"

Norah took deep breaths to calm herself down and stop the shaking, while Chris wrapped his arm tightly around her shoulder. It was 3:00 a.m., and she and Chris were on the couch. It almost felt like old times, with Chris taking care of her at odd hours of the night, but before it would have been her drunk from a night out, whereas this was from yet another dream–another memory–of a past life.

"This can't be happening," she cried.

They had such a great time at dinner that evening, all you can eat Korean BBQ, that things were almost feeling normal for Norah. They laughed at their stuffed bellies and how they would sleep as if they were in a food coma.

"But you told me you've seen them before. Why is this one so bad?"

"Because if I am still seeing past lives, doesn't that mean I was right about being *wrong* about the Bryers? Getting their forgiveness wasn't the Lesson I needed to learn."

Where in the hell was Celeste when she needed her?

Norah took a deep breath and told the story once more.

THE YEAR WAS 1718, NORAH REMEMBERED SEEING A NEWS-paper as vividly as if she were sitting there now, holding it. It was another dream, but so much more real than when she dreamt about Luisa. It was more like her times as Eugène and August.

The grief was still immensely heavy, even after all these years. Thomas walked the streets of London, as he so often did those days, thinking of the life he and Milly might have had.

Thomas fell in love with her the moment he saw her all those years ago, and she with him.

They were so young, and it was reckless. Sure, men he knew did it all the time. Courted and bedded a woman before asking for her hand in marriage. Some he knew did so without ever honoring their actions.

But he was never that kind of man, and Milly was not that kind of girl. Thomas made his way down along the Thames River, lost in thought. A ferry whistled somewhere in the distance, and a cool breeze brushed at his cheeks.

They *were* in love.

He couldn't marry her, of course, his parents would never allow it. Such a silly thing to think at this age, a man now grown. To think his parents wouldn't allow him to be with the girl he loved simply because she wasn't born to a suitable enough family. Even more silly was his fear of losing his inheritance and all the comforts it had afforded him.

The life they would have had together. He played it over and over again in his head through the years. Was he that young and foolish? Was he simply too scared to go against his father, or was he truly such a loathsome character to have cared more about money than love? No, Thomas had always longed for a family of his own, ever since he could remember. A wife he loved and who adored him. A home full of children he would care for. Ultimately, he was too cowardly to stand up to his father when Milly and their child needed him most.

Milly fought him fiercely over giving up the baby. She even insisted she could have raised it on her own, which even today

Thomas knew was a preposterous thing to think. Her family would have disowned her, and she would have been all alone with a child to care for. But even now, as he rationalized the rational, his heart ached.

Thomas watched absentmindedly as a woman carried a baby in one arm and held the hand of a toddler with the other, as they crossed the street toward what he could only presume to be their home. Another woman, who looked to be a maid or nanny, walked closely behind trying to help guide the little one in. He let out a grand sigh and continued on his walk.

Thomas' father offered Milly their home in which to have the baby, with the hopes that she would be more comfortable, and that his staff would be there to assist. He even offered to have his own doctor present to deliver the baby. It was the least he could do. After all, once done, he would take the child to a new home, never to be seen again.

Milly wouldn't allow it. She said she refused to take charity from a man who refused to accept her and her child. If she was only going to be afforded a few short moments with her baby, those moments were going to be in a place of comfort, and not with watchful eyes full of judgment.

Thomas decided far too late, pacing his home frantically waiting for news of how Milly and the baby were doing, that he would fight to stay with her. If he couldn't convince his parents that she was a good match, then they would just have to start a family on their own. They'd have a proper wedding, a proper home together, with a proper family. Starting with this little one.

In the end, none of it mattered. Milly died in childbirth, and Thomas' father had the baby adopted straight away. Thomas never even got to meet him.

He had other romantic opportunities, but never at love. He eventually became one of *those* men, but never without regret. No one ever did compare to Milly. To the life he built within his head.

There were a number of years, not long after the child was born, that he tried to look for him. His fear and dependency on his parents were masked entirely by his anger over losing Milly. But to no avail. His father refused to help him, believing it was for his own good to just let it be. Despite his every effort, Thomas never found him.

He turned and walked back along the river, streets bustling as always. It was never a quiet walk within the city, but the fresh air and movement always helped Thomas clear his head.

If he had done the right thing from the start, Milly would have never died, and his child would have never grown up not knowing the love his mother would have undoubtedly given him.

Before going back inside, he picked up a newspaper from the stand across the street from his home. The boy would be turning thirty-five that year.

CHRIS LISTENED INTENTLY, ARM STILL GRASPED TIGHTLY around her shoulders.

"I don't understand," Norah said. "It's as if all I've ever done in all of my lives is hurt people. It's all different scenarios, but the same results. I hurt those who love me. How do I learn what to stop when it's all been so different?"

Chris finally unwrapped his arm from her shoulder. "Can you remind me of each life? Just a brief bit about what happened?"

Norah ran through each, from the latest with Thomas, then to Luisa and how her carelessness of falling in love lost them everything, to August and all the harm he caused with his work, to Peggy and betraying her friend, and lastly Eugène, being so careless and self-involved that his only son died alone.

"And now this life," she sobbed. "My carelessness and selfishness caused Sam's death. Is that it? Am I too selfish to move on from this life lesson?"

Chris lifted Norah's chin, the moonlight coming from the window shone just bright enough to see the softness in his gaze. He said, "Norah, you haven't been selfish in this life. You were a college student, then you were building a career. From what I heard, you were an amazing friend to Sam. He was fighting demons beyond you."

Norah shook her head. Her chest felt tight with emotion. "I don't even care if this is it for me. Fuck, I don't even know if I believed in an afterlife before all of this, and now that I have all these other lives filling me up, I am okay to be done. Honestly, if nothing else, I'm tired. This isn't about me, it's their lives I ruined, it's all of them I owe, and I don't know how to make up for it."

"Norah, it's okay for it to be about you; it is your life. It's okay that you had a moment to yourself, not knowing Sam was going to need you. You have to know this was not your fault, right? From what I've heard about these lives, none of those were your fault, either. Thomas was young and thought listening to his father was the best thing to do. Alvaro was the villain in Luisa's story, Peggy was protecting her mother, that science was brand new for August, he was learning along with the world, and didn't know any better. From what you said, he even stopped when he did learn. And poor Serge, Serge was an accident. Norah, it seems like the only thing you're at fault for here is not forgiving *you*." Chris gripped her tightly by the shoulders and forced Norah to look into his eyes. "You need to forgive yourself."

NORAH WENT THROUGH HER WEEK FOCUSING ON EVERY sensation she felt.

A small part of her expected to feel a tingle or some chills as she pictured a judge and a gavel somewhere in the sky, declaring her fit to pass through to the afterlife of her choosing. A big part of her felt ridiculous for even having the thought.

But wasn't all of this ridiculous?

She didn't know for certain that forgiving herself was the Lesson she needed to learn, but when Chris said those words to her, it was like it all clicked. The relief she felt after hearing him tell her that she needed to forgive herself, that it wasn't her fault, was as if a weight of ten thousand pounds had been lifted from her shoulders.

She wanted to be angry that no one had directly said those words to her, that no one ever shook her out of her own self-loathing enough to tell her that it was okay to forgive herself for living her life. Just like Maureen said, it was Sam's choice to have done what he did, that no matter what she would have done, he himself would have needed to be the one to stop it.

In reality, she never gave anyone the opportunity to save her from herself. She wallowed in her own self-pity and self-hate, convincing herself she didn't deserve to let herself live.

Since he came back into her life, Chris was Norah's rock, and she thanked Celeste every day since, hopeful she was listening, for bringing him back to her. The night that she dreamt of Thomas, they stayed up that morning talking for hours. At the very least, being there to witness the aftermath of Norah's memory pushed him to truly believe her past lives were real. They talked in greater detail about each of the lives she had seen, and he walked back through each, emphasising all the ways in which she shouldn't blame herself.

In late sixteenth-century London, it was normal to get caught up in societal differences; at that time in history, it was the norm to adhere to the family's demands. Louisa falling in love with the wrong person and not knowing their true intentions didn't make her a bad person. A young girl torn between her best friend and protecting her mother wasn't a bad person, and neither was a young doctor who followed his mentor blindly, truly believing he was making a positive difference in society.

And lastly, the life that Chris saw as being difficult to forgive oneself for—but one he insisted she needed to—was Eugéne. A war vet whose unknowing negligence led to the untimely death of his child. All sad stories, but all ones she couldn't take direct responsibility for. She needed to forgive any part she felt she had in it.

Norah would never be able to forget the feelings that came with remembering those lives, but they were getting easier to step outside of, which helped for her to see Chris's point. She appreciated the ability to see the stories from a different angle, ones that, when stated, seemed so simple. It was allowing yourself to climb through those feelings to a place where you can see it wasn't your fault.

Sam was different. Harder. This was *her* life, the very real life she was living at that moment. Sam was her best friend and her responsibility.

But thanks to Chris, she was getting there. The Bryers were helping too, simply by being back in her life. She had a lot to be grateful for, and she knew it. And while the desire to have a drink was certainly there, somewhere deep in the back of her mind, the *need* was becoming a distant memory. For Norah, the direction of her life was on the right track for the first time in a very long time.

Only one thing was missing.

Celeste. She wished she could talk with her, not only to confirm that she was on the right path, but to see her friend again. She missed her terribly.

As Chris had put it before, Norah simply needed to live her life the way others did. She may never know what her afterlife holds for her, but she could have hope. She could have faith. She could obsess over all the possibilities of learning or not learning her final Lesson, or she could focus on doing her very best through this one last life.

Norah laced up her shoes and quickly stretched. She and Chris had been running before work all week, and her body was pleasantly sore. She took a deep breath as she walked outside into the crisp morning air, taking in the quiet. Chris stood waiting for her on the sidewalk, and she greeted him with a quick kiss hello before they took off at an easy jog, side by side.

Sam would have been proud.

# CHAPTER 48

## Celeste

I think she's got it!" Loretta ran towards Celeste, long red hair trailing behind her as if she were running from fire, excitement exuding from her.

Loretta was the Guardian assigned to temporarily watch over Norah's Soul.

Celeste still held on to the hope she would be allowed to remain Norah's Guardian after the Council made their final decision. Benny may have lost all hope, but she refused. She was relieved when she learned it was Loretta who would be Norah's Guardian until everything could be sorted out. Loretta was always helpful with the questions Celeste had through the years. She had always been friendly with incoming Trainees, never treated them as less than. Celeste found it easy to see why the Council assigned Loretta as Norah's Guardian.

Temporarily.

Celeste stuck closely to the building those days, hoping to catch a whisper or two from anyone passing. It was wishful thinking. No one aside from those involved would know anything, but she was too restless to sit at home.

On this day, Celeste had been lying on a blanket reading a book in the field across from the Council building, trying to stay distracted. She was there for a very real and very terrifying reason. It was the day she and Benny would receive their sentencing from the Council.

Loretta skidded to a halt when she reached Celeste. Celeste stood, matching her excitement.

"Norah?" Celeste asked. "Do you mean Norah learned the Lesson?"

"I think," Loretta panted, trying to catch her breath. "The thought is there. She was talking with Chris, and he said something that made a light go off for her. She's moving in the right direction, and I think she's going to learn the Lesson."

Celeste jumped up and down, pulling Loretta into an embrace and causing them to jump together.

Celeste hadn't reached out to Norah, too afraid to break any more rules while awaiting the Council's decision. She was also banned from checking in on her, but Loretta kept her regularly updated; it was the only reason she hadn't gone totally insane.

"One thing, though," said Loretta when the jumping settled. "She did see her first life that centered on this lesson, Thomas. Which was the last life for her to see, right?"

Celeste nodded. She had hoped that since she was no longer around Norah that the memories would stop. Loretta must have noticed a look of concern on Celeste's face because she said, "The realization came after she saw it, so maybe now that she's learning the right Lesson, they'll stop?"

Celeste made a noncommittal hum. "But you're saying she hasn't fully learned the Lesson yet?"

"You know how this Lesson goes. It's considered the hardest because Self-Forgiveness is so difficult for many Souls. One minute, she'll feel at ease, and the next, she'll convince herself it was all her fault again. It's easier to blame yourself, to be bogged down with guilt, than to accept what happened and move on. Guilt allows people to stay in the past, as much as they know it's better not to. Still, the thought is there. Norah is trying to forgive herself, and that's a huge step."

It was great news. It was everything Celeste wanted to hear. But without knowing how much of a direct influence her actions had on this realization, she didn't know if this meant Norah's Soul was okay now. Did seeing the lives drive the realization too much, or will the Council consider her working it out on her own?

"Don't stress, okay? She'll get through to her afterlife. I'll keep you updated." Loretta squeezed Celeste's arm. "I thought this would be good news leading into your meeting with the Council." Celeste returned her squeeze with a tight smile. "You're going to do great. Good luck!"

Celeste turned back to her spot and reached down to retrieve her blanket and book. She *should* be happy, but instead she just felt more dreadful. Even if it was good news that Norah was on track to learn her Lesson, Celeste's future was still undecided. She wished she were back in the pet store surrounded by puppies. Puppies would make her feel better. Their meeting with the Council wasn't for a few more hours, so she decided she would wander over to the dog afterlife area and have a visit.

She hadn't heard from Benny at all that day. She had hoped to walk in with him again, but she was certain his nerves were more on fire than hers. He had more to lose than her in all of this.

*Maybe* more to lose. Celeste stood to not only lose her opportunity to earn her full Guardianship, but if her soulmate didn't make it to her afterlife, both Norah *and* Celeste would cease to exist. She never had a reason before now to picture her existence without Norah, and now that there was a very real possibility, she understood why the soulmate left behind could fade away. Celeste simply couldn't imagine a place without her.

She wasn't giving up hope. Norah was going to officially learn the last Lesson, and all of Celeste's worry would be for nothing. It was possible the Council would see this was all a mistake and go easy on Celeste and Benny.

If nothing else, she hoped they'd go easy on Benny.

"CELESTE, BENNY, WELCOME. ALTHOUGH I WISH IT WERE under better circumstances." Kinsley stood in the center, behind the long table, as the rest of the Council sat in their respective chairs. "Once again, Benjamin, sorry to see you on that side of the table."

Benny gave a stoic nod.

Each time Celeste entered this room, she liked it less and less.

"We have received word that your Soul has begun the spark of learning their final Lesson. We can't say for sure they will come to the full realization, but given how they fared in their last five lives, this is a great improvement." Kinsley paused, awaiting a reaction from Celeste and Benny, but received none.

"It is difficult to say whether or not they would have learned this at all if it wasn't for Celeste's interference, but with them still needing the time to work through some self-doubt, along with the fact that we cannot fault the Soul for Celeste's actions, the Council will not penalize the Soul when the time comes to review whether or not they learned the final Lesson."

Celeste felt herself breathe for the first time since entering the room. She placed her hand to her heart and whispered, "Thank you."

Kinsley directed her attention toward Celeste, and in a rare moment of visible agitation, said, "That does not automatically mean the Soul will pass through, Celeste. Norah may have a long life ahead of her, but any number of things can happen. She could die tomorrow, and we'd be unable to say for certain she learned the Lesson. She could experience another hardship that pulls her right back into her uncertainty. All possibilities that you will no longer have any part in."

An iron fist squeezed Celeste's heart. She prepared herself for this; if she were truly honest with herself, she knew that ultimately the Council would never allow her to continue being

Norah's Guardian. Still, she held out hope that they would see her acts of desperation as just that. A desperate attempt to make sure Norah passed through, and nothing for her to gain.

Her actions should have been seen as going above and beyond in her job, really.

"Celeste," Kinsley continued, her typical air of poise back in its place, "the Council hereby revokes your Guardianship."

Benny stepped forward. "She is in training; she didn't know the full consequences of her actions. I should've prepared her for that. Don't punish her for a mistake I should have caught."

"We understand mistakes happen, Benjamin, and you're right–Celeste is still in training. But she knew this entire time who her Soul was. She's hidden it not only from the Council, but from you, for *centuries*."

Celeste stole a look at Benny long enough to see his cheeks grow pink.

"And then for her to go even further and disregard your direct orders *not* to interfere, and what's more, to involve Silas, another Trainee. While the Council appreciated Celeste's taking full accountability for her actions and requesting no punishment be brought to Silas, her actions cannot go unpunished. Not only could this situation have been avoided, but Celeste had ample opportunity throughout the entire ordeal to speak up."

Kinsley cleared her throat and took a long look down the table on either side at all of the Council members. "Celeste, there is a reason the Council is only revoking your Guardianship and not banishing you from the Guardian afterlife area or applying a, let's say, harsher punishment."

Reginald planted a firm grimace on his face.

*Even more grimacy than usual.*

He either disagreed with Kinsley's ruling or disagreed with not imposing a harsher punishment. Celeste assumed the latter.

"The reason that this Soul can see their past lives after interacting with you is the same reason I strongly assume that once you connected with this Soul as their Guardian, it would have been remarkably difficult, if not impossible, to keep yourself away. You see, this Soul is your—"

"Soulmate," Celeste interrupted.

"Ah," Kinsley paused, no doubt taken aback that Celeste ruined her grand announcement. "I suppose I should have guessed you would have figured this out."

Celeste decided it was best not to mention Silas.

"So you understand what this may ultimately mean for you?" Celeste nodded solemnly. "The Soul could either pass over and join you in whatever afterlife you both choose to create, or they do not pass on, and you disappear. There's a possibility you carry on, but it is likely that you will be unable to stay here—in any afterlife—without your soulmate."

Celeste's eyes stung with tears as she stood quietly, head bowed.

Muriel's voice floated from the far end of the table. "What we can do is trust that this Soul has a lot of life left to live to help solidify this final Lesson for her. As such, we must trust in the process, and in Loretta to do the excellent job we know she will do."

Trust in the process. Celeste almost laughed.

Reginald, never one to contain himself for long, rose from the table. "And what happens if this Soul goes and blabs about all of this to the world?"

Kinsley rolled her eyes, and Celeste yearned to laugh at her annoyance with Reggie, but the turning of her stomach wouldn't allow it.

"I'm being serious," Reginald said. "It took us eons to get to a place where we could shepherd all the hearsay; people would believe anything in those days. There was once a time, before the intrawebs, when someone's neighbor would just be thought of as a little kooky. That was alright. But now, with the instant messaging and social-whatcha-ma-call-its, it's easy for word to quickly travel to the masses! Who knows what's going to happen?" Veins popped out of Reggie's neck, emphasizing his agitation.

"We've dealt with worse," Muriel said, sounding bored with the whole situation. "We need to focus on what we can control now. Right now, Celeste, what we can control is you. Pulling you from Guardian training."

Celeste swallowed hard and stepped forward, placing herself in line with Benny.

"I understand. I broke a lot of rules, and I should have come to you all as soon as I realized I knew the Soul. All of this would have been avoided had I just trusted the process. I am sorry for the harm I have caused to the Council, to my Soul, and most importantly, to Benny." Celeste turned and faced him, and to her relief, he faced her back. "You trusted me to do the right thing. You trusted me to listen to your guidance and not interfere with the Lesson directly, and I am sorry I went against you."

Warmth washed over her as Benny smiled back softly, the corners of his eyes crinkling.

"Which does bring us to you, Benjamin," Kinsley said. She turned to him directly. "We need to discuss your punishment."

Fiddlesticks. The last thing Celeste meant to do was draw attention to him.

She stole a quick glance at a still-boiling Reginald, assuming his anger meant good news.

Kinsley said, "Be it a little late, and it shouldn't have happened in the first place, we appreciate that you came forward. We have decided to suspend you from being a Mentor to the next round of Trainees, resuming with the following rotation. Your other Trainees will be dispersed among the other Mentors. You will keep your seat on the Council. However, you are on probation for the same length of time as the next Mentorship rotation."

Benny's shoulders sank in relief. Celeste could practically see air leaving his lungs, and she wished she could hug him.

Reginald sat back down heavily into his seat and crossed his arms about his chest. "Ridiculous," he mumbled.

"Reginald, we discussed this as a Council. Benjamin has been a stellar member up until this point and has always proven to be an excellent Mentor. As we stated earlier, mistakes are understood here."

Benny ignored him, instead addressing Kinsley and the other members of the Council.

"Thank you," he said. "I promise I won't let you down. I appreciate the second chance."

The Council members—well, all but Reginald—smiled reassuringly at Benny. The shift in the mood of the room emboldened Celeste.

"May I ask, if Norah and I are soulmates, why didn't I know there was more to our connection? I felt a strong pull that seemed more intense than other Guardians, and I did realize I knew her in more than one life after some time," her face grew pink at that admittance, "but it seems like something we both should have just...known."

"You would have felt the loss of a piece of you when you arrived in your afterlife," Kinsley explained. "When you saw all of your lives play out, you saw all the people you've shared those lives with. However, for soulmates specifically, it is intentional that you don't remember that one particular Soul that you carried with you. Although you probably felt a bit of a loss weighing on you. Just like it is imperative for all Souls to truly learn the Seven Lessons on their own, it is imperative that soulmates have the ability to live their lives, learn their lessons, and fulfill their own path when their other half passes."

Celeste had discovered that she'd known Norah's Soul in more than one life, but she guessed that was due to spending so many lives watching over her. If she hadn't become her Guardian, she would have lived her own afterlife never knowing, allowing Norah to move through the remainder of her own lives.

Kinsley continued, "Norah has been able to continue each life, one after the next, because she gets to still be human without a tie to another, which would, potentially, prevent her from doing so. Love, close friendships, all of it is still very much a part of her lives, although I am sure she has felt a little unsettled in all of them. I'm willing to bet you, too, have felt like a bit of an outsider here, tied more to your work than relationships with other Guardians?"

Celeste nodded.

"Typically, the first s oulmate t o pass g oes i nto t heir own afterlife, and when the second passes, both experience a rush of undeniable connection. You find each other. You reunite. However, if one half of a soulmate passes but is unable to come to an afterlife, the pair is not reunited. The final separation becomes unbearable for the remaining Soul. You either settle somewhere in your afterlife together, or well, you do not."

Celeste knew of the possible outcome, but to hear Kinsley describe it made it feel so *real*. A heaviness settled deep in her chest as she choked back a sob that was trying to escape.

Ezekiel spoke, sounding flummoxed, "Truthfully, you're the first Trainee of your kind. In fact, no Guardian has ever been assigned their soulmate, let alone gone and interacted with them on Earth. This is a first for us."

At the mention of her training, Celeste took a deep breath and ventured another question. "Will I ever be able to reapply to become a Guardian? Not right away, of course, I understand I need to step away for a bit. Oh, and, well, if I am still around and all. Also, if my soulmate is eligible to become a Guardian." *This was certainly all very complicated.* "Could I reapply? Eventually?"

"Celeste," Kinsley said. "You have a huge heart, and you care deeply for this job. We do see that. For now, though, focus your attention on the afterlife you want. Go relax. Read a book. Play with puppies. I hear they are always looking for volunteers in the Dog afterlife area." Kinsley winked.

Once out of the room, Celeste turned to Benny. He looked like a kid waiting to open the beautifully wrapped present in front of him. "It's okay." She smiled. "You can celebrate."

Benny's entire face lit up. "I shouldn't be so relieved given your outcome, but that could have gone far worse for me."

"You can absolutely be happy with your outcome. But I do feel terrible you have to give up being a Mentor for now."

Benny dismissively waved his hand. "Ah, that's okay. I'll miss it, that's for sure, but I'll get to focus on Council-only duties. I'll stay on my best behavior, and I'll get right back in with the round of Trainees after that. I'm happy to keep my seat on the Council, and focus on what I *can* do rather than what I cannot."

"And hey," Celeste added, "at least Silas doesn't get what he wanted."

"Yes, he doesn't get to slide into the Council, because I haven't been kicked out!" Benny beamed. "But, you know what? When the time comes, I will vote for him honestly. If he deserves to pass his training, if he does ever have the opportunity to sit on the Council, I will not hold any of this against him."

"Benny, he blackmailed me to try and get you off the Council."

"And you broke the rules because you thought it was the right thing to do, and I broke the rules trying to help you. People make mistakes, and after all, we are only human," he said, nudging Celeste with his elbow.

She hated to admit it, but Benny was right about Silas. They were all just doing what they thought was best.

"What are you going to do now?" he asked.

Celeste shrugged. "I don't know. I honestly hadn't thought of it. The moment I got here, I wanted to be a Guardian, and the moment I was assigned my Soul, my only focus was on getting them to their afterlife."

Benny squeezed Celeste's upper arm. "You'll be great at whatever it is you decide to do. Kinsley is right: take this time to enjoy *your* afterlife. It will all be okay, Celeste. Norah has time in this life to figure it all out. She'll make it through."

She and Benny went in opposite directions: he back to work, she back to her place. She'd have to move out of the Guardian quarters, but there was a silver lining—she'd get to put her flair into whatever home she ended up in. All the pinks and purples and bright colors she could think of. It was going to be beautiful. And it gave her something to look forward to.

Celeste forced a smile as she walked home.

# CHAPTER 49

## Norah

ONE MINUTE NORAH WAS CLEANING, PREPARING FOR her and Chris to have a night in together, and in the next instant, sadness settled in. A flood of memories with Celeste came to her: the first time they met when she spilled coffee on her, their lunch dates and walks, the flight to California. Little snippets played in her mind like a movie trailer of their friendship. Norah thought her heart might explode.

She had missed Celeste before, moments of wishing she could call her and talk with her, but this was different...more permanent.

Earlier that day, while she was at work, Norah walked around the corner toward her desk. Her head was down, buried deep in the paperwork Dr. Ross handed her to file, when a familiar voice jolted her. "Hiya, stranger."

"Billy," she exclaimed. "How the hell are you?" She looked around for Dr. Ross before correcting herself. "How are you?"

"I'm great," he said with a smile. "Doctor just wants some bloodwork done. How are you? We've been missing you down at the bar."

"I'm doing pretty great." His genuine smile at her words filled her with mixed emotions. She hadn't thought of all the regulars at the bar in some time. "It's really good to see you, Billy," she said. And she meant it.

He leaned in close, her on one side of the desk, he on the other, "I said that we miss you, and we do, but now that I've set eyes on you...boy, am I glad you haven't come in. You look good, kid. I always knew you were too good for us."

Norah cleared her throat, trying to find the words to respond. Billy filled the silence, waving his hand in front of him while he said, "Some of us have reached the point of no return. You have your whole life ahead of you. And when you fall back down, and I've been around too long to know that's inevitable, all you gotta do is get back up. One foot in front of the other. Day by day. Whatever cliché they throw around–it's thrown around for a reason. Just get back up. You're too good not to, Norah."

Norah wanted to say something, but she had no idea how to respond. Luckily, she didn't have to. Barb called Billy up for his appointment.

"Thank you, Billy," she managed before he walked away.

"You better drop off some of those brownies soon, though," he shouted as he walked back.

Norah held onto that high the remainder of the day. But when she got home and began to clean, her mind drifted, and the wall of doubt hit her heavily. Would Billy be so proud of Norah if he knew why her life had taken a wrong turn in the first place? Would Sam be upset to see her moving on without him? Would he agree with Chris that she needed to forgive herself? Yes, he would—she knew Sam, knew he loved her and would want to see her happy. She had acted irrationally to think he would have wanted anything other than happiness for her. It was unkind to his memory. But the old feeling crept back into her like a ghost she couldn't escape.

She desperately needed to talk to Celeste.

Chris walked through Norah's front door holding an arrangement of spring flowers in one hand and snacks in the other: a bag of Twizzlers, Mike n Ikes, and Doritos for her;

Peach Rings and cheese puffs for him. He kissed her hello, then stepped back to take a good look at her.

"You okay?" he asked.

"Yeah, I'm good." Chris cocked his head and raised his right eyebrow. "Okay, honestly, I'm missing Celeste a bit."

Chris nodded knowingly. "Wish I had gotten to meet her."

"Oh, now you believe me?" Norah teased.

"Kinda hard *not* to after what I watched you go through," he said, wide-eyed. He pulled Norah into a tight hug, kissing her softly on the forehead.

"I wish you could meet her, too," she said, wrapping her arms tightly around his waist.

She couldn't articulate her exact feelings. When Celeste first left, it felt like missing a friend who had moved away. As if she were still there, just a phone call away. It all hadn't quite sunk in fully that Celeste was *gone,* gone. A jolt of sadness hit her only moments before Chris walked in, and it felt like losing Sam.

"Before we start the movie, is my green hoodie here? It's my most—"

"Most comfortable, I know. Yeah, it's in my room—on the dresser." Norah smiled and tapped Chris on his lower back, nudging him along.

He went searching for his hoodie while she arranged the couch pillows on the floor, pulling throw blankets down to create a giant bed.

Norah wriggled around, shaking her whole body, hoping to shake the funk she was in, and tried to focus. This night was about her and Chris. He deserved her full attention.

She knelt down to adjust the blankets and pillows, fluffing where needed. Her mind, ever the betrayer, drifted to Celeste, and Norah hoped for the millionth time that she was okay. When she stood, the dizziness and the haze came rushing to her, and then the now familiar, all-consuming feeling of falling into another memory.

*Fuck.*

And then the darkness settled in.

IT WAS UNLIKE ALL THE OTHER MEMORIES. IT WASN'T
one life she visited, walking in different but familiar skin as her
story played out. But rather, she sped through many, many lives
all in one go. Norah watched in awe as every life she had lived
prior to Thomas played out in rapid fire.

*A mother cradling her daughter, the love so intense her heart
beat through her chest like a drum. A man and a wife holding
hands walking along the road, a comfortable and pure love
pouring from them. A brother and a sister sharing a laugh. No
one else could ever make either of them laugh that same way,
their whole bodies vibrating.*

*Two best friends growing up together, a lifetime of shared
adventures and secrets that died along with them. Two lovers
forced apart, yearning after each other for a lifetime. Both
ended up with the wrong person, neither able to find true happiness without the other.*

*A man who saved a woman's life by rescuing her from an
anxious horse, never to see each other again. The man thought
back to that moment each time he wrestled with the value of his
own life. A child and an old man who bonded over their love of
stories, helping heal each other beyond comprehension. The boy
found a safe place in the old man, and the old man found a purpose in the boy.*

All these lives swirled before her. Lives full of love, passion,
fear, anger, warmth, heartache, joy, fun, happiness. Norah experienced every possible emotion in a single intense moment.
Seeing all the different lives and all the different people left
her with more clarity than anything she had ever experienced
before. The different languages, races, ages, and genders held
no meaning; only the feelings that each life invoked mattered.

She could discern which life led to which lesson—Kindness, Humility, Empathy, Generosity, Temperance, and Honesty, making all the connections to what helped her learn them along the way.

Each life, and each lesson, and they all had one thing in common.

NORAH SLOWLY FOUND HER WAY BACK TO THE PRESENT, regaining her senses. She felt the softness of the pillow bed below her, and strong hands gripped her arms tightly, shaking her awake. "Norah!" Chris shouted, worry thick in his voice.

She blinked her eyes open several times before sitting up, her vision clearing as she looked around the familiar space. Chris placed his hands on her back and gently helped her up to a sitting position.

"Jesus, Norah, you scared me. What the hell happened?"

Norah tucked her knees into her chest and dropped her head between her legs.

"I know Celeste," she choked out. She tried to wrap her head around what she had just seen.

Chris swallowed hard. His voice was full of worry as he said, "I know you do."

"No, no, I mean I've *always* known her. Every life I've ever lived, she's been there." Chris rubbed her back encouragingly. "In one life, we were husband and wife; in another life, hundreds of years later, we were mother and daughter. Different people, different places, different lives, but in every life, we were connected. There were even lives we barely knew each other, but impacted one another's lives. An action of mine in my life that caused a thread of impact on hers. Up until Celeste's final life. At that point, I guess I was born into this life, and she moved on. That must have been when she became my Guardian. She told me I was her first Soul she looked after. She had to have known she knew me."

"Holy shit," Chris said, "it's like she's your—"

"Soulmate," they said simultaneously. The gravity of their words settled around them both.

Chris left Norah still seated on their makeshift floor bed to go get her a glass of water, while her head continued to swirl. Being soulmates explained so much. How comfortable Norah felt with Celeste from the beginning, she could talk to her about anything, how easy it was to become friends at a time when Norah pushed everyone else in her life away.

Chris returned, water splashing as he sat down and handed the glass to her.

"This is all just too crazy," he muttered. "Do you think being soulmates is why you can see your past lives?"

"It has to be, right?"

"I don't know." Chris shrugged. "Maybe all Guardian Angels are their Soul's soulmate."

"No, they aren't supposed to know their Souls—remember?"

Chris nodded as if this were the most mundane conversation any two people ever had.

"So, I'm not trying to be a dick or anything, but if Celeste is your soulmate, what's that mean for me? Like, should we not be together?"

Norah burst out laughing. The sensation was in complete battle with all the other feelings she had been experiencing; it almost felt forced.

"I don't think it's like that. We weren't romantic in all of our lives. Actually, I don't think we were romantic in most of our lives. Being soulmates seems to be more about the person who was continuously there, having a connection with someone that makes a tremendous impact on both of your lives, time and time again."

Norah left out that, for her, the relationships she'd had with her soulmate-with *Celeste*-felt more authentic than any relationship she'd had with anyone else in the world, even Sam. But she didn't want to hurt his feelings.

She also thought of Sam. But she knew this was different. In this lifetime, Sam was and would always be her best friend. Just like Chris, the love and care for one person didn't take away from the love and connection of another. But Celeste was different; their connection transcended lifetimes.

One of the most beautiful things about being human, though, was that love came in infinite supply.

# CHAPTER 50

## Celeste

Loretta sat beside Celeste on her new front porch, facing the endless lake that sat rippling lightly with the soft breeze. Just beyond her porch, where her land met the lake's shore, a hammock chair hung from the branch of a giant peepal tree, ready and waiting for Celeste to climb in with a good book. Roger, Celeste's German Shepherd, lay sleepy at her feet. He was a good boy who missed his owner terribly, but Celeste was a good foster mom until he was able to be reunited with him.

"Wait, you need to repeat that," said Celeste.

"Norah saw every life the two of you shared together. It was one giant flash of all memories. All in one go."

"She saw lives before this life's Lesson, before she needed to learn self-forgiveness?"

Loretta beamed and nodded. "Yep! You were in all the lives prior to this last Lesson. This is so neat, right? Have you ever heard of this happening before?"

Celeste had a split second to decide if she should tell Loretta everything. Technically, no one ever said she wasn't allowed to, or that she had to keep it to herself. Loretta had been coming to see her every day to keep her up-to-date on Norah, which Celeste greatly appreciated. And, once again, the Council never said she couldn't, but it still felt as if Loretta was risking something by sharing updates on Norah with Celeste. Celeste wasn't going to do anything with the information, of course. Breaking rules was a thing of the past. Yes, no more breaking rules.

Celeste said, "Umm, Norah and I are soulmates. It's kinda what got me into this mess."

Loretta gaped at Celeste. Voice full of disbelief, "A real soulmate? I mean, she and Chris did call it that, but you are *real* soulmates? Do you have any idea how rare that is? I mean, it's so rare it didn't even cross my mind. Sure, people cross paths with the same souls in different lives, but a soulmate...that comes with building a connection over multiple lives. That doesn't just happen in one single lifetime. That's commitment. It's why they are so rare; people don't often have that sort of devotion to one another."

Loretta sounded exhausted by the concept, like it was work to keep the soulmate connection. Not in one life did Norah feel like it was work. Perhaps that's why Celeste missed what they truly were to each other. To everyone else, soulmates seemed unachievable, but to her, it was just *them*.

A shadow crossed Loretta's face. Celeste knew instantly she pieced together the problem having a soulmate might mean for her. Loretta said, "Well, there's nothing else for Norah to see. Since she's seen all of her past, the lives have to stop. Maybe she needed to just wrap it up. She can move on. She can finally focus on learning the final Lesson."

Celeste nodded in agreement and reached down to pet Roger. She needed to allow Norah the time and space to work through the Lesson and trust the process. The way she should have done.

"Hey," Loretta said, her face lighting up. "Do you think that's why Norah has struggled with this final Lesson?"

Celeste's eyebrows met in the middle. "What do you mean?"

"She had you with her, her soulmate, to aid her in learning all other Lessons, but when you moved on and you weren't with her, she struggled. "

Celeste squeezed Loretta's hand, at a loss for words. To think of Celeste being with her as the reason Norah was able to learn the other six Lessons in her previous lives helped to relieve the blame she was placing on herself for how hard it had been for her to learn the last one.

"Oh, I nearly forgot," Loretta jumped in excitement, which caused Roger to bark and Celeste to jump. It was a whole thing. "I located Sam for you."

Celeste shot up out of her seat. Roger barked again...and it was a whole thing. "And?"

"He's about a year old, born in Sweden to a lovely young couple. Howard is his Guardian. Hard to say, of course, but Howard says he thinks he'll be just fine."

Celeste breathed a sigh of relief.

"Wanna show me what you've learned on the piano now?" Loretta asked.

# CHAPTER 51

## Norah

"Hurry up!" Norah shouted from her living room. "I'm coming," an exasperated Chris called back.

Norah reached for her toes, getting in one final stretch as she waited for Chris to get ready. "We've gotta get on the trail to make it back in time. I promised Barb an early lunch today—she's got somewhere she needs to be later."

"I'm sure her cats are willing to wait for her," he teased from down the hall.

They'd talked a lot the past few days. About her past lives, about her next steps, and how to move on. About what would happen if Norah didn't move on to her afterlife.

Chris encouraged her to live the way she always had, focusing on this life as if it were her only one, doing the best she could to be the best she could, without looking for it to grant her a ticket anywhere.

There were moments Norah felt strongly that he was right. After all, if it weren't for Celeste, she would have gone about her life in blissful ignorance. Well, maybe not *blissful*. But there were times she felt the weight of her knowledge so heavily she could barely breathe. More and more often than not, though, she would do that dangerous-but in this case beautiful-thing that humans do, and get too caught up in the craziness of the day to think about what it all meant.

Norah found herself staring at Chris in awe, as if seeing him for the first time.

His genuineness, his pureness, his support, and his faith in her. There were moments she became angry at herself for the way she had treated him over the past couple of years. She owed it to him to do better, but she was also learning to give herself grace. She was a grieving friend and was learning how to navigate a world without him. As long as she did her best not to cut Chris out, they would be okay. Ultimately, Norah realized that she might never know what the final Lesson was, might never hear Celeste tell her exactly what it was she needed to do, but she also realized that focusing on that Lesson was preventing her from moving forward in life. And she had already wasted too much of her life wishing she could change the past.

Norah thought about Celeste and their link to one another; the clarity that came with knowing who Celeste was to her. Chris teased her continuously about the connection at first—Norah was certain there was some insecurity to it—and reassured him that she was happy to have him by her side in this life; in the here and now. It was understandable. She wasn't quite sure how *she* would handle hearing he had a soulmate waiting for him somewhere. How could she explain all the different ways a person could love someone?

Of course, they didn't actually know if what they suspected was true, if Celeste really was her soulmate. Secretly, Norah loved the idea of knowing that someone was always there for her, and that she'd always be there for someone else. Someone she shared so many lifetimes with, so many memories, and who knew her in every form. If soulmates were real, she knew without a doubt that it would be her and Celeste.

"Besides," she had told Chris, "we have no idea how any of this afterlife stuff works. If you had told me there was any kind of an afterlife a year ago, I would have laughed. At this point, I wouldn't be surprised by anything."

She bent down to touch her toes for one final stretch when Chris's voice carried down the hallway. "What is this?"

He walked into the living room and looked down at his palm, a curious look on his face. He held up a little round golden pendant, the shape and size of a quarter.

Norah's eyes grew big. She'd completely forgotten about the pendant and the note she found in her carry-on bag.

"It's warm. Like, it's actually letting off heat."

"What?" she asked, reaching for the pendant. She placed a thumb and forefinger on either side, just as Celeste's note had instructed.

"*Norah,*" Celeste's voice came shouting out of the pendant. Norah shrieked and dropped it on the floor.

"What the fuck was that?" Chris asked.

"No idea, but that was definitely Celeste's voice."

"Celeste?"

Norah looked at Chris, stunned, unsure what to do.

"Pick it back up," he encouraged.

Norah reached down, grabbed the pendant, and Celeste's voice came right back.

```
"Norah, it's me, Celeste. I shouldn't be reach-
ing out, I've got myself—and Benny—into
enough trouble already—"
```

Chris mouthed, 'Who's Benny?' and Norah shushed him.

```
"I won't be able to send another message. The
pendant connected to the one I left you isn't
mine, and I kinda needed to beg to use it, so
I have to return it. But I needed to tell you
how sorry I am for leaving the way I did. I'm
sure you are still upset with me, but I am also
sure you are wondering what is going on, and
I didn't want you to worry." Norah could hear
```

Celeste take a deep breath before continuing. "My Guardian duties have been revoked, and you've been assigned a new Guardian. Don't worry, she's wonderful. You are in good hands. She's been keeping me up-to-date on you. I am so happy you and Chris worked things out."

Norah stole a glance at Chris, and they both smiled.

"I'm sorry for interfering in your life. I should have trusted that you'd pull through without me. Live this life the way you want to, without fear for what it might mean in the end. Continue to be the great person you are, know that you deserve love and happiness. Everything is going to be okay. Oh, and Sam is on to his next life and doing wonderfully so far. I just thought you should know."

Chris and Norah stood together, unmoving. Sam was okay. Chris rubbed Norah's lower back, and the weight of his touch gave her a needed sense of grounding.

"Well," Chris said, breaking the silence. "At least now I know for sure my girlfriend's not crazy." Norah gasped in fake horror and playfully slapped Chris on the arm. "What?" He laughed. "You have to admit *I'd* be crazy for not doubting all of this, even just a little bit."

"Yeah, imagine how I've been feeling." Norah flipped the pendant back and forth in her hand, lost in thought. "Sam," she whispered.

Chris wrapped his arms tightly around her and kissed the top of her forehead. "What are you going to do?" he asked, pulling away to look at her. "Can you send her a message back? And you have a new Guardian now? What's that about?"

"I don't know." Norah buried her face in Chris's chest. "She told me that she couldn't tell me the Lesson I needed to learn, and she also said it wasn't typical for Guardians to interact. I think she broke some rules coming here, and now she's in trouble. Damn, I really hope that's not the case. I wish I could make sure she was okay, too."

"Don't you dare blame yourself," Chris said, pointing at her sternly. "If Celeste is in trouble, it's not on you. You didn't ask her to come down to Earth, break rules, or be here with you."

Norah sighed and said, "I know, I know." After a long pause, she looked up at Chris, tears welling in her eyes. An all too familiar ache, one she spent the last three years trying to get rid of, crept into her. The feeling of loss for yet another. She knew it to be true, but needed to say it out loud. "I think she's gone for good." Norah pressed her lips together and bit back the tears that brimmed her eyes. "Maybe this is a good thing? I need to move on. She's okay, and Sam's okay. That's all that matters."

# CHAPTER 52

## Celeste

Silas and Reginald walked along the garden path, both with their hands clasped neatly behind their backs, faces set in hard stone as if discussing the most serious of serious topics. Celeste tried her best to stifle a laugh, but was a moment too late. Silas glared in her direction.

So much for blending in. It had been just under a year since she was removed from Guardian training, and while she missed it terribly, she did not miss adhering to the Council's stringent rules. No longer required to wear all white, Celeste's new wardrobe was full of the most vibrant colors, but each time she came to visit, she needed to ensure she was in boring old white. She'd stick out like a sore thumb otherwise, and she couldn't have that.

She hung back while the two finished their conversation. She was in a bit of a hurry, but couldn't resist taking the time to talk with Silas. It may have been a while since they went toe to toe, but it was still fun to know that while she didn't exactly win in any of this, neither did he. She couldn't imagine how she ever found measly Silas threatening.

Reginald looked in her direction, and her heart skipped a beat. It would take some time for her subconscious to remember she didn't report to the Council any longer.

"What are you doing here?" Silas asked as he approached. Reginald walked off in the other direction, his glow barely visible in the sunlight, and yet her eyes burned with PTSD.

She turned her attention to Silas. "Just thought I'd say hi. Wanted to check in and see how you were doing."

Celeste noticed that once Silas learned she held true to her word, writing a letter to the Council in defense of him, and once Benny reassured him, several times over the past year, that he saw a lot of potential in him, Silas became a little more bearable to Celeste. Of course, neither could help themselves when it came to, let's say, their playful banter.

"I just saw Benny," Celeste said. "He said he hasn't seen you at any of the Council meetings lately? Oh, wait, so sorry," she said, slapping her palm to her forehead. "I was thinking you attended those for some reason."

"Ha ha. Very funny, Celeste. How's your Soul moving along? Oh, right, you're no longer a Trainee."

Celeste simply smiled in response. It took her some time to get used to the freedom of being in her own afterlife. Sometimes she missed being busier, and she missed her sense of purpose, for sure, but most of all, she missed Norah. For the most part, she was getting used to it.

For the most part.

It took everything in Celeste to return Silas's half of the pendant after she recorded her final message to Norah all those months ago. The pendant was Celeste's last link to Norah; she knew it was the right thing to do—and she was determined to do what was right. When Norah made her way to their afterlife, Celeste wanted to be sure returning to the Guardian afterlife wasn't completely off the table, unless it was by choice.

Silas asked, "What are you doing here, anyway?"

Celeste responded, "Just seeing an old friend."

She was coming from seeing Benny, but was now headed to the Guardian Tower. She and Benny met up for weekly brunches to stay in touch; they quickly became a highlight for

Celeste, and she suspected Benny enjoyed them just as much as she did. Brunch that day was a little rushed, as she had somewhere very important to be.

Silas and Celeste said their goodbyes with bright smiles that were perhaps more real than either would ever admit.

Celeste made her way over to the Guardian Tower, following along the remainder of the garden's path, through the pink peonies bursting with notes of sweetness.

She stopped first within the entrance to the Tower, to grab a bag of cheddar popcorn and chips from the vending machine. The chips were for her friend, her only payment for these special visits. She made her way past the communal meeting place she had met Silas a couple of times before, and smiled at having all the sneaking around behind her now. She then went up to the fourth floor via the long, winding staircase, beautifully wrapped in nothing but fresh air, allowing everyone to be surrounded by blue sky, sunshine, and greenery instead of being stifled by walls.

She tossed the bag of chips on the desk beside her ginger friend and asked, "How's our girl doing today?"

Loretta shushed her. "How many times have I told you? You can't let everyone know you are here."

Celeste shrank into her shoulders and took the seat next to Loretta. "I'm sorry," she said. "But it's not like we aren't completely exposed here, anyway."

"We don't need to flaunt it. I don't know if we'd actually get in trouble, but I don't want to find out."

Celeste rubbed her hands together in anticipation and squealed. "I'm just excited. It's a big day."

At this, Loretta allowed a squeal as well. "Me too! Are you ready?"

The start of the morning began with Norah awakening in her apartment to a giant gift basket filled with a new floral teapot, with matching tea cups, and a variety of teas. The basket was placed there with the help of Loretta, and included a little note written on lavender stationary that read, "Remember, a

good cup of tea can solve almost any problem. You've got this."
Norah placed her hand to her heart, inhaled deeply, then looked
up. "Thank you," she whispered.

From there, Celeste and Loretta *oohed* and *ahhed* over
Norah in her white dress, Chris in his tux. Loretta had to con-
jure up a second box of tissues during the vow readings—the
first was used up as they watched Norah get ready. She'd tucked
a picture of Sam into her bouquet, and Maureen placed the
pendant from Celeste around her neck as a final touch.

Loretta and Celeste shared a little slice of dark chocolate
cake, swirled with raspberry purèe and topped with cream
cheese frosting. An exact replica of what the wedding guests
were having. Even Loretta couldn't help herself as they playfully
blew their own bubbles while the newlyweds left the ceremony.

They decided to give the happy couple their privacy once
the evening wound down. They had boundaries.

Celeste asked Loretta all the questions she couldn't ask
while they watched the wedding play out.

"How is Norah's return to her residency match process
going?"

"Chris hadn't quite convinced her, yet."

"When are the Bryers moving to South Carolina?"

"That has never even been discussed."

And lastly, "When are they going to have babies?" Celeste
squealed.

Loretta sighed, "Again, Celeste, they don't even know if
they *want* kids."

When Loretta announced that she really did need to get back
to work, reminding Celeste that Norah was not her only Soul,
Celeste asked one final question. "Can I come back tomorrow
and check on Barb and Dylan?"

"Their Guardians have everything under control, I promise."

Carlos and Wade, Barb and Dylan's Guardians, would oc-
casionally allow Celeste to sit with them on their check-ins, as
well. Celeste said as she stood to leave, "I just like seeing them.

I never get to hear Barb's cat stories anymore, and I want to see how Dylan is doing as shift lead." Her eyes gleamed with pride.

"I will ask them if you can come by in a couple of days, that way your visits won't be back-to-back. And only if I get to come say hi to Roger soon."

Celeste playfully saluted. "As if you can't come see us anytime you want to."

She thanked Loretta again for letting her watch the wedding before leaving.

She'd stop by tomorrow, just in case.

# ACKNOWLEDGEMENTS

I held to the concept that writing was a solo hobby for far too long, but I now have a new love and appreciation for the Acknowledgement sections, tucked deep into the very back of the book when really they should be front and center. This book would have never been written if it weren't for the incredible support my family and friends have shown me.

My sisters, Amanda Foster and Melissa DiCocco, whose love and support are without limits. From my very first attempt at writing to this latest book, to quite literally, every ridiculous hobby I've tried in between, you have both been there as my test subjects, my cheerleaders, and my sounding boards. Thank you both for being early readers, never making me feel crazy or too much, and for giving me all the love and support you do. I think I can finally forgive you both for the relentless teasing when we were little; you've made it up to me tenfold.

To Casey Lewis and Jenell Kosmicki for also being such tremendous beta readers. You both provided priceless feedback by filling in gaps and clearing up confusion in ways that are impossible to see when you are deep in the story. It is a huge task to take on someone else's work and provide such strong support, and I cannot thank you both enough. Casey, thank you for loving Celeste the way you do. If no one else enjoys the story, your love for her has made all this work worth it. Jenell, my gratitude for your support goes far beyond this book. Thank you for always being there for me in all facets of my life.

To Nikki Nally for not only reading and providing valuable insight to Norah specifically, but also, most importantly, for the most stunning cover art I could (or couldn't have) ever imagined. You were a dream to work with and are truly, truly talented.

To my editors, Lilly Fredrickson and Gigi Nally (www.gillycritique.com), thank you for making this story clean and seamless. I was able to dive more into scenes, push myself to explore more of all of the characters, and pull together a much stronger story because of you two. Thank you both!

To Jon Ellis, the best partner anyone could ask for. From bringing me coffee to making me breakfast, and your endless patience and support through all my meltdowns, I couldn't have done it without it.

To my Writing Gal Pals, thanked individually here, but as the best writing group in the whole world, deserved its own shoutout. From meeting at Writeshare, to our quiet afternoons writing, to our podcast, to businesses started, weddings, and birthdays. Our group has blossomed into a true friendship that I don't know what I would do without. The motivation, accountability, and support are unmatched. Thank you for your support, and thank you for allowing me to be a part of all of your journeys, as well.

www.ingramcontent.com/pod-product-compliance
Lightning Source LLC
Chambersburg PA
CBHW051305130726